ROSEMARY WHITTAKER

The Cinnamon Snail

ROSEMARY WHITTAKER

Also by Rosemary Whittaker

Sunshine State
The Wattle Birds
The Feijoa Tree

Copyright © 2011 by Rosemary Whittaker

All rights reserved. This book or any portion thereof may not be reproduced or used in any manner whatsoever without the express written permission of the publisher except for the use of brief quotations in a book review.

First printing, 2013
Second impression, 2013

ISBN-13: 978-1491294758
ISBN-10: 1491294752

Published by Rosemary Whittaker
rosemarywhittaker.wordpress.com

Initial cover image and interior design by Scarlett Rugers Design
www.scarlettrugers.com

About the author

Rosemary Whittaker is a British-born author. Since leaving university, she has lived in the United States, New Zealand, Australia and Denmark. Her experiences in these countries are reflected in her recent novels.

For more information, visit Rosemary Whittaker's blog at rosemarywhittaker.wordpress.com.

About this book

Everything has fallen into place for Kate Merrit. She is dating the most handsome and charismatic man she has ever met. Her future plans are uncertain, but they most definitely include Christian.

His job in London ends sooner than either of them expected and he has to return home to Copenhagen. Kate knows there are new challenges and experiences ahead. But she has no way of knowing just how much this move will turn her world upside-down.

This book is a work of fiction. Names, characters, places, and incidents are the product of the author's imagination or are used fictitiously. Any resemblance to actual events, locales, or persons, living or dead, is coincidental.

Acknowledgements

My deepest thanks go to Donald, who was with me when this project started and, amazingly, was still there at the end.

Thanks also to Nicola Probert, who gave up her time on holiday to read the manuscript in its early stages and provided much honest but friendly criticism.

Thank you to Jacky Wilkins, whose original painting and enthusiasm inspired me greatly.

And not least, my grateful appreciation to *Jorden Rundt*, the cafe that eventually became *The Cinnamon Snail*. I am grateful for many excellent lattes and the friendly staff, who never disturbed me as I sat and wrote — www.cafejordenrundt.dk.

To my daughter, Beth, who makes my life wonderful in any country.

Chapter One

'Please be out,' I beg silently as the intercom shrills and echoes up inside Marie's flat.

Christian and I are waiting outside the flat at eight o'clock exactly. Christian hates being late for anything. He likes to extract the maximum enjoyment from every situation. Possibly all Danes do. He rings the bell again and smiles at me. 'Great, you have brought the flowers.'

I nod and wave the orchids, creamy and delicate in their cellophane jacket.

'Wonderful. Marie loves orchids. That was a clever choice.'

'What wine did you bring?' I ask, not because the name will mean anything to me but because I want to return the compliment.

'Pinot Noir and Sauvignon Blanc. You can't go wrong there, can you?'

I shake my head. If he had said a bottle of Blue Nun and one of Chianti, I would have been none the wiser.

The buzzer shrieks and he leans towards it. 'Marie, it's not terrorists — it's us. Now let us in, we're freezing out here.'

The door clicks and swings open and I follow him up the stairs. Jeremy and Marie are standing in the doorway. His arm is around her shoulders. I notice she has had her hair freshly highlighted and I push my own hair behind my ears before she can see that it is still just the same boring colour, despite the card she slipped threateningly into my hand the last time we met.

'Darlings!' She leans an inch or two towards me and wafts a breathy kiss in my direction. I know the drill now and waft one back. The first time I met her and she leaned in, I kissed her cheek and she jumped as though I had shot her.

'Kate.' Jeremy takes advantage of the fact that Marie now has both arms round Christian's neck, to wave at me, shrugging his shoulders to show he can't get near. I don't care. He and I aren't exactly kindred spirits. If Jeremy and Marie weren't Christian's friends, I would happily never see either of them again and I suspect the feeling is mutual.

Marie unpeels herself reluctantly from Christian and steps back.

'Darling, you get more handsome each time I see you. Come in, come in. Dinner's ready. And that's a lovely necklace, Kate,' she throws over her shoulder as she disappears into the reception room behind. I have learned to refer to it as *The Space*.

Jeremy takes my coat and hangs it in the concealed nook behind the door. 'Drinks, anyone?'

'I'll have my usual, thanks.' Christian sinks into the white leather sofa and waves at me to join him.

'What about you, Kate?'

'Sounds good to me,' I say.

Dinner at Marie and Jeremy's is always a bit of an ordeal but Christian loves them both, so we meet up at least once a month, either at their ultra-minimalist flat in Belgravia or at a nearby restaurant in Knightsbridge. The food at the restaurants is invariably pretentious and the prices eye-wateringly laughable but I prefer those evenings to the ones at their flat, when I spend the whole evening terrified that I will smash or maim one of their boring but priceless minimalist artefacts. At a restaurant, there are always waiters and other diners around to distract attention from me and the fact that I have absolutely nothing to say to these people, nor they to me. They tolerate me as a hanger-on for the sake of getting hold of Christian for the evening. Everyone loves him, me included. He is witty and well-read and moves effortlessly between the groups among which he finds himself. On top of that he is decorative, unbelievably and unfairly decorative. Even if he sat silent like me, scrabbling frantically for something to say, he would be welcome simply for the golden glow he casts across the table.

Marie pops her head round the door. 'Nearly ready, darlings. Did I tell you that Milla and Rupe are coming too? They'll be a little late.'

'Fantastic,' says Christian. He loves crowds.

'Wonderful,' I add gloomily. Milla intimidates me even more than Marie. It isn't just her endless legs and her immaculate hair. It's her air of confidence, the certainty that whatever happens, she is all right, everyone will love her and she will succeed at anything she tries. Whenever she is in the room, I feel myself subsiding into a huddle of self-consciousness and I try not to speak in case I embarrass myself. Luckily, Christian is always happy to do the talking for both of us. He never tries to be the centre of attention but somehow, when he is in a room, people cluster round him, warming themselves at the flame of his gregariousness. They like how unassuming he is about his achievements, his looks and his charisma. He draws people out so they feel good about themselves too.

'Here's your akvavit, Kate.' Jeremy hands it to me with a lifted eyebrow.

'Great,' I say, taking a sip and choking. 'I thought your usual was a martini,' I hiss at Christian out of the corner of my mouth.

'Yes, it is, but Jeremy keeps a really good bottle of akvavit so I always have that when we come here.'

I take another sip and he sees my face and laughs. 'Hold on for one minute while I finish mine and we can change glasses.'

He touches my cheek and I brush his fingers with my lips. He is a rock on occasions like this. I wouldn't get through them without him. He is never knowingly unkind and, if he knew how uncomfortable I was, he would probably insist we didn't come here again. But I know how much he loves to socialise so I am not about to spoil things for him by admitting how much I hate group events.

'You finished that one quickly, Kate. Another one before dinner?' asks Jeremy as he passes by. I am sure I don't imagine the sardonic gleam in his eye.

'No thanks but I will have an orange juice if you've got any.' I push my empty glass into his hand.

'I'll just go and see.'

I hear him go into the kitchen and rummage around. That's just the sort of place this is. If I asked for absinthe or a White Russian for breakfast, it wouldn't be a problem but asking for orange juice is like demanding a chocolate cream pie at a Weight Watchers meeting. I don't follow him to offer any help.

Marie never lets anyone into her kitchen on these occasions and I have my suspicions as to why. Her kitchen is as minimalist as the rest of the flat and frankly I am surprised she can even make toast in it, let alone a five-course dinner for six people. Not that she would want to make toast anyway, because she is on a wheat-free, dairy-free, everything-that-tastes-of-anything-free diet.

Jeremy emerges at last. 'Will tomato juice do you? Don't tell Marie but I took some from the special carton she keeps for Bloody Marys. She has it delivered specially from Harrods. Southern Italian, organic tomatoes ...'

'... crushed by the feet of ten virgins at dawn?' interrupts Christian. He looks amused. 'Next time, Kate, get Jeremy to make you a martini.'

I take a sip. 'This is lovely. Sorry to put you to so much trouble, Jeremy.'

'Don't worry. Marie won't notice it's gone. She's too busy ...' He stops abruptly.

'Serving up?' I suggest and he nods gratefully.

'Come on through. It's time to eat. Milla and Rupe may be late so they said to go ahead and start without them.'

In the event, a series of shrieks from the door signals the arrival of Milla and Rupe. They waft into the room on a cushion of air kisses and *'darlings'* and I notice without resentment that Jeremy pushes enthusiastically past Rupe to kiss Milla. She looks as annoyingly gorgeous as ever with her glossy, chestnut hair falling neatly onto her shoulders and her wrap dress accentuating her slender curves. When I wear a wrap dress, it spends its evening gaping wider and wider at the top, exposing far more than I ever intended and always on an evening when I haven't worn decent underwear.

Once we are all sitting again, Marie emerges from the kitchen with a loaded tray. 'Ta-*da*!'

Christian jumps up to help her pass the bowls around and everyone dips in appreciative spoons.

Milla tastes hers. 'Lobster bisque! Marie, you are *so* naughty. You *know* I can't resist this and it just puts pounds on.'

I lay my spoon down guiltily, uncomfortably aware that the waistband on this skirt has been too tight for months. But it's the one I was wearing when I first met Christian and I have a sentimental attachment to it. I leave the rest of the soup and sit in silence while everyone chatters about what a marvellous cook Marie is. She dips gingerly into her bowl of bouillon without croutons and smiles at their praise.

By the time we have moved through monkfish and noisettes of lamb and are on our second helpings of chocolate mousse, I have thrown caution to the winds. I can always starve tomorrow. I am not wasting this meal. Marie of course hardly touches anything. Milla has a little of the fish but pushes the lamb and the chocolate mousse around. Christian glances over at me and grins. 'I am glad to see one healthy appetite at the table. This meal deserves to be appreciated.'

I immediately feel as though I have swollen to a size eighteen. 'Marie went to all the trouble of... erm, so I thought ...'

'I agree. Does anyone want the last portion of mousse? Lucky for me.' He disposes of it in two quick gulps and leans back. 'Marie, you are the absolute best chef I have ever met.'

I flinch. I cooked him tuna pasta last week and he said he loved it. But I realise he is just being polite so I add to his praise. 'It was delicious, all of it. Thank you.'

'Rupe? You have been very quiet,' says Christian. 'Everything all right?'

'Everything's fine. Bloody hoo-hah at work today. Management threatened to cut the bonuses.'

'That was predictable.'

'It may be predictable but we're not standing for it and we let them know that. You'd think we were baby-killers instead of investment bankers.'

'But surely ...' I stop myself just in time and he ploughs on.

'We're the economic lifeblood of this country and they'd better remember that. We earn our bonuses and we need every penny of them just to get by.'

I stare at the tablecloth, willing myself not to make a scene when Christian is having such a good time. Rupe's last bonus, the details of which we heard at nauseating length at an identical dinner party round at their flat, was approximately twenty times my annual salary. I sip at my coffee and try to think of something cheerful to distract myself.

'Kate?' Marie fixes me with a beady eye and I cringe, wondering whether she is about to draw me out to make me look stupid or make her usual thinly-veiled digs at my relationship with Christian.

'Uh huh?' I reach for his hand and look her straight in the eye.

'I was thinking that you and Christian must have been together now for ... about three months, is it?'

I stare at her frostily. She knows as well as I do how long we have been together. 'Eight, actually. We met at his Christmas party. I was Becca's guest.'

She looks amazed. 'That long? It doesn't seem it. We lost our single man when you came along.'

Christian squeezes my hand before I can reply. 'But you gained a wonderful new friend in Kate.'

'Of course.' She doesn't sound convinced.

He turns to me. 'You know, I thought you were Irish when I first saw you across the room, with your dark hair and those deep blue eyes.'

'Dorset, actually. I suppose it's in the same general direction.'

'Wherever it is, I couldn't take my eyes off you.' He lifts my hand to his lips and kisses it.

I flush with pleasure and Marie shoots me a filthy look. I smile at her as blandly as possible.

Jeremy stands. 'OK, enough of the small talk. Brandy everyone?'

Milla beams at him. 'Not for me, darling. I'm *pregnant*!' She pats her flat stomach.

All the men jump to their feet and kiss her again while Marie shrieks happily from her chair. Rupe looks extremely pleased with himself and I swallow my resentment at his crassness and smile at him.

'Congratulations.'

He puffs himself out. 'Thanks, but you can see that this year's bonus is only going to come in the nick of time. Babies are bloody expensive things. Trust funds, private education, tutoring, nannies. It's not something to take on lightly.'

I think of the children I see around our way, many of them from single-parent families, where it is a daily struggle just to pay the heating bills and feed everyone a decent diet.

'It's not easy,' I agree.

I look over at Milla and soften. Her face is glowing with joy and excitement. It isn't the baby's fault it will be a rich kid and it certainly didn't ask to have a jerk like Rupe for its father. Looking at his smug, red face, I almost feel sorry for the baby. I am happy for Milla at least. She may be perfect but that isn't her fault. It's the luck of the draw. She will have the perfect pregnancy and the perfect lack of stretch-marks and the perfect lack of sickness and the perfect baby. I wonder why I feel so resentful when I am fairly sure my body clock hasn't even had the cogs put in, let alone started ticking.

Christian kisses Milla warmly again before sitting down. I wish for a moment that he wasn't so tactile. It's probably another Danish thing, I reassure myself, and you can't legislate for cultures.

I start to gather up the plates, forgetting for a moment Marie's ban on guests in the kitchen. Everyone is still gathered around Milla, asking questions, laughing. I push through the door to the kitchen and look for the dishwasher. It's hidden behind a gleaming door and I open the washing machine and then the fridge before I find it. The fridge seems to be bare of anything but bottles and a chunk of brie. As I put the last of the plates into the dishwasher, the door behind me bangs open. It's Marie and she looks annoyed.

'I asked you all to stay out of my kitchen.'

'Sorry — so you did. I was just helping.'

I look round at the gleaming work surfaces and the shining hob that hasn't seen a saucepan in months. The swing bin catches my eye. It hasn't been closed properly and the edge of one shiny silver box protrudes. I can just make out the words. '*Clarke's Catering.*' I jerk my eyes away from it and see Marie staring at me. She looks panicked.

'I'm impressed,' I say. 'I always mean to wash up as I go along but I never manage to. You're much better organised than I am.'

Her face relaxes. 'It just takes practice. Shall we go out to join the others?'

I follow her into *The Space* where everyone is now drinking brandy. Christian hands me a glass. 'Everything OK?'

'Everything's fine.'

I take a huge gulp. Marie and Jeremy have their good points and Christian loves them. I simply must stop being so shy and ungracious around them. By the end of my second glass of brandy, it doesn't seem that difficult. Their faces are blurring into a pleasant haze and I am totally relaxed. It takes a moment for me to register that Christian is on his feet.

'As this is an evening for big announcements, I should tell you that I have one too.'

Everyone's eyes flick towards me in shock and Marie's mouth falls open. I sit up straighter. We didn't get engaged, did we? I am fairly certain I would remember that but I check my fourth finger just to be sure. Maybe he is going to propose to me. I turn expectantly towards him but he doesn't catch my eye.

'This is the last week of my assignment. The Copenhagen office has cut it short unexpectedly. We have landed a big project over there and all the hands need to be on the deck.'

I drain my glass and look round at everyone. Their faces have fallen and no one speaks for a moment. In fact, I think Marie might be going to cry.

'Say something, someone!' says Christian. He catches my eye and lifts his glass towards me in a half salute. I stare at him numbly. Jeremy turns and looks at me before he stands and raises his glass.

'To Christian, our very good friend. May the road rise to meet you.'

There is a chorus of agreement and everyone drinks. I look vaguely towards my empty glass, reach over and refill it. He might have chosen a less public place to tell me. But that's Christian. He's an original and this is part of what I love about him. But I can't believe this is all happening so suddenly. I sit for a while in a dream as the chatters swells and drifts around me. When Christian comes in with both our coats, it doesn't register for a moment. He pulls me to my feet and does up the buttons for me.

'Are you all right?' he whispers.

'Fine, it was just a bit of a shock. I mean, I knew something like this was coming sometime but ...'

'Can you walk downstairs?'

'Of course I can. I'm not that shocked.' I try to smile at him.

'You've had a fair bit to drink.'

'Hardly anything.' I take his arm and aim a kiss at Marie's left eyebrow. 'Lovely afternoon, thank you, darling. We should do lunch next week.'

He steers me towards the door and turns on the top step to kiss her goodbye.

'Better go straight home to bed, Kate darling, or you'll have a sore head in the morning,' trills Marie and I glare at her. It's plain that she doesn't like the thought of anyone but her sharing a bed with Christian. That's just tough. I am quite sober enough to make my own decisions. It's been a bit sudden, that's all.

I wonder how I'll like Denmark.

Chapter Two

It is almost noon by the time I finally climb back into reality. I am at home. When I check, I am alone. Christian must either have left already or he didn't stay over after all. I lie for a while and stare at the half-closed curtains. It looks like a nice day. September so far has been a wash out, all gales and lashing rain, so an Indian summer would be perfect before the chill of October and the dreariness of November. I hate November — nothing but freezing cold mornings and endless rain to look forward to, but still too early to start thinking about Christmas. Even January and February, although depressing, aren't so bad because spring is lurking behind them, however reluctant it might be to appear.

After half an hour of lying still and wishing I had the energy to get up and get some painkillers and a drink, I force myself out of bed. It is Saturday and I wonder what I had planned. Christian probably has something organised. Christian! I sit back down on the bed. Something about him is niggling inside the deepest recesses of my brain. Did we have an argument? Is that why he isn't here this morning? The thought doesn't feel quite right and anyway, Christian never argues. He is perfectly happy with disagreements. Although he rarely changes his mind, he doesn't expect me to either. Sometimes I would really prefer to have a shouting match but his way is probably better. Culture probably comes into it too — I always tell myself that when we see things differently. But if we didn't have a row, why is he so strongly in my mind? He can't be ill. He was very cheerful at Marie and Jeremy's last night. If her caterers have poisoned him, then why don't I feel ill, except for a thumping headache and a dry mouth?

As I sit and stare at the line of autumn gold pushing itself through the edge of the curtains, I go back through last evening bit by bit. Something about the kitchen and Marie being annoyed with me? Rupe's stupid bonus? That can't have bothered Christian. He may not be on a banker's salary but he has a pretty good job with his firm. Milla? Of course, she's pregnant. She told us all last night. I have a vision of her patting her flat stomach and beaming round at us all. Mystery solved.

Except it isn't. As I make my way to the kitchen and fill the largest mug I can find with water, something is still worrying me. Why would Christian care if Milla is pregnant? I put the glass down with trembling hands. He doesn't want to start a family, does he? I have a vague recollection that he and I talked about getting engaged — or someone else did. Did we talk about children too? I grab at the memory but it slips easily past me and disappears. I hadn't considered getting engaged this young but I think about it for a moment and it doesn't seem so awful. It seems to happen to most people eventually, so why not now? Maybe people get married younger in Denmark.

Denmark! I choke down the last gulp of water and lean back against the counter. Whatever is bothering me is to do with Denmark and not about getting engaged at all. I let my mind go blank and sure enough the memory slides in, uninvited, and sits there watching me. I inspect it. Christian made an announcement too, something about going back there soon. I can't quite remember why or for how long but at least I won't look so stupid now when I see him. I relax and rinse my mug before heading to the bathroom for a shower.

By the time I am clean and dressed, I am feeling better and quite hungry, even after Marie's five course meal last night. I remember that I planned not to eat at all today but the thought no longer appeals. Starve a something and feed a hangover, or whatever it was that Mum used to say. Just as I open the fridge door, the phone goes. It's Christian and he sounds as cheerful as ever. 'How is your head this morning?'

'It's fine,' I say cautiously, feeling it to check. 'At least, it is if I don't shake it too much.'

'In future you must stay away from Jeremy's akvavit. It doesn't suit everyone.'

'I hardly touched mine,' I remind him. 'You had them both.'

'Then it must have been the brandy.'

'I don't think so. I don't even like the stuff. I had a couple of glasses of wine with dinner and that was it.'

He sounds even more amused now. 'OK, whatever you say. Can you manage any food?'

'I was just about to get some breakfast,' I tell him with dignity.

'It's almost one o'clock so shall we make it lunch? I can pick you up in ten minutes.'

I close the fridge again. 'Lunch would be fine but nothing too spicy. I think I ate too much rich stuff at Marie's.'

'Just something light,' he promises and rings off, laughing.

I make my way back to my bedroom and look through my wardrobe for something nice to wear. Christian always dresses much more smartly than me. He wears his expensive suits with an easy air and never looks over-dressed. I always feel wrong in comparison, either too casual or too smart for any occasion.

'Why should that matter?' asked Christian one evening when I confided this to him. 'Dressing is all about what makes you feel comfortable, not what other people think is suitable.'

That would be fine if I looked as good as he does in everything he wears or if I had his charisma and confidence. He could turn up for a black-tie dinner in ripped jeans and every other guest there would feel over-dressed. His confidence is one of the things I love about him. He makes everyone feel better just by his being there. I choose my smartest pair of jeans and my favourite T shirt and add a jacket as a gesture at smart casual. I can always tell him I thought we were going to get a sandwich and eat it in the park.

He smiles and kisses my cheek when he arrives and pushes a huge bunch of roses into my arms.

'What are they for?' I ask. Not the most gracious question but I'm feeling a little disorientated today.

'Why do they have to be for anything in particular?' he counters. 'They are just pretty and they reminded me of you.'

I give him a quick hug and push my face into their delicate, pink petals. 'Sorry. They're perfect. Thank you.'

Becca emerges from her room while I am rummaging round for a vase. She is still in her Winnie the Pooh pyjamas and I nudge her. 'I didn't know you were here. I thought you must have gone out. Christian's here so you might want to hide those pyjamas.'

'Why?' She blinks at me sleepily and wanders past me into the hall. 'Hi, Christian, how's it going?'

He kisses her. 'My favourite architect. And those pyjamas are fantastic. Very postmodern.'

'Well, I thought so.' She waves a hand at us both and disappears into her bedroom.

I stare after her as she goes. How can she be so relaxed, so uncaring about what anyone else might think of her? If I emerged into the hall in tatty Pooh Bear pyjamas and found her boyfriend standing there, I would die of shame. Not only does she not seem to care but no one else does either.

Christian takes my hand. 'Ready to go?'

'Where are we going?'

'There is this great noodle bar near to the office. I thought we could go there.'

Noodles sound safe enough so I nod happily. 'Isn't it a fantastic day?'

'The best. It is what I will most remember about England, these crisp mornings and warm afternoons in autumn.'

What he will most remember? The memory of him making an announcement about a visit home flickers back into my mind, but it is still hazy. I decide to wait until we are sitting down so that I can ask him properly.

Oodles of Noodles is only twenty minutes' walk away. By the time we arrive, my head has cleared almost entirely. The owner has pushed some of the tables out onto the pavement and people are talking and laughing in the warm, autumnal air. We sit down under a huge striped umbrella.

The Cinnamon Snail

'If this was the South of France, we could do this practically all year round,' I tell Christian as I settle into my chair.

'Maybe, but then you would be eating frogs' legs and not noodles.'

'I would not. They must eat other stuff too.'

'Indeed they do — snails and garlic and horse meat and ...'

I slap at his hand. 'Shut up. My head's not up for it today.'

'A bowl of Harry's noodles and you will be a new woman.'

'How do you know the owner's name?'

'A bunch of us from work come here sometimes for lunch.'

'Oh.' I concentrate on my menu. Christian's life always sounds so much more interesting than mine. Even his lunchtimes sound fun. Mine seem to consist of day-old sandwiches stuffed with whatever I can find first thing in the morning. I'm always running late.

Harry is standing by our table. 'Something to drink? Oh, hi, Christian. Just two of you today? That makes a change.'

'I managed to get the prettiest one all to myself for once,' says Christian, closing his menu.

'Uh huh.' Is it my imagination or does Harry sound doubtful? 'You two ready to order?'

'Shall we have the ginger chicken?' Christian asks me. 'Harry makes the best I have ever tasted.'

'Sounds good,' I say. It saves me ploughing through the entire menu and choosing something that I hate when it finally turns up.

'And to drink?' asks Harry.

'Kate? The house red is very good.'

'Do you by any chance have orange juice?' I ask and Harry frowns in surprise.

'Of course we do. Orange and mango, orange and apple or just orange?'

'Straight up.'

'Got it.' He looks at Christian. 'House red for you, mate?'

'Fantastic.'

Harry disappears and Christian takes my hand. 'Congratulations on managing to order an orange juice. I hear it can be quite hard to find in north London.'

I laugh at the thought of Jeremy sneaking Marie's precious tomato juice from under her nose last night, while she was busy unwrapping and hiding the catering boxes.

'What is she like? Honestly, Christian, did I tell you that I went into the kitchen afterwards and it was completely spotless? There's no way in hell she ever ...'

'It was a lovely evening, wasn't it?' he interrupts and I flush darkly. I had forgotten how loyal he always is to his friends. He never utters a word of criticism about them and neither does he expect me to.

I change tack quickly. 'Yes, it was great. I was just going to say how clean it all was. I make a horrible mess whenever I try to cook.'

He takes my hand and smiles as my blush subsides. 'We are not all the same and that is OK. They have been so kind to me while I have been here. I am going to miss them.'

I am glad he has raised the subject. With a little careful probing, I should be able to tease out the mystery of this visit to Denmark — and hopefully without him realising I don't have the faintest idea what exactly it was that he announced last night.

I dig into the pile of steaming noodles in my bowl and the hot, fragrant sauce banishes the last of my headache. 'You're right, these are amazing. What were you saying about missing Marie and Jeremy?'

He puts down his chopsticks. 'Naturally I will — Milla and Rupe too. What did you think, that I would forget everyone as soon as I left?'

'No, of course not but you'll be back. Milla will probably ask you to be godfather to the baby. She loves you. She must be due sometime in the spring.'

'I don't think so. She will choose someone British.'

It is my turn to lay down my chopsticks. 'Someone British? Why on earth should she? Even under this government, there's no rule that says someone who was born in another country can't be a godparent. Don't be silly. Everyone here loves you. I bet they do ask you.'

'We won't argue about it.' He takes a slug of his wine.

'No, because I'm right.' I finish the last of my noodles and grin at him.

'And you?' he asks. 'Are you all right with all this?'

'Fine,' I lie airily. 'Of course you want to visit your family. I would too in your position.'

I am hoping he might take the chance to invite me to visit too. I would love to meet his father and brother. In fact, if he and I are going to stay together, I will have to meet them sometime. But I don't want to get ahead of myself. If he needs to make this visit alone, to get his homeland out his system and find some closure, I won't get in his way.

'I must say, you are taking this better than I thought you would. Thank you so much for understanding.' He lifts my hand and kisses my wrist. Something in his eyes makes me uneasy.

'There's nothing to thank me for. Did you really think I'd kick up a fuss about you wanting to visit your family and friends? You don't know me very well.'

He stares at me. 'I don't understand. You were there last night when I made my announcement.'

'Yes, you said something about a project at work and that you need to visit to help them out. I'm really sorry, Christian but I think I was a bit tired or something. I didn't take in all the details.'

He leans back and waves at Harry. 'Two filter coffees please, one black.'

I don't speak while we wait for the coffee to arrive. Images from last night swirl through my head — Milla glowing, Marie drinking far too much as usual and flirting with Christian, me feeling fat and unattractive, the tomato juice, Rupe's bonus and finally, coming faster and faster into focus, Christian standing up and raising his glass towards me. I can see him quite clearly now, his mouth moving, saying the words I still can't hear. I can see his face, not open and friendly as it usually is but wary, calculating, even slightly nervous.

Harry places our coffees in front of us, instinctively giving the black one to Christian, and I wait until he has gone before looking up. My hands are clasped around the cup for warmth, so tightly in fact that the cup jiggles noisily and the creamy brown liquid splashes into the saucer.

'You didn't say *"visit"* did you?' I whisper and I can no longer help the shameful tears prickling at the back of my eyes, before they slide down my cheeks and splash onto the table.

He shakes his head.

'But even today, you've let me go on thinking ...' I can't go on.

'That is not fair.' He sips at his coffee and I am annoyed to see his hands are perfectly steady. 'I told you all very clearly last night what my future plans were. It's not my fault that you had so much to drink that you didn't take it in properly.'

It's a fair point so I wait for a moment for my voice to steady again. There is never any point trying to have a row with Christian. He just becomes cooler and more detached until I calm down.

'Is this a permanent move?' I ask at last, trying to sound as though I feel nothing but a mild curiosity, instead of fighting a sensation that my entire world is crashing down around my head.

'I am afraid so. They only sent me on assignment for six months and I have overstayed that by another eight. I have told you several times that one day I must go back. You must remember that.'

For a minute, I wish he had never overstayed, that he had gone home when he was meant to instead of staying the extra months to meet me and break my heart, but I can't. Christian is the best thing that has ever happened to me and my life will never be the same after meeting him. I can't regret that. Besides, there is still hope. He hasn't mentioned me coming too but perhaps the idea hasn't yet occurred to him. I could even be the one to suggest it. But even before I have finished this thought, I know it wouldn't work. Christian makes his own decisions. He won't ever be swayed by anyone else. He needs to think of it for himself. I study his face, waiting for it to break into a huge smile, for him to tell me it's an April Fool and of course he wants me to go along. But the minutes lengthen as he stirs his coffee and he doesn't speak. Despite all my hoping and desperate planning, I know in my heart of hearts that he isn't going to.

Chapter Three

When I get back to the flat, I open the front door very quietly in case Becca is still around. Much though I love her, I don't think I can face her matter-of-fact approach at the moment. All I want is to lie on my bed and howl for the rest of the weekend. As I make for my bedroom, she appears from the kitchen.

'I just finished arranging those flowers you dumped in the sink.'

'Thanks, Becca.' I keep my face averted.

'They're really gorgeous. They must have cost a fortune. What is it, some anniversary or other for you guys?'

'No, it was just ...' My voice cracks and she looks at me in alarm.

'What's wrong?'

'Nothing, I'm just a bit hung-over.'

'Fair enough.'

She goes back into the kitchen and I make a thankful dive for my bedroom, where I fling myself on the bed and hide my hot face in the pillow, waiting for the flood gates to open.

'It's just that I've seen you with hangovers before and this isn't one of them.' She has followed me into the bedroom and sits next to me on the bed.

'I'll be fine.'

'I'm sure you will — but you're not fine right now, are you?'

She strokes my hair and that finally does it. Mum used to stroke my hair when I was a little girl and howling into my pillow because someone hadn't picked me for their team or I was bottom of the lowest set in maths again. I slump back down and start to cry in earnest. Becca doesn't mind. It's one of the things I like most about her. She is totally and utterly unflappable. If the flat was burning down, she would wander into the street in her ratty old pyjamas and perch on the wall to wait for someone to come. She never gets flustered about work deadlines. If people don't like her or are unkind, she shrugs comfortably and moves on. In fact, the only thing I have ever seen her even mildly stressed over, is Jon in IT. She has nursed a secret crush on him for months but never done anything about it. I have urged her repeatedly just to get it over with and ask him out. If anyone has the personality to take a rejection, she has, but she refuses point blank.

She sits with me for what seems an age, stroking my hair, murmuring soothing nothings, just waiting. When I finally gulp and sit up, she pushes my hair back off my face and looks at me thoughtfully. 'Water, or something stronger?'

'Just water, please,' I hiccup. She nods and leaves the room. I catch sight of myself in the wardrobe mirror and flinch. My eyes are almost swollen shut and my face is a mass of blotches, like strawberry ripple ice-cream.

She returns with the water and I sip it gratefully. 'Thanks, Becca.'

'No problem.' She curls her legs under her on the bed and leans against the wall. 'Is it a row, a break-up, an arrest for insider trading, or another woman?'

I snort in spite of myself.

'It's all I could think of off the top of my head,' she explains. 'But give me a minute and I'll come up with some more.'

'Don't bother.' I sit up properly and start combing my fingers ineffectually through my hair to make it lie back down. 'It's none of those. He's going back to Denmark.'

'For good?'

I nod miserably.

'Are you going too?'

I shake my head and feel my eyes start to brim over again.

'So you *have* split up.'

I hate the way she says it, matter of factly, as though it is no more important than ordering a cappuccino.

'No, we didn't split up.' I say it as firmly as I can. Denial is definitely the best way forward here. There are a million chances for me to put things right. It's not as though we had some huge row. For once I am thankful that Christian doesn't do rows. This is all just a misunderstanding and he hasn't had time to think things through yet. He probably thinks I wouldn't want to move to a strange country, that it would be far too much to ask of anybody.

'So, you're still together?' She's ruthless but I know she doesn't mean to be. She just has a passion for facts, for order and reality.

'Not exactly,' I admit and it hurts even to hear myself saying the words.

'You're going to have to help me out here.'

Her face is faintly amused and I resent it. This might not be the tragedy for her that it is for me but she knows how I feel about him, how completely in love with him I am. She ought to understand the devastation I am feeling now. But if she's determined to be obtuse, I will have to make her understand.

'I know he always said he was going back ...' I pause and watch her face for any indication that she might side with me. She doesn't react. She never does. I plough on. 'I mean, he always said it wasn't permanent, him being over here. I just thought that ...'

'You thought what exactly?' she prompts me.

'That he'd want to take me with him.'

She pulls her knees to her chin and considers this before answering. When she does, she doesn't even try to take my side, even though I'm crying. To be fair, she doesn't take his side either. 'Did he ever say that he was planning on taking you with him?'

'No, but he didn't ever say he wasn't planning on it either. So that could mean anything.'

'I've never said I'm going to try out for the Bolshoi ballet. Do you spend time picturing me in a tutu? He always said he was going back, didn't he?'

'Yes.'

'He never once mentioned you coming too?'

'No.'

'Yet now you think he was leading you up the garden path?'

'We're a couple. Couples make decisions together.'

'All evidence to the contrary. It seems to me that you have two choices. Either he saw you as a couple but he thought he'd spelled out his plans and you were happy to go along with them and have a "just for now" relationship. Or else he never saw you as a couple. It's your choice.'

'We so *were* a couple.' I am close to tears now.

'Then he obviously communicated his view of things and you didn't communicate yours. I really don't see how you can blame him for that.'

'I communicated without words. People in love have a special unspoken language.'

'Next time I suggest you get it in writing.'

She doesn't say it unkindly but I know there is no point in arguing further. She has applied her own ruthless brand of logic to the situation and there will be no moving her. If I want to attempt any further self-justification, it will have to be in secret. She stretches and grins at me. 'Would you like me to drop it now?'

'Please.' I smile at her gratefully through swollen eyes. Until I can figure out exactly where we stand, I don't particularly want to discuss it with anyone, even Becca. When we left the noodle bar, Christian said he'd ring me later. That doesn't sound like someone who has entirely split up with someone else. And he said there would be a farewell party. I need to find something incredible to wear, get my hair cut into a proper style for once and possibly even highlighted. He just needs reminding of all he is losing. As I think about this, I feel more cheerful. He must be in turmoil, leaving his friends, going back to a place he hasn't lived for over a year, where he will have to revert to speaking his other language. I mustn't be too hard on him. In fact, I feel a bit guilty that I haven't thought more about him and been more supportive. I could have offered to help him with all sorts of tiny things, packing and passports and bottled water and whatever else he's going to need over there. I feel better already, planning, thinking more rationally about the whole thing.

By Wednesday, I haven't heard from him and I am beginning to panic. He is leaving on Sunday so the party must surely be arranged for Friday or Saturday and I need to make plans. Eventually I try ringing his number, though even I know this isn't the greatest idea. I am almost relieved when it drops through to his answer phone. After much thought, I decide I am going to have to call either Milla or Marie. I weigh up the options. Milla is less in your face and definitely isn't making a play for Christian but then I run the risk of getting the awful Rupe and hearing about his bonus yet again. In the end, I call Marie. Jeremy answers and sounds surprised to hear me. I keep my voice light as I ask for Marie.

'She's not here. Are you OK?'

'Fine, I'm fine. Why wouldn't I be?'

'No reason. Can I help you with something?'

'It's nothing really, just that Christian said there was going to be a farewell party for him before he goes and I haven't been able to get him on the phone. Of course he must be terribly busy, so I thought I'd check with you two in case you've heard anything.'

There is a long silence. He must know whether or not he has heard anything, unless Marie keeps their social diary and only announces at the last minute where he is going and what he should wear. She is quite capable of it.

'Shall I call back when she's home?' I ask at last and I can almost hear him jump.

'No, don't do that. It's on Saturday at eight.'

'Great,' I say in relief. That gives me time to get my hair done and go shopping with Becca. 'Where is it?'

'It's here,' he says and I feel a jolt of surprise. I thought it would be at some big restaurant somewhere.

'Great,' I say again, less certainly this time. Surely someone was going to tell me. But of course, they must have expected Christian to have invited me and he has probably been too busy to make calls like that.

'I think Marie was going to call you,' he says and I nod, even though he can't see me.

'That's fine. Can you let her know I'd love to be there? Is there any special wine you'd like me to bring?' It hits me when I say this that, while I've been with Christian, I haven't had to worry about things like choosing hostess gifts or making arrangements. The thought makes me feel single for the first time since I met him. But of course it doesn't mean anything. There is no reason I can't be helpful and take more of the burdens off him while he's so stressed.

'Nothing particular that I can think of,' says Jeremy. 'I'm pretty well sorted on the alcohol front so why don't you bring some soft drinks? Orange juice, things like that. There's bound to be someone who wants to drink that stuff.'

I ignore the note in his voice when he says *that stuff*. It was really quite thoughtful of him to remember.

'See you at eight sharp,' I tell him and ring off.

The next few days whirl by. Becca and I go out on Friday to the shopping centre near us which stays open until late. She is looking bored even before we get through the giant revolving doors and I have to promise her we will alternate clothes shops and book shops.

Her face is resigned. 'And something to eat? I haven't had anything since breakfast except horrible greasy canapés and some champagne.'

'What on earth were they for?' I ask, scanning the directory for clothes shops.

Her face changes. 'Oh, Kate, I'm sorry, it was Christian's leaving do this lunchtime. But it was pretty awful,' she adds, seeing my face. 'It was just boring old farts from the fifth floor making speeches and banging on about the wonderful work he'd done for our clients.'

'I bet he has,' I say loyally.

'I suppose. Then they presented him with a stupid bronze cast of the Little Mermaid, of all things. Can you imagine? It would be like giving me a model of the Tower of London if I left. I don't know whose stupid idea that was.'

'What did he say?' I am trying to imagine him, standing there in his smart suit with one of his lovely pastel coloured shirts, giving a witty speech, with all the women hanging on his every word.

'He gave a very nice speech, actually. He said that having The Little Mermaid as a gift would remind him every day of the links between his homeland and what he has come to think of as his adopted country. Everyone thought it was wonderful.'

'I wonder if he'll give a speech at the party tomorrow,' I muse and she frowns.

'Kate, are you absolutely sure that this is a good idea? I mean, isn't it just going to hurt you more? If you like we could go out to the theatre or something and have a takeaway afterwards. We haven't done that for ages. It would be fun.'

I feel guilty when she says this. We used to have a lot of evenings like that together. Ever since Christian came along, I have spent most of my spare evenings with him. But that's natural. When friends pair off, they are bound to spend more time with their partners. If she and Jon had ever got it together, I bet I wouldn't have seen her for dust. She is watching me so I smile cheerfully.

'We'll have more evenings like that once Christian has gone back. But for now, I just need to see him, spend some time talking to him, and sort things out.'

'It's not the best place to talk, is it? A noisy party with Marie screeching at everyone and loads of people getting drunk.'

'Maybe not but it's all I've got. It's not Christian's fault that your stupid firm moved him at such short notice. Anyway, I thought maybe he and I would go out for dinner or something afterwards. The party can't go on forever.'

She shrugs. 'OK, whatever you say. Let's get this shopping over with, shall we?'

Becca is a real star. She walks past the bookshops without a second glance, accompanies me in and out of changing rooms and gives me as much advice as I am prepared to listen to.

'Definitely too tarty,' she says as I emerge from one dressing room in a plunging scarlet silk dress.

'No, it's not. It just shows my ... assets.'

'Christian's already seen your ... assets, hasn't he?'

'Well, yes, but no harm in reminding him.'

'No sense having them fall out in front of everyone though, is there?'

'They don't.' I give an experimental hop. 'Oh, I see what you mean. Let's keep looking, shall we?'

By the time we have found the perfect dress, I am exhausted and she has that far-away look that means she is eyeing up all the crap design features of the shopping centre, and mentally semtexing and rebuilding it. We find a coffee shop and order cappuccinos.

'You're sure it's the right dress, Becca?'

She sips at her chocolaty foam. 'I am sure. It's nice, even I can tell that.'

I pull the edge of the dress out of the bag and stroke the silk. It is heavy and matte and it drapes beautifully. It is also in my very favourite deep teal. I can't go wrong with this. For once, this is an occasion for which I am going to feel perfectly dressed.

'Thanks, Becca. I'd never have gone in that snooty little shop without you.'

She raises her eyebrows. 'I don't see why not. They want to sell their stuff, don't they?'

I look down at my faded jeans. 'Not to me, just to people like Joan Collins. That assistant's face when we walked in. Did you see it?'

'I wasn't looking specially. Have we finished now?'

'Just shoes and underwear.' I finish the last bite of my pain au chocolat as she groans.

'I'm all shopped out. Honestly, Kate, this evening was more than I do in an entire year.'

'You're always in book shops.'

'That's not the same. That's not shopping.'

'Tell you what. I can manage the shoes and underwear by myself. Meet you in Waterstones in an hour?'

She slouches gratefully off and I wander round for a while longer, picking out some silky cream underwear that actually matches. I never usually bother but this dress seems to demand it. I find some black shoes with a rather higher heel than I usually wear but Christian is tall. I will still look fragile and dainty beside him, or at least smaller than him, which will hopefully make him feel protective.

On Saturday afternoon, I have an appointment at Anton's. I finally phoned the number on the card that Marie gave me and the woman who answered said they didn't have an opening for weeks. When I reluctantly mentioned Marie's name, she said they could probably fit me in for a quick wash and cut but no highlights — so I settled for that.

When I arrive at the salon, I catch sight of the prices and gasp in horror, mentally reviewing the week's purchases so far. I sit with a magazine and wait, frantically trying to calculate how much is in my bank account after last night's shopping trip. This isn't the sort of place where you want to stand at the desk and argue, while the assistant snips up your card with a huge flourish and the perfectly-coiffed customers raise perfectly-groomed eyebrows. Eventually a man arrives and flings a rainbow coloured cape round my shoulders.

'Kris at your service, darling. How can I transform you today?'

'Erm ...' Is this guy for real? I stare at him without speaking. He has the weirdest bleached blonde and pink hair, all spiked out on one side. He had better not be planning anything like that for me. My hands fly protectively to my head and he laughs. He has very kind eyes beneath the eyebrow piercings.

'It's your hair, darling. You tell me what you're after. I am just your handyman.'

I suppress images of topiary and stare at my reflection without hope. He breaks the silence.

'What's his name?'

'Christian,' I say without meaning to but he has caught me off balance.

'What has he been up to? Off with another woman?'

'No, it's not like that at all. He'd never do that. It's just that he's going home to Denmark and he hasn't asked me to go with him — yet.'

'I see. So I need to give you a hairstyle that will knock him off his feet and make him buy you a ticket immediately?'

'Something like that.'

'Then let me at it.' He waves his scissors wildly and I dodge. 'Just kidding, my pet.' He runs his hands through my hair and grimaces. 'I'd like to slice some layers through this, give it some more bounce. And you're crying out for a fringe, just a half one. And these ends. Who cuts your hair, your flat mate?'

He laughs heartily but I ignore him. Becca only cuts it when I have messed up and can't get both sides to match. He sweeps me off to the basins and leaves me in the care of what looks like a twelve year old girl, who washes my hair so nervously that I don't have the heart to tell her the water is stone cold.

Kris combs my hair and then straps on a tool belt stuffed with enough implements for him to perform brain surgery. I watch him like a hawk as he starts to chop and chip, slice and razor. I relax when I see how little he is taking off the length. By the time he comes to the blow dry, I am almost asleep. It's been a rough week and I find the scent of the papaya volumising lotion and the roar of the dryers all around, very soothing. He finishes drying my hair, whips off the rainbow cape and spreads his hands. 'Voilà!'

I stare at myself in the mirror. It's amazing. My hair is still shoulder length but it curves gently round my chin at the front. The back, when he brings me a mirror to check, swirls into gentle waves.

'I love it. Thank you so much.' I feel tears pricking at my eyes. It feels as though someone has taken care of me, taken the trouble to give me a lift in this crappiest of all crappy weeks, and I am unbelievably grateful.

'Not a problem, my darling. You look sensational. The man's a fool if he doesn't burn his ticket and throw away his passport on the spot.'

'Just asking me to go with him would do fine.' I stand and tilt my head from side to side to see the shining waves form and reform perfectly.

He touches my forehead with a dubious finger. 'Just a suggestion — two eyebrows is the usual allowance. Better than one, don't we think?'

'Oh, yeah, I'll have a go at them.' I pick up my bag and reach for my purse.

He scribbles the price on a piece of paper. The list seems to go on and on, everything from the shampoo girl and next door's weekly food and electric bill, to replacing the state of the art curling tongs. No wonder they write it down I think, as I watch him add it up. I wouldn't be able to say the total out loud with a straight face either. He hands me the paper and I am grateful to see I have just enough in my account to pay him. I hand over my card. While he is swiping it, I search through my purse for change for a tip. I am horrified to find I only have two pound coins and a piece of chewing gum. While the receipt prints, I wonder if it would be more insulting to offer the two pounds or nothing at all. I decide that, if it was me, I'd like even a small tip so I hold out the coins.

'I'm so sorry but this is literally all I have.'

'How are you getting home?' he asks.

'Bus ... erm, walking,' I say.

He pushes the coins back into my hand and closes my fingers over them.

'You're not walking home with that hairstyle. It needs to stay perfect and not bring eternal shame on me. Keep the money and get the bus but I'll make you a deal. You come back when you get engaged and bring me a huge bottle of champagne.'

'I promise,' I say, hoping that putting it into words isn't bad luck.

I wave goodbye and walk to the bus stop, feeling my beautifully blow-dried hair swish and flip in the breeze. I have the dress and shoes, I have the hairstyle and Becca has promised to do my nails. For once in my life, I have all the bases covered. If this doesn't work, nothing ever will.

Chapter Four

We arrive outside Jeremy and Marie's at eight fifteen precisely. I don't want to look too eager but I am acutely aware that I only have this one evening to talk to Christian and put everything right, so I will have to swallow my pride and just go for it. I have dragged Becca along too, grumbling and complaining. She took a lot of persuading but I told her it was payback for me coming to her Christmas party and that I couldn't do this alone. She agreed at last but I couldn't persuade her to dress up.

'No one's going to give a stuff what I'm wearing. I don't know any of them except that awful Marie and who cares what she thinks?'

'Come as you are then,' I said grumpily. 'As long as you don't wear those old Winnie the Pooh Pyjamas.'

'Darling!' She imitated Marie's high pitched voice. 'Don't you know they're just the *latest* thing?'

She stands on the doorstep with me now and swings her carrier bag back and forth irritably.

I nudge her. 'Careful, you'll break the drinks.'

'It's only cartons of juice. Is that bloody woman going to let us in? It's freezing out here.'

She leans on the buzzer again and after a minute Marie answers. 'Hello? *Hello?*'

'Let us in you stupid woman, before we die of cold,' shouts Becca.

The phone goes dead and I wait for the door to click. Nothing happens.

'One more minute and I'm going home.' Becca aims a kick at the door and I stop her.

'The tenancy association will be out here if you don't stop that. They're always poking and prying.'

'Good, they might let us into the warm while they interrogate us. Ring again.'

'You are having some problems?' The voice behind us is amused. I swing round to find myself face to face with Christian. I had expected a few minutes to prepare myself for meeting him and I feel annoyingly flustered. His smile is as warm as ever as he hugs me and I find myself wondering if I imagined our lunch at Harry's. He turns to Becca. 'Lovely to see you again.'

'Yeah, whatever. Get the stupid cow to let us in, will you? I'm freezing my bits off out here.'

He raises his eyebrows and presses the buzzer. Marie's voice shrills out into the night, suspiciously this time.

'Hello?'

'Marie, sweetheart, there are thirsty guests on your doorstep. Will you not let them in?'

'Darling! Come on up.' She lowers her tone to what she fondly thinks of as sotto voce. 'Be careful, there was some madwoman trying to get in earlier.'

The door clicks and he holds it open for us both. I push Becca up the steps. 'Madwomen before beauty.'

When we reach the top of the stairs, the door is open, *The Space* is already full of guests and I see a huge bowl of Jeremy's special punch on the glass and steel table. I automatically step behind Christian and let him go in first. I am not sure I can face her alone. She beams at Christian.

'Sweetheart, you made it.' She leans in for a prolonged hug and runs her hands slowly down his back. She catches sight of me over his shoulder and jumps visibly.

'Kate? I didn't think ... did you two come together?' She gives Christian a suspicious look.

'No, we met on the doorstep when you were not being so hospitable.'

She looks relieved to hear that we didn't arrive as a couple. I push Becca forward. 'You remember Becca, Marie? Jeremy told me you were going to call and invite me so I thought you wouldn't mind if I brought along a guest.'

'No, I ... of course.' She beams vaguely. Then her eyes narrow as she takes in every detail of Becca's jeans, faded and torn in a DIY rather than a designer way, and topped off with a pale blue T shirt and hoodie.

'Come on in.' She turns her back on us and shepherds Christian into *The Space*, shouting at the top of her voice, 'Look who I've got, everyone — the guest of honour. Now the party can *really* start.'

I feel both proud and resentful as a roar of voices greets her announcement. If I was in a foreign city for a year, I would put serious money on it that no-one would be able to gather even a quarter this number of people at a farewell party for me, and all apparently devastated.

I take off my own coat and hang it behind the door and stand for a minute, feeling exposed and foolish. I glance quickly round the room to check that everyone is smartly dressed and for once I seem to look all right. I look round for Becca and finally see her at the far end of the room, going through the very few books on the minimalist chrome shelf. By the appalled look on her face, I can guess that Marie and Jeremy's reading tastes don't match hers.

Milla sees me standing in the middle of the room and immediately comes over. She holds my shoulders and scans my face earnestly before air kissing me.

'Super to see you again, sweets. I was so sorry to hear about you and Christian. We all were.'

Hear what about me and Christian? I wonder. And who is this '*we all*'?

'Oh well, you know,' I say awkwardly as she shows no sign of letting go. 'It's not as though Denmark is a million miles away. It's hardly more than an hour by plane.'

Her hands drop to her sides. 'But I heard ...'

'What?' I hold her gaze until her eyes drop.

'I heard that ... he'll be very busy for a while. Yes, that's it. Very busy and he probably won't make it back over here for a long time.'

Really? Is *that* what she heard? I keep my chin up and look her squarely in the eye.

'His friends will have to go over and visit him instead, won't they?'

'I suppose so.' Her eyes flick wildly round, looking for help. 'I'll just go and see if Rupe is ...' She disappears before I can speak.

I am glad I spoke up for myself. She can't possibly have heard anything that I haven't. What was between me and Christian was private and he would never break a confidence. He is as loyal to me as he expects me to be to his friends and I like him the more for it. But it's clear that both Milla and Marie have made the assumption that we have broken up for good. That's their problem. If they can't see that it is possible to have a perfectly civilised discussion and keep a relationship going even when you don't live in one another's pocket, that's too bad. And it won't be for long. I am perfectly prepared to move to Denmark as and when Christian asks me. First though, I have to nudge him into realising it is even a possibility.

I head into the kitchen in search of a drink. As the canapés are on silver trays tonight, and marked with little flags with the caterer's logo, I assume it is OK not to keep up the pretence of home cooking. Maybe not, though. Marie is peeling the cling film off a tray of mini bruschetta. When she sees me, she swings round as though she has been shot.

'Kitchen rules, Kate. How many times?'

I look round for the juice I brought. 'Sorry, just looking for a drink.'

Her face creases in annoyance as she wags one manicured talon at me. 'In *The Space*. Jeremy's running the bar.'

I back towards the door, wondering whether I ought to make another polite comment about her wonderful organisation but she spares me.

'Off you go and please don't come in here again. You have no idea of the level of sheer hard work it takes to produce food for so many people.'

'I really don't.'

I wave at her and back out. I wonder if she wants me to feel guilty that she has had such a supposedly hard day in the kitchen and all for the sake of my boyfriend. But I don't care. They could easily have met at a restaurant. Anyway, she couldn't have made it any clearer that she no longer considers Christian my boyfriend. Cats and cream spring to mind. When I finally reach him, I find Jeremy mixing cocktails and pouring shots. He looks surprised when he sees me.

'Kate, you came!'

I decide to carry the battle into his territory. 'Why does everyone seem so surprised? Of course I came. It's Christian's last night here.'

'But you and he ...'

'Have been seeing each other for eight months.' I abandon my quest for orange juice and help myself to a large glass of wine.

'But that's all over now, isn't it?'

'Because he's moving to Denmark?'

He looks puzzled. 'He told Marie ...'

I lean forward and speak as clearly as I can above the noise. 'I don't know what you think he told Marie or what she thinks he told her or what Milla thinks Rupe told everyone at work. Christian and I are the only ones who know what's going on in our relationship and he would never talk about me behind my back. Got that?'

He doesn't answer. He is looking over my shoulder. I turn to find Christian standing behind me, swaying in time to the music. He doesn't look at all perturbed. The din in here is so loud that I doubt he could have heard anything anyway.

'I came to ask the prettiest girl in the room for a dance before someone else snaps her up.'

I give Jeremy a triumphant glance. 'Hold my wine, will you, Jeremy?'

I take Christian's outstretched hand and turn into his arms. He puts his hands on my shoulders, I put my arms round his neck and we sway gently to the music. Thank goodness it's a slow song. I bury my face in his shoulder. He always smells so good. He is wearing a pink shirt tonight, open at the neck, and on him it looks great, masculine yet relaxed. I imagine Rupe wearing it, his brick red neck straining at the collar and clashing vilely with the pink. As we dance, I see a few faces turned towards us, mostly female, and I smile to myself. This will show them. Marie has emerged from the kitchen and looks as though she has bitten on a very large lemon. That's just too bad. She married Jeremy and now she is stuck with him. He might be a lot richer than Christian but I wouldn't swap with her for anything. Jeremy is boring about wine, drones on endlessly about his job and never seems to notice what his wife is up to, even when she's clearly lusting after someone else's boyfriend. Christian would never be like that, I think, snuggling closer and looking up at his face, trying to impress every line of it in my memory for the next few weeks until I see him again. He leans towards me and I see Marie's eyes narrow in frustration. I smile at her sweetly.

'Shall we go outside?' he whispers in my ear and I nod happily. He unlatches the French doors that lead to the balcony and we slip through. I close them behind us in case Marie decides to follow.

It is cold outside and I shiver in my silk dress. It felt warm enough when I was trying it on in the heat of the shopping mall but it's actually lighter than I thought. But no way will I go back in for a jacket and give Marie the chance to dive outside and satisfy her insatiable curiosity. I would never get rid of her again and this is my hour, not hers. This is my time to tell Christian how I feel and how I would give up anything and everything for us to be together. He sees me shivering and peels off his jacket without speaking. It's an intimate gesture but he doesn't wrap it carefully round my shoulders and kiss me as so often before, just passes it over and looks out across the city.

'It's beautiful, isn't it?' I want to give the conversation a romantic twist as soon as possible before the others take it into their heads to join us.

'Kate, I was chatting to Milla just now. She seems to think we are still together.'

'What did she say?' This conversation isn't going in the direction I had planned.

'Nothing much but I had the impression she thought I was treating you badly, being less than honest with you. Is that how you feel?'

'No.' I try to say it as cheerfully as possible. 'I mean, we haven't really talked about the future, have we? I thought we could just ... sort of ... see how it went. Take it one step at a time.' I pull his Hugo Boss scented jacket more closely around my shoulders.

'Kate, when we had lunch, I told you how it was. It seemed better to be honest even though you didn't want to hear it and I really don't see how I could have made it clearer. I am going back for good and we cannot continue to see each other.'

'But *why*?' I burst out. 'It's not that far and I could visit.' I could relocate there too, I want to say but even now, something stops me. The idea has to come from him. It's just the way he is.

'I think visiting is not a good idea. It was lovely while it lasted and maybe, if I had been staying ... but things have worked out differently and I think it is better for us both to go on with our separate lives.'

'But I love you.' I hate myself as soon as the words are out but I had definitely planned to say them to him sometime tonight and time is running out.

'I love you too. But I can't really see you ...'

'See me what? I can do whatever you like. What can't you see me doing?'

I could hardly be spelling harder for an invitation to join him if I went down on one knee.

'If I am being honest, it is just that I cannot see you fitting into my life in Denmark. You have your life here and it suits you. You belong here. I have my life there with all my friends and family and I don't see you having a place in that. I shall always think of our relationship here as being perfect for the time we spent together here. But it wouldn't, what do I say ... translate? So we should leave it there and keep the memories.'

'I want more than memories, Christian. I want a future.'

'So you should but it is not with me. The sooner you understand that, the less painful it will be. Now shall we go in?'

And this is the moment that I finally realise he means it. He isn't messing me around. In his mind, it's over. He is just too kind to walk away until I accept it too. I lift my chin. All I have left is the opportunity to hide how I feel, to show a little dignity and class and let him see just what he is losing.

'I bought new underwear especially for tonight,' I hiss and gesture in its general direction. '*And* shoes, *and* this dress. It cost me a fortune. And you haven't even commented on it.' I wipe my eyes on my sleeve and he grimaces and passes me a handkerchief.

'I'm sorry. It's a lovely dress, even if ...' He waits while I blow my nose and then defiantly stuff his handkerchief back into his jacket pocket.

'Even if what?'

'Nothing. It's a lovely dress.'

'I'm not moving from this spot until you tell me.'

He shrugs and scratches his ear. 'It's not very ... *you.*'

'Too classy?' I stare at him aggressively and my heart melts when he laughs and takes my hand just as he used to.

'Not too classy. Not too pretty either. But somehow it looks as if you are trying to be something that you are not.'

Great - I spend an entire month's wages on a dress and the person I wanted to win back by wearing it, doesn't even like it. My eyes fill again. He doesn't seem to notice.

'We should go in. There is a cake I have to cut, Marie says. And I should say a few words.'

'I'm not coming in.'

He takes my elbow. 'Yes, you are. I'm not leaving you out here all alone.'

'Don't worry, it's the first floor. I'd probably only break my legs if I jumped.'

'But such nice legs. What a waste.' He pulls me into his arms and kisses me briefly. 'I won't forget you, Kate.'

I push him away. 'Yes, you will. You'll forget me as soon as some blonde Scandinavian tart bats her eyelashes at you. You're a rat, Christian. You've had your fun and now you're going to swan off somewhere else and start all over again.'

I pause for breath. He doesn't look angry, just amused at my outburst. I cast around for something to throw at him, some comment that will really hurt. I move to the door, stop with my hand on the doorknob and turn.

'By the way, that stupid cake you're going in to cut now, the one all covered with roses and Danish flags. It's *shop* bought, so there! And so are the canapés.'

I don't wait for his reply but push my way through the suddenly silent crowd. I don't care that they're all staring. I don't care that the tears are pouring down my face. I will never see any of them again anyway.

I pull my coat from the stand and walk straight past Jeremy to the front door. Becca is there, not doing anything, just leaning against the door, looking bored. She straightens up when she sees me. 'Come on, hon. I've got a taxi.'

'How did you know?'

'It's been out there all evening just in case.'

She grabs my arm and steers me out of the door. Jeremy follows us, looking worried. She stares him down.

'Fabulous party, angel. We *must* do it again sometime.'

And she marches me on and down the stairs, where I fall sobbing into the waiting taxi.

Chapter Five

I wake about two o'clock on Sunday afternoon. I didn't sleep until after it began to get light. I lay without crying, staring at the ceiling and wondering how a chapter of my life could have been so casually ripped out without me having any control over it. That is one of the worst things about this whole sorry mess - I don't seem to get a say in any of it. Christian made up his mind without telling me, made plans for the rest of his life without including me and then announced them as a done deal. In fact, everyone else seemed to have more idea about what was happening than I did. A little voice whispers that, had I not downed so much wine and then three glasses of brandy at the dinner party and so been oblivious to his speech, it might have helped. And he did try to make things clear at *Oodles of Noodles* but I didn't want to hear. I tell the little voice to shut up. However clearly he might have tried to tell me we were over, the fact remains that he didn't try to talk to me first or ask me what I wanted for our future, so I have every right to feel angry.

Arrogant, domineering ... my thoughts stop there because, whatever he may or not be, arrogant and domineering isn't it. He knows what he wants and he sets out to get it but he is never unkind, always thinks the best of people, never wants to hurt anyone and is happy for everyone else to go after what they want. Apart from me of course. All I want is him and that's the one thing I can't have. It seems that there is a line drawn around him that I can't cross and no amount of pleading on my part is going to change that. Tears begin to leak from my eyes at this thought. As if on cue, Becca puts her head round the door. She is holding two cups of coffee and I nod silently. She perches on the end of the bed and hands one to me.

'At least you haven't got a stonking hangover to deal with too. Small mercies.'

'I wish I did have. It might take my mind off the rest of it. And stop me remembering last night too clearly.' I break off and grimace as I think back to standing with Christian on the balcony, practically waving my new underwear at him, pleading with him to reconsider.

'You'd only have to face it in the end. Better get it over with now.'

She stretches her legs out on the bed and wraps her hands around her steaming mug. She isn't being unkind, even I know that. It's just the way Becca works. She looks at the facts, lists them, analyses them and then either acts or moves on. For the first time, I wish I was more like her. It doesn't usually seem as though she has as much fun as I do but, just now, I would settle for the less pain. I brush my eyes with my hand and take a gulp of my coffee. I look at her suspiciously. 'Becca, is this Irish?'

'Just a tiny bit.'

'How can it be a tiny bit Irish?' I demand.

'How should I know? Isle of Man, maybe? I thought you needed it. Just a kick-start.'

'Whatever.' It is actually very warming and I drain my mug without arguing further.

'What are we doing today?' she asks as I hand her the mug.

'Doing? I don't know what you're doing but I'm lying in bed and thinking about everything I've lost and wondering what I did wrong and why I'm such a total loser.'

'Not a hope.'

She grasps my wrist and pulls me upright. She may look small and fragile but Becca is surprisingly strong. She also rarely loses arguments. She just powers on with her viewpoint until people crumble. To be fair, she always sifts and sorts the facts first, so her viewpoints have a rationale to them, unlike mine, which I pull from the air and defend to a greater or lesser extent, depending on whom I am talking to. In that respect, she is more like Christian but he is far more charming and persuades people into accepting his point of view by sheer force of personality and people skills. Becca would rather die than charm anyone so you have to really get to know her as I do to appreciate her qualities, her doggedness, her total loyalty and the soft centre she would rather die than let anyone suspect is there.

Today though, it's not happening. She is not going to persuade me to get up and face the day, to pretend it's no different to any other one. I don't know exactly what time Christian is flying but I know the airline he always uses. As soon as I can get rid of her, I am going to look up the flight times and find out what time he is leaving. Then I am going to pull the duvet over my head and howl as I think of him boarding the plane, slinging his bag into the overhead compartment, smiling at the stewardess, easing his long legs under the seat in front and lying back, doubtless thinking more of what lies ahead than what he has left behind. He will be planning, making lists, looking forward to meeting his friends and family again. I picture a huge crowd at Copenhagen airport, all gathered round the arrival gates with balloons and champagne, celebrating just as wildly as everyone at the party yesterday was mourning.

I let my mind wander for a moment and imagine a different and much better scenario where he follows the crowds reluctantly to the gate and down the ramp and is just in the act of swinging his bag into the locker when he stops. His face changes and he makes his way swiftly back down the aisle. Perhaps I should be at the airport all ready to meet him. As he starts to apologise, I lay a finger on his lips. 'It doesn't matter. I know you were foolish and inconsiderate and made a terrible decision because you didn't listen to me but none of that matters any more. It's you and me who matter from now on, you and me and our wonderful future together.'

He is just sweeping me into his arms when Becca nudges me. 'Yeah, we're spending the day together, like it or not. And nowhere near Heathrow.'

'I have no idea what you mean. I'm having a shower and then getting back into bed. Sorry, I know you mean well but I'm staying in bed today. There is no way I am going out with you and pretending that nothing has happened.'

I put my nose in the air and stalk off to the bathroom. I slop back after my shower, wrapped in a towel and yawning, to find my bed completely stripped and my laptop cable and battery missing.

'Becca, what the hell ...'

'Too late. The sheets are in the washing machine with your pyjamas and you're not using your laptop today. We're going out, so get dressed.'

'Over my dead body.'

Half an hour later I follow her out onto the street. It is the most glorious autumn day, which only adds insult to injury. An occasion like this demands thick fog and preferably a thunderstorm. I slouch along the road after her, not speaking. She ignores my mood.

'Are you hungry?'

'No.'

'You must be. You didn't eat anything at the party.'

'What are you now, my mother?'

'I'm hungry. Come and keep me company while I have something.'

'If I must.'

I glance at my watch. We push in through the revolving doors of the shopping centre and for a moment I consider letting the door swing round and carry me out again. With so many bookshops on this floor, Becca will never even notice. But I follow her in. Even I can see that I'm behaving like a petulant five year-old, when all she's trying to do is help me. She ignores the bookshops, which in itself is above and beyond the call of friendship, and makes straight for the food hall. We sit at a white plastic table and she pulls out her purse. 'What would you like? It's on me.'

'Honestly, Becca, I couldn't swallow a thing.'

'OK.' She pushes her way through the crowds and comes back ten minutes later with a tray of sweet and sour pork and two cappuccinos.

I watch her cut the first piece. 'That looks nice.'

'Buy your own.' She waves towards the stand and I shuffle off sheepishly. She's tough. I sit back down with my plate and delve into the pork. After the first few mouthfuls, I must admit that I feel better.

'Thanks, Becca.'

'There's nothing to thank me for. I'm sorry you're feeling so let down.'

'Not just let down. My heart is broken.' I wave a dramatic hand at the crowds around me. 'Look at them, all getting on with their lives. I'll never be like them again. There's a part of me that's always going to be missing. I'm ... maimed, I suppose.'

She lays down her plastic cutlery and looks around dispassionately. 'I don't see that's such a problem. I can't see anyone here who I'd particularly want to be.'

'That's just you, isn't it? You do your own thing and you don't care about anyone else.'

'That's a bit harsh. I care about people. I just don't want to change myself to be like them.'

I struggle to explain to her what I mean. 'Look, it's like this. This is me.' I put a square of pork on my plate. 'And this is Christian.' I pick the most perfectly-shaped piece and put it on her empty plate. 'And this,' – I take the salt shaker and pour a stream of salt in a wavy line across the table between the two plates – 'is the ocean that now divides us.'

I wipe my eyes and stare at her. Surely now she will understand.

'I hope you're going to clear that up when you've finished making such a mess.' A middle aged lady in a flowered tabard stops wiping the table next to us and glares at me. 'I'd expect that sort of behaviour from some of the yobs we get in here but you two should know better.'

'Sorry.' I hastily sweep the salt into my hand and dump it on top of Christian's head.

'Minimum wage I get and then people like you make a deliberate mess.' She gives her table one last, vindictive swipe and stalks off.

'Does it really matter if there's an ocean between you?' asks Becca. 'He's made it quite clear what he wants and it would be quite a lot harder for you if he was still around. You might not go to Marie's any more but you'd be bound to bump into him when you visited me at the office or went to a café or something. That would be far worse, seeing him all the time, perhaps with someone else.'

She doesn't pull her punches. She never has done. I ignore the ridiculous suggestion that he would be seeing someone else if he was still living in London. He only dumped me because he was leaving. Otherwise we would still be together. I try to explain it to her yet again.

'Don't you see? If he was still around, there would be a chance to talk, explain things, show him what he was missing.'

'Wasn't that what last night was all about? And that didn't seem to work out very well.'

'It was too rushed, that's why. He was in turmoil. Look at it from his point of view — he was stressed because his employers suddenly announced he had to move country and he had to pack and say goodbye to all his friends. It can't have been easy for him. So he had no time to think about us and our relationship, let alone make plans for our future. It probably just seemed the kindest thing not to involve me in all that turmoil, to cut the knot altogether rather than string me along and hurt me. That's at least as plausible as what you're saying. What do you think?'

'I think you'd have a great future writing romantic fiction. Kate, he's always known he was going back one day. He's had plenty of time think about what he wants in the future. He's been seeing you for eight months. That's long enough to have made up his mind whether or not you and he have a future. He's leaving on his own. Doesn't that tell you something?'

'You wouldn't be like this if it was Jon,' I say huffily. 'And I'd be a sight more understanding.'

'You want me to string you along with pretty stories about how he's going to pine for you and realise he's missed you and how he'll jump on a plane home and rush into your arms?'

'Not exactly but it's quite possible that once he's settled, had some space and got his head in order, he might have second thoughts. I think I'd be crazy to give up hope straight away.'

'It would be more logical and less painful.'

'Love isn't logic.' I look at her smugly, having scored this point.

'Which is probably why half of all marriages break up. He's gone and he's not coming back so he's not going to get all these so-called chances to see what he's missed. There's nothing you can do about that so the sooner you accept that and move on, the better it will be for you. You can't change yourself, and neither should you, and you definitely can't change the situation.'

I stare at her in shock as the point of what she has just said sinks in. She is right that I shouldn't change myself. Even I know that isn't the answer. But it might just be possible to change the situation. Why didn't that occur to me earlier?

'Thanks, Becca. You're a good friend.'

She frowns at me. 'I know that look. Have you been listening to a word I've said?'

'I really have. I heard all of it and it made perfect sense. You're very logical.'

She pushes her chair back and stands, still looking suspicious. 'If you're sure. What now?'

I beam at her happily. 'How about looking in some of the bookshops?'

'Really?'

'Yes, you came out clothes shopping with me. I'd like to come book shopping with you. I need something good to read to take my mind off things while I'm getting over him.'

Her suspicious look is fading and I see the familiar glow in her eyes, the one that most people get when they see an amazing handbag or pair of shoes. I can see that her mind is drifting away from me and my immediate problems, which is good. Until I get home and think things through properly, I'm not that keen on discussing them with anyone else.

'If you're sure, there's a new biography of Mandela that I wouldn't mind taking a look at.'

'Great, I'm all yours.'

I pick up my bag and link my arm through hers. Before we leave, I lean over and move the piece of pork that represents me, right to the very edge of the plate, where I leave it to consider whether or not to dive off the edge.

Chapter Six

I wake on Monday morning with a lightness in my limbs and a feeling of energy I haven't had since Christian broke the news of his departure. I throw some bread into the toaster, flick the kettle switch and lean against the counter, humming and mentally ticking off items on the list I made last night. Becca wanders in and looks at me suspiciously.

'Why are you so cheerful?'

'Another day, another set of opportunities,' I say as I pour the milk into my coffee. I sound like the less grumpy nuns from the Sound of Music but I don't care. I grab my toast and sit down at the table to scoop out the last of the raspberry jam.

She frowns. 'Don't put the empty jar back in the cupboard.'

'Sorry, I'll pick up some more on the way home.'

'I'll be late tonight. Some new client who can't make it in until about 7 p.m. Jerk!'

'What are you going to wear?'

She looks down at her jeans and open-necked shirt in surprise. 'This. Why do you ask?'

'Well, you know, a new client. I thought you'd have to get all smartened up.'

'This *is* me smartened up.'

She looks offended so I backtrack quickly and give her an encouraging nod. There is no sense in alienating her. It will be bad enough when I have to tell her what I'm planning. She won't mince her words and I am not looking forward to it. But she'll come round. She always does.

I dump my plate and mug in the dishwasher and make for the front door.

'I'll be back about nine if you need to talk about Christian or cry or anything,' she calls after me and I feel guilty again. She is the best friend I have ever had and I feel terrible about deceiving her. But it's not totally a deception, I tell myself as I head for the bus stop. It's just not worrying her unnecessarily about things which may never happen.

I arrive at work twenty minutes early and make straight for Personnel. It is just my bad luck that only Julie is there at this time of the morning. She is irritable and sour and seems to make it her personal object to obstruct every request anyone makes. I smile at her anyway. No response.

'Is Mr Pearson in yet?'

'Nah.'

That's typical Julie. *Nah*. No attempt to find out how she might be able to help or to offer further information.

'I'd like to make an appointment to see him, please.'

'I don't have his calendar.'

'Could you get it?'

'Not until the computer's back up.'

The Cinnamon Snail

'When will that be?'

She sighs heavily. 'I don't know, do I? When the computer man gets here.'

'Oh, you mean it's down?'

'Catch on quick, don't you?'

I would like to lean across the desk and pull her hair hard but that is not going to get me my appointment so I smile at her again.

'Any chance you could write my appointment request on a piece of paper and put it into the computer when it's fixed and then send me an email?'

'All appointments go in the computer direct. We're not in the dark ages.'

I give up and turn away. 'Thanks, you've been very ... something.'

I arrive on the third floor and look round the electrical goods with distaste. I can't imagine how I have worked here for two years. Christian always said I was wasting my time. But, after graduating with a degree in English, I looked around for ages for these rosy opportunities that automatically come to all graduates and make their massive student loans worthwhile. By the time I had applied for every job in London that specified it needed a graduate, I was running out of money and was pleased to find temporary Christmas work in Sawley Brothers, selling electrical and white goods. When they offered me a permanent position, my finances were in no state for me to refuse and I have been here ever since, growing more disillusioned with the job market and wondering whether I ought to take another loan and go back to university to get a teaching qualification. So far, the thought of even more debt has put me off - that and seeing some of the children who live nearby, as they walk home after school. They would have me for breakfast. Once Christian came on the scene, I put everything on hold. I spent all my spare time with him and wouldn't have had time for another course even if I was convinced I wanted to do one.

So I have hung around for far too long in limbo, selling useless electrical appliances to people who think they will make their disappointing lives better. But no longer. If Christian's departure has done anything, it has galvanised me into action. I lay awake last night and had a vision of myself coming up to retirement, still selling dishwashers and electric carving knives to rude customers. Even worse, developing the same sort of enthusiasm for them that Caroline, my floor manager, possesses. You might not think it was possible to get excited about a fridge whose door can be hung either way round, but you would be wrong. She went wild when I showed her a new delivery of bread makers that can also make jam and I honestly feared for her blood pressure the evening the rep came round to show us the electric egg boilers. My conscience sometimes pricks me sluggishly as I see her flitting round the department, straightening, inspecting, memorising all the amazing new features. I would love to have a job that I felt so passionately about. But it is never going to be this one, so handing in my notice will actually be doing her a favour. She can stop handing me citrus juicers with a hopeful look as though this time, finally, a low-energy light bulb will go on in my head and I'll have a juicing eureka moment.

I wander along to the staffroom and pull my overall from my locker. Someone had the bright idea of giving the sales staff in our department black overalls patterned with bright yellow bolts of lightning. Caroline, instead of ripping them up and stuffing them into the nearest food processor as any normal person would have done, was delighted with them and even added a few design suggestions of her own as accessories. I glare now at my stupid gold badge, also in the shape of a streak of lightning, that bears the motto she thought up - '*We'll serve you quick as a flash!*' — and head out onto the shop floor.

'I was hoping you'd be early. And *jolly* well done for that, by the way.' Caroline appears from behind a bank of fridge freezers. She has always reminded me of a PE teacher on speed and she thinks her staff thrives on praise, even at eight thirty on a Monday morning. Personally, I thrive on silence and very low lighting.

'Good morning. Did you have a nice weekend?' I ask her, determined to be as nice as possible during my notice period, to make up for the two years of unenthusiastic grunts I have directed toward her. She looks a little surprised but smiles widely and shows me her gums.

'Super, thanks, and an even better Monday. Look at these!' She gestures widely to a stand in the centre of the department and I follow her gaze.

'Vacuum cleaners.'

'Oh, you tease. What are you like?' She pulls me by the elbow until I follow her across the floor to the stand. 'Bagless *and* ultra-low energy consumption. They didn't think we'd get a delivery until next week but I pushed and pushed and kept ringing and in the end they switched our store to the top of the delivery list. Doesn't it just show you?'

What someone will do just to shut you up? I slap myself mentally. It's only a month. I can manage to be nice for a month — maybe.

My resolve wears thin over the following few hours. In between customers, she keeps pushing glossy leaflets into my hand, exhorting me to read them and memorise the star selling points. She even tries to make me take one with me to my coffee break.

'The rest of the staff is going to be *so* interested. Remind them all about their staff discounts. That ought to do it.'

'I think I'll leave it to you,' I call over my shoulder as I rush away. 'You do that sort of thing so much better than I do.'

I leave her standing there, looking gratified. I wish I had been a bit nicer to her these past two years. It clearly doesn't take much. When I get back, I'll ask her to explain the massage chair settings again.

I queue up in the staff restaurant and pay for my coffee and Danish. I'm pleased to notice that the word *Danish* on a packet doesn't reduce me to tears. I'm making progress. I sit at a table with the new guy from accounts.

'How's mad Caroline?' he asks through a powdery bite of sausage roll.

'Oh, don't call her that. She's just a bit over-enthusiastic. She's got these new vacuum cleaners. You go back to accounts through our department, don't you? Can you just stop for a second and admire them? Tell her that you're thinking about buying one.'

He snorts a fresh shower of pastry crumbs across the table. 'Yeah, that'll happen. Last time I hoovered my flat was when my parents came for Christmas.'

'Go on. Just take a look and say how nice they are.'

'D'you want to go clubbing tonight?'

'No, thanks, I'm going out with my boyfriend,' I lie.

'Oh, well.' He bunches up his plastic wrapper and looks around for a bin. I take it from him.

'I'll do that. You go and admire.'

I come back onto the shop floor to find Caroline beaming. 'You'll never guess what? James in accounts just stopped by. He couldn't take his eyes off the new cleaners. I told you, these will just sell themselves.'

I nod and smile and the morning passes. As soon as it's time for lunch, I go back to Personnel and ask Daisy if I can see Mr Pearson.

'Is it urgent?' she asks and I wave an envelope at her.

'Don't tell anyone,' I whisper, 'but I'm handing in my notice.'

She takes the envelope and grins. 'You need to give that to me, not Mr Pearson. Sorry to break it to you, love, but he probably doesn't even know who you are. I'll deal with this, get your forms and things ready and you can pick them up tomorrow morning.'

'Oh, er, thanks.'

It all seems a bit of an anti-climax to be honest. I wasn't exactly expecting Mr Pearson to beg me to stay or to tell me that the future of Sawley Brothers' electrical sales hangs on my expertise and practical know-how, but a few expressions of regret would have been nice.

'Got a better job, have you?' asks Daisy, skimming through my letter and filing it.

'No, nothing like that. It's just that my boyfriend has moved to Copenhagen and so ...'

'Ooh, you lucky thing. I love Belgium, me.' The phone rings and she gives me an encouraging wave, mouthing, 'See you tomorrow.'

That was a damp squib. I hope Becca takes the news just as well. I have a nasty feeling that she won't. Just to give myself the best possible chance, I clean the kitchen, open a bottle of her favourite red and order two pizzas for nine o'clock.

By the time her key finally clicks in the lock at ten past, I have had two glasses of the wine and am feeling ready to face her.

'What a complete arse,' she says as she dumps her bag and coat in the hall. 'Stupid man wanted a whole office designed for about a quarter of what we charge. 'Try an internet download,' I told him. They have some great programmes for designing square rooms and square windows for square people.'

'You didn't really?'

She yawns widely and slumps at the kitchen table. 'Why not? He could have looked up our prices before he wasted my time. What's on this pizza?'

'I've got one Hawaiian and one cheese and bacon.'

'It'll do if you couldn't find anything more interesting.'

She pours a glass of wine and flips a piece of pizza in half. I wait until her mouth is full.

'I had an interesting day.'

'Caroline finally stuck her finger in a socket, did she?' She reaches for another piece.

'She's not that bad.' I wonder if I have really been that mean about Caroline over the years.

'OK, what happened?'

I lift me chin and breathe deeply. 'I handed in my notice.'

She chews for a minute. 'Why?'

I am taken aback. I had expected an explosion. But Becca is nothing if not fair minded and I recognise her *marshalling all the facts* face. The difficulty is that none of the facts are going to lead to us agreeing on my plan. The best I can hope for is a reluctant acceptance.

'I thought about what you've been saying to me for years. This job isn't leading anywhere and I'm not using my degree.' That ought to work. She's very pro further education.

'No, you're not. But I suspect you're not going back to college?'

I wave this aside. 'Student loan to pay first. But I've been thinking. I really ought to be planning for the future and broadening my outlook, trying new things and places. Those things would all make me more employable.'

She ignores my hopeful smile. 'And where exactly is all this broadening going to take place?'

'I thought ... Denmark?'

It's out and she can take her best shot. It's not as though it's any of her business so I don't really care. But I brace anyway for the withering criticism.

'Is there anything I could say that would change your mind?' She pushes away the empty box and pours another glass of wine.

'No, not really.'

'OK.' She seems to drift off for a moment.

'You're not angry?'

'For goodness sake ...'

'I mean, upset?' I amend.

'Would it make any difference if I were?'

'I'd hate it.'

'You'd better stop worrying about other people pretty quickly if you're going to do this.'

'I suppose.'

'I don't need your rent. I probably won't even advertise the room, so it'll still be there if you need it.'

'You're a star, Becca, but don't get into difficulties over it.'

'I won't.'

'I'll be here another month.'

'I supposed you would.'

I relax a little. It hasn't gone as badly as I thought but it doesn't feel right for Becca not to offer an opinion but to sit there so calmly. It feels as though the natural order of the universe has been turned upside down, even if it is to my advantage. I look her in the eye. 'What do you really think?'

'You need a lobotomy.'

'Right.' I settle back in my chair, feeling better.

The month passes increasingly quickly. When he left, it felt like an age before I could possibly see Christian again and I tried not to think about it. But the days begin to spin by ever faster as I realise how much there is to do, until suddenly the last week is here and I am trying to hold back the hours with both hands, as panicked as a child who has broken something expensive and is waiting for their parents to return home.

I am finishing work on Friday and during the morning I become gradually aware that Caroline is planning something. She keeps sending me to other departments with truly bizarre errands. Even I could come up with better excuses to get rid of me. But I use the time to say goodbye to the people she sends me to speak to and to avoid learning the specifications of the automatic pasta maker that almost sent Caroline into orbit when it arrived on the shelves this morning.

At three o'clock, I say goodbye to Jess in children's toys.

'Tell Caroline no, we don't happen to have any spare filters for the display tumble dryer,' she grins.

'She'll be devastated. Well, I'll be seeing you.'

'Sooner than you might expect.' She winks and races off to separate two tussling children before they rip the neck off the giant giraffe.

The bell goes at five fifteen to warn the last customers that we will be closing soon. I sell what I profoundly hope is my last ever electric can opener and Caroline appears behind me.

'Why don't you go and ... er, change to go home now?' Her voice is higher than ever and her cheeks are pink. 'I can manage the last few customers.'

'OK, I'll do that.' I walk stiffly away, trying to look casual and unsuspecting but feeling like some terrible actor from a straight to video movie.

I give her twenty minutes. I change into my jeans and sweater, check in my locker for the usual loose change and half eaten packets of toffees, slam it for the last time and walk out of the changing room. I make my way back onto the shop floor, wondering what on earth she has planned. I wouldn't put it past her to have arranged a demonstration of heated towel rails just to cheer me up on my last evening. I recoil from the thought of Caroline in a tiny cheerleader's skirt, zooming into the department on an electric hostess trolley, juggling blenders. The floor is suspiciously empty and the lights are out. They are never out. I start to walk towards the door as slowly as possible, to give her a chance to do whatever it is she insists on doing. I only make it as far as the countertop dishwashers when the lights go back on and I hear Caroline's excited voice.

'Surpriiiiise!'

She is joined by a few rather unenthusiastic cries of *'Surprise'* and I turn to find her bounding towards me, beaming. I am rather touched to see that her eyes are full of tears.

'Your face, you should have seen it. Totally priceless, wasn't it everyone?'

A few people nod and I pin on a smile and prepare to be jolly.

'You lot! I had no idea that something like this was being planned.'

Something like what exactly, I wonder, looking quickly round the department in case there is a stripper about to jump out of the 10kg washing machine. Caroline points to the enormous cake perched next to the till.

'We've got you a cake in the shape of a café sandwich press. I made it myself. It was the first thing you ever sold unsupervised.'

I am glad she has told me what it is instead of making me guess. It is flat and square and white, which doesn't narrow things down much as far as electrical goods are concerned. But I am incredibly touched that she would remember the first thing I sold under her anxious eyes.

'It's wonderful, Caroline.' I finger the liquorice wire stuck onto the back of the cake and admire the slice of marzipan emerging from the interior.

'Who is she, exactly?' I hear one of the men ask his companion and Caroline frowns him down.

'We've all contributed to a farewell gift and it was left to me to choose it.'

A foot spa, I bet myself, or a toaster oven. Please let it not be a trouser press. Christian gets all his stuff dry-cleaned.

She hands me a large, uneven parcel and I rip it open gingerly. It is a beautiful bright red heated throw and I beam in relief.

'I hear it's very cold in Denmark in the winter.' She looks at me anxiously.

I keep a straight face. 'I hear that too. It's absolutely perfect. You couldn't have chosen better.' I really mean it and I hug her warmly.

'Can we go yet?' asks Megan from haberdashery. 'Only, I'm meeting Pete.'

'Don't forget your cake.' Caroline slices it into chunks and wraps one in a piece of kitchen roll.

'Cheers.' Megan waves at me. 'Bye then ... erm ...'

'Kate. See you.'

The others disappear as quickly as possible with their cake and I help Caroline clear up.

I produce a small, wrapped parcel from my bag. 'That was so nice of you. This is just a little something to say thanks for putting up with me.'

She wells up again. 'Don't say that. You've been lovely. Far nicer than the last man they gave us.'

If I've been far nicer, I wonder who on earth they landed her with before.

'Go on then, open it. You can change it if you like.'

I had thought of buying her a necklace or some earrings but decided in the end to stick to an electrical theme just to be on the safe side.

'It's an electric flosser,' I say awkwardly as she stares at it in silence. 'I didn't think you had one yet.'

'An interdental cleaner,' she breathes. 'I've had my eye on these for ages. How did you know, you clever thing?'

'Lucky guess, I suppose,' I mumble. It was actually the only thing in the shop with a plug that I hadn't heard her say she had already bought.

'I love it. I'll always think of you when I'm ...'

'Spitting?'

'Silly.' She pushes my shoulder as we head towards the lift. 'It's something to make my life a little easier, just like you've always done, even if you didn't realise it.'

'I'm glad. I hope they find you someone much better to replace me.'

'If they were that good, they'd send them somewhere else.'

She presses the button in serene unconsciousness of what she has just said, and I hide a smile.

As an epitaph to my time at Sawley Brothers, it is probably as appropriate as anything.

Chapter Seven

I am leaving for Copenhagen on Monday morning and the weekend is pretty much taken up with last minute arrangements. I decide to leave a lot of my stuff at Becca's until I am more settled. It is such a short flight that I expect to be back for Christmas and I can collect some more things then. On the Sunday evening, Becca gives me the address of Christian's office.

'I don't like this one little bit,' she warns me. 'If it weren't for the fact you could easily find it on the Internet, I wouldn't give it to you.'

'Don't be such a misery. It's not as though anyone could blame you for anything I might do.'

'Christian could.'

'Since when have you cared about what he thinks? You don't even like him.'

'That's not fair. I said I didn't fancy him and you seemed to take huge offence at the thought. But he's OK on the whole.

He's a nice guy and he's always been friendly enough to me. I certainly don't think he deserves any of this.'

'Any of what?' I roll up the red throw and scrunch it into the last remaining crevice in my suitcase.

'Being stalked.'

I look up from where I am sitting on my case, trying to force the zip shut.

'Stalked? That's a bit dramatic, isn't it? If it was George Clooney, it might be stalking but I've been going out with Christian for nearly a year. How is that stalking?'

'How is it not? Would you be going anywhere near Denmark if it wasn't for him?'

'Maybe not but I've been thinking for a while that I'd like to travel more and see the world while I'm still ...' I stop abruptly, hoping she won't notice the unfinished sentence.

'Single,' she supplies, reaching round and dragging the zip shut. 'Now, that I *could* see. If you took a year off and travelled a bit before deciding what you wanted to do, I'd support that. But that's not what you're doing, is it? You're going to Denmark simply to hang around vaguely in the hope that Christian might notice you and change his mind.'

'You make it sound so pathetic. If you want to put it another way, I'm off to pursue my dreams, to snatch at my last chance of happiness. I'm taking risks and giving up everything to follow my heart.'

'Yeah, giving up white goods and electrical appliances. What a sacrifice.'

She straightens up and looks at me with something like pity and it touches a nerve. I glare at her. 'How about you? What have you given up to follow your heart? How about you chasing your dreams for once, without being so hopelessly stuck in society's conventions?'

'Kate, architecture *is* my dream. It always has been.' She looks at me in amusement and my eyes drop. OK, bad example but what has she ever risked in the pursuit of happiness?

'Maybe that's so, but what about Jon? You haven't risked anything to follow that dream.'

'Give it up, hon. I'm quite happy as I am. What will be, will be. I suppose I could go and sit outside his house every morning and stare at him when he comes out. Do you think he'd notice me then?'

I laugh in spite of myself. 'OK, you do it your way and I'll do it mine. The difference is that you have no idea what it would really be like to be with Jon, whereas I've had a relationship with Christian and I know exactly what I've lost.'

'I can live with my situation. Go on then, weigh it.'

I shove the case onto the bathroom scales and wince as the needle shoots up more than six kilograms over the luggage limit.

'What are you going to take out?' she asks.

I shrug. 'Nothing, I've only got the bare essentials as it is. Those scales are crap anyway. Every time I weigh myself they register way more than I really am. I did that low fat diet for a whole week before last year's Christmas party and they said I'd put on a kilo. That couldn't possibly be right so I'd say they weigh about, what ... twenty percent over?'

'Whatever. Let's hope the airline scales do too. Want to go out?'

'Why not? There's nothing left to do until I pack my hand luggage tomorrow morning and I don't want to sit here all evening and stare at the walls.'

'I could model my pyjamas for you,' she offers and I laugh.

'Save them for Jon. He might be the type.'

We go round the corner to *Grape To See You*. It is a would-be cutting-edge little wine bar that is entirely out of place in our neighbourhood. We are more of a burger and kebab locality. But there is almost never anyone there so we are sure of a quiet drink.

Phil waves at us as we enter. 'Laydeez!'

'Two glasses of champagne, please,' says Becca.

'Pushing the boat out, aren't you? What's the occasion?'

'I'm moving away,' I break in quickly, before she has a chance to say anything shaming about stalking.

'No, that's awful. You two are my best customers.'

'It's not saying much,' says Becca.

He shrugs. 'Things will look up. It always takes a while to get established. Go and find a table and I'll bring it over.'

We sit at a corner table and I stare around. 'I'll miss it here.'

'It's still not too late.'

'I won't miss it that much. Just think, this time next week I'll be ordering a drink at some trendy little bar in Copenhagen.'

'In what language?'

'Christian says everyone there speaks English. But I've already found a language school. It's free.'

'Aren't you jumping the gun a bit? Why don't you see how it pans out first?'

'I don't need to see how it pans out. If Christian and I get back together, I'll be there permanently and I'll need to speak the language. I've learned one phrase already.'

'Hit me.'

'Jeg elsker dig.'

'Oh, no, don't tell me …'

'*I love you.*' I grin at her bit shamefacedly. Maybe it is jumping the gun a bit but I want to be prepared when he finally comes to his senses. And the shock of seeing me might just make him realise what he has been missing.

'It could come in handy getting that drink if you run short of kroner. Speaking of drinks ...'

Phil arrives and places the two champagne glasses in front of us. 'On the house. Good luck with the move.'

'Phil, you'll never make a profit if you keep giving away drinks.' Becca pushes a note into his hand and he nods.

'That wasn't very gracious,' I hiss at her once he's gone.

'He's got a failing business. He can't let his heart rule his head like that.'

I ignore the not-so-subtle subtext. 'I thought it was a lovely gesture.'

We sip the champagne and I laugh. 'He didn't let his heart rule his head. He's given us the really crappy stuff.'

She drains her glass. 'Phil, over here. Refills, please and none of this rubbish next time.'

He grins and reaches into the fridge. I watch the cork fly high into the air and wonder if I should keep it as a memento of my last ever evening in London. She follows my gaze.

'Don't even think about it. You're way overweight on your luggage. Anyway, you don't want to be taking along junk that you don't need.'

'True, I'm starting a completely new life. Aren't you going to make a toast?'

She stares down at the pale foam creaming over her glass and down the stem. 'I wouldn't know what to wish you.'

'How hard is it to make a toast, Becca? Why not wish me love, everlasting happiness, success with the man of my dreams ...'

'And a whole stack of Mills and Boons? No, I'll drink to you finding your way.'

I pull a face but drink anyway. It isn't the most enthusiastic toast ever but she was never one for words. Anyway, Christian *is* my way so we are on the same page really. I drain my glass in one gulp and think of his eyes and his smile and the feel of his finger tracing my face before he kisses me. I'm not really giving up anything in making this journey. I'm losing nothing and gaining everything.

I set my mobile to wake me at some unholy hour and it breaks into an uneasy dream where I am swimming across the North Sea with the Danish coastline receding further and further with each stroke. I am going down for the third time when the alarm shrieks in my ear and I thump at it. I don't want to wake Becca. She offered to come to the airport but I refused, telling her I wanted to do this by myself. It was partly true but I was more worried that her disapproval would cloud my departure and I want everything to be positive today. It's a whole new chapter in my life and I need to feel energised and excited by it.

I tiptoe to the shower and then pack my hand luggage. I put on my thick winter coat, even though it is bright and clear outside. It will be colder over there. It also means I can put two very large paperbacks into the pockets and not have them weighed as carry on. I take one last look round the room where I have spent the last two years. It has few memories of Christian. He rarely stayed here overnight. Why would he, when he had a gorgeous flat with an outsize Jacuzzi and a balcony overlooking the water? But it has happy memories of the year before he arrived, memories of me and Becca when I first came to London. We have had some great times here.

I shut the front door very quietly and set off towards the bus stop. As I round the corner, I take one last look back and am almost sure I see the corner of Becca's curtain twitch. If she is there, she doesn't wave. She's an oddball. She's impossible to predict, refuses to do anything that anyone else expects of her and is totally maddening. But she is also the best friend I have ever had and now, as her window disappears from sight, I feel completely alone. I lift my chin and force myself to smile as I think of Christian. Once we are back together, he might be open to the possibility of coming back to live in London and then I can see Becca again. But that's all for the future. Right now, all that matters is seeing him and getting this whole mess sorted out.

I take the bus to the coach station and board the coach for Stansted. It's quite a hike but the flights were so much cheaper from there that I had no choice. I have just enough money in my savings account to get me through the first month. After that, I need to find a job and somewhere to live. Or to have moved in with Christian, says a little voice, but I'm not taking anything for granted, whatever Becca may think. I want Christian to see me standing on my own two feet and coping alone in a foreign country. That way, he might be able to see me fitting into his life.

I wait apprehensively in the check in queue at the airport, inching my case further and further forward. When I get to the front, I squat down and heave it onto the belt, trying to look as though it is almost empty. The woman looks at my red face in amusement and then at the scales.

'You're a bit overweight there, love,' she says and I stare at her, affronted, until I realise what she means.

'Not that much, surely?' I say and give her a pleading smile.

'Is there anything you don't want in there, something that you could leave behind?'

'No!' I almost shout it at her. 'I'm starting a whole new life in Denmark and I need every single thing in it. Do you have any idea how hard it is to start a whole new life with just one suitcase?'

'I really don't.' She smiles sympathetically and attaches a luggage label. 'Don't blame me if the baggage handlers won't touch it.'

'Thanks so much.' I take my boarding pass and swing my backpack onto my shoulder, hoping she doesn't take it into her head to weigh that too.

Once I am through security, I relax. They have taken my shampoo and my bottle of water off me but it could have been worse. I buy a coffee and sit for a while on a chair, waiting for my flight to be called.

A pleasant-faced woman leans over and taps my shoulder. 'Excuse me. I can see by your boarding pass that you're on my flight. You need to get the train right now.'

'Train?' I look down at my boarding pass and then up at the screen.

'Yes, it's the penalty for having a cheaper ticket. Come on, I'll show you.'

I trail after her through the shops and onto a little train. Christian always flies business class on short flights and first class on long haul flights and I can't imagine anyone ever buying him a ticket which required him to get a train. I follow the woman up the escalator and along to the gate where an anxious-faced man is pulling a stretchy band across the door. He glances at our tickets and motions us through. 'You're the last. We were about to take your luggage off.'

'Sorry,' I gasp over my shoulder and run down the ramp after the woman. We enter the plane in a cloud of disapproval.

Once we have taken off, the stewardesses come round to take orders. I shake my head. 'I've only got Kroner.'

'We take both currencies if you want something.'

I settle for a packet of crisps and look at the unfamiliar coins she gives me in return.

'There you go. Enjoy your snack.'

'Your English is very good,' I say as I pop the bag open.

She gives me an odd look. 'I'm from Clacton.'

'Oh.' I settle back and crunch loudly to avoid the amusement of the passenger next to me.

It seems to take no time at all before we are losing height again. The day is still bright and clear so I have a great view of the coastline as we sweep down over it. It isn't until the wheels finally find the runway that it hits me. I am on foreign soil now, not just out of my comfort zone but out of my country. I have no job, no place to live and no one in the entire place to care whether I live or die. No one except Christian of course. As he has no idea I am here, that hardly counts. I walk down to the exit, wishing I could sit back down and wait for the plane to make the return flight. But that would be the coward's way out. I can't quit before I have begun. I lift my chin. There are no reasons at all for me to stay in London now, but one huge one for me to be here. I just need to keep my eyes on that.

'*Jeg elsker dig,*' I whisper to myself as a reminder, and walk through the shops towards customs.

Chapter Eight

I step out of the airport and onto the concourse and look around me. It is appreciably colder here than London at the beginning of October. The light seems brighter too. Tiny pieces of white fluff scud along the vivid blue above me and I drag a refreshing gulp of air deep into my lungs. A row of fountains play and skip along the concrete and I see the remains of pink and red summer flowers in huge planters all around. I stand for a while, breathing deeply and looking around, until my head feels clearer. I follow the crowds back inside the airport and buy a train ticket for the city. I hesitate at the top of the two travelators, turning my ticket round and round in my hands and wondering which way to go. A businessman cannons into me from behind and his trolley skins my ankles. '*Undskyld.*'

I stare at him. 'Erm ... Copenhagen?'

He switches seamlessly into English when he sees my blank face, and points. 'You will want to go down there, not here.

This way you will end up in Sweden.' He propels his trolley around me and runs down the ramp.

I stand and let my travelator carry me unresisting down to the darkness of the station below. I look in uncomprehending panic at the strange names flicking over on the board above my head. How on earth will I ever pronounce them? Some of them have letters I don't even recognise. A grey train skims into sight and whispers to a stop beside me. I look for a door handle and feel stupid when a child next to me pushes a glowing button and the door hisses and swings open. I heave my bags on board and find a seat.

The journey into the city takes about twenty-five minutes and gives me time to calm down and take stock. I am not going to survive for very long here if I am thrown by every little thing that is unfamiliar or that I don't understand. I need to relax and take things one step at a time, to go with the flow. In fact, I am so busy meditating on the flow that I almost miss my stop, despite its being announced in both Danish and English.

The station, when I emerge into it, is massive and clearly very old. I stare for a while at the sweeping girders supporting the roof, before making my way past the shops and cafés and out onto the main street. I am glad now that I put on my thickest coat. The light is fading quickly and the dusk sucks the last of the sun's warmth from the air. People hurry past me with their hats pulled over their ears. I go back inside and into the nearest shop to show them my piece of paper. The woman there produces a leaflet with a map of the city centre and traces my path for me. I thank her and walk as quickly as is possible with a heavy case to drag, around the corner and onto the street. My hotel, which I picked at random from my guide book because it said it was clean and moderately priced, is a tall, narrow building about five minutes' walk from the station. I bump my suitcase wheels up the three steps, collapse into one of the armchairs near the reception desk and wait for someone to arrive. Five minutes later, a man passing through the hall sees me.

'*Goddag.*'

'Hello.'

'Hello. Are you being looked to?'

'Not really. I'm having a bit of a rest after the walk here.'

He nods, bangs the bell as he passes and goes through a swing door. A woman arrives and greets me pleasantly. Christian wasn't boasting when he said that most Danes speak perfect English. As this woman talks to me fluently about the services the hotel provides, I feel faintly ashamed that my only other language is a tiny bit of schoolgirl French. Her badge says she also speaks German. I resolve to go down to the language school tomorrow and get started on Danish so that I don't spend all my time here at a complete disadvantage.

She hands me a key and asks if I would like help with my luggage. I shake my head. I have no idea about tipping rates and I don't want to embarrass myself any further today. I start towards the lifts before looking back.

'Is the water drinkable?' I ask her and she looks surprised but smiles politely.

'Definitely. I do not think you need have worries about that.'

I am glad when the lift doors slide shut to hide my burning cheeks.

The room is tiny but very clean and comfortable. Although I am in the middle of a busy city, I can't hear any noise. I am completely exhausted by the early start and all the emotion so I wash my face and unpack a few things then lie down for a quick nap.

It is completely dark when hunger wakes me. I stretch and sit up. I should have brought some food with me but any extra weight in my case might have caused an entire luggage handling strike. I will have to go out and find something instead. It will be a good experience. If I can find food by myself in a foreign city without speaking the language, that will prove I can survive here.

Luckily there is a different woman on the desk when I go back down to the lobby.

'Good evening,' I say quickly to set the language rules right away. I am beginning to realise that *'Jeg elsker dig'*, although romantic, won't be my go-to phrase as far as getting basic essentials is concerned.

'Good evening. Is your room comfortable?'

'Yeah, great thanks. I'm looking for somewhere to eat this evening.'

'Our restaurant is open.' She waves toward the swing doors.

I have already seen the prices on a leaflet upstairs. I would be bankrupt in two days if I ate here but I don't want to offend her.

'I'd like to stretch my legs a bit. Is there somewhere in town that you can recommend?'

'Certainly. There are a few lovely restaurants around Tivoli.'

'Expensive?'

'Not very. Maybe about five hundred kroner if you have three courses and wine.'

Five hundred kroner? What planet does this woman live on?

'I was actually thinking of something a little cheaper. I don't need three courses.'

'Do you like Italian food?'

'Yes.'

This is true. Becca and I always order the best pizza from a place not far from us. They do a great quattro formaggi, which is my favourite, and she loves ordering the really weird combinations, such as peach and pear with blue cheese. She ends up picking the weirder things off but says it's more interesting than always ordering the same old thing. Watching her ploughing through her anchovy and pineapple pizza last week, I had to disagree.

The woman persists. 'There is a lovely little place where they spin ... grind ... no, that is not right. They push their own pasta out freshly.'

'Sounds lovely. Is it pricey?'

'Maybe four hundred kroner.'

'I was really thinking of something a bit cheaper.'

She rests her chin on her elbows. 'I have a suggestion. Why do you not give me your budget and I will tell you.'

I think my way mentally through my purse. I changed one hundred pounds into about a thousand kroner at Stansted but that needs to last. I can't possibly eat my way though it in two meals. But I don't want to sound too mean or provincial either.

'About 100 kroner maximum?'

I am sure I don't imagine the smile that flickers across her face before she suppresses it.

'There is a McDonald's just across from the head train station.'

'Sounds good.' I tilt my chin and walk defiantly across the lobby to the door.

It is definitely far colder outside at this time of day and a light frost sparkles on the pavement ahead of me, lit by the street lights. I walk faster and reach McDonald's in less than ten minutes.

It is warm and inviting. As I wait in line for a burger, I look around me. There are people milling all around, perched on seats, talking and laughing. To judge from the number of languages being spoken in here, I am not going to find myself the only foreigner in Copenhagen.

I sit at a free table and open my paper wrapper. It isn't very cosmopolitan to go to McDonald's on my first day but I'm starving. I can take some risks tomorrow and investigate all the little out of the way cafés down back streets, the ones that tourists never find. Maybe I will discover one that even Christian has never heard of and I will take him there for a candlelit dinner so he can ask me to get back together with him.

I sink my teeth into my burger and remember Becca. I haven't contacted her all day and she must be going out of her mind with worry. I dwell briefly on the thought of her pacing the flat, chewing her nails, and I grin. She is either not home yet or else is slouched in front of the TV, flicking channels and eating a takeaway. I dial her number and feel a thrill as I hear it ringing. It is a thread that reaches all the way between Copenhagen and London, connecting my new life with my old. I jump when she answers it and picture her by the hall table, picking up the receiver.

'Hallo?'

'Becca, it's me.'

'Who's *me*?'

I deflate at once. 'It's Kate.'

'Just kidding. You've taken your time calling.'

'So you *were* worried?'

'Not particularly but I thought you might be.'

I swallow the last piece of pickle. 'I'm fine. The journey was fine. The hotel is fine.'

'Sound a complete nightmare.'

'I don't have that much credit so I can't talk long but I wanted to let you know I'm safe.'

'That's good to hear.'

'How are you?'

'You really want to waste your credit on hearing about my day?'

'I might do. Then next call I can reverse the charges.'

'What are you planning for tomorrow?'

I feel a warm glow. She might pretend to be brusque, but underneath she really cares.

'Not exactly sure. I need to get some groceries. Becca, the prices here ...'

'I know. I was over there.'

'What? When were you here? Why didn't you tell me?'

'I don't know. A couple of years ago, the winter before you graduated. I was working on a big project with the Copenhagen office and they thought it would be easier to have me actually on site for a couple of months.'

'You could have told me.'

'It never occurred to me.'

'So you already knew Christian over here?'

'No, I may have met him but not to remember. It's a big firm. But I remember things being pricey. I had an expense account so it didn't really matter.'

I bite back a sarcastic retort. It isn't her fault that she is so good at her job and is paid ten times as much as me. She never flaunts it and, apart from books and takeaways, I don't know what she spends it on. But I must admit that being on an expense account would make things a lot easier for me right now. Never mind, it is just one more obstacle to battle for Christian's sake. I wouldn't want things to be too easy. If a prize is worth winning, it ought to cost something.

'I'll find a supermarket tomorrow and get some stuff. I have to go to the town Hall and get one of these ID number things.'

'CPR number.'

'Yes, that's it. How do you know?'

'I had to have one. Even for two months. Don't try to do anything without it. They'll never cope. The system will go into meltdown and life as we know it will never be the same again.'

'I'll remember. And I'll go into the language school when I've got that number thing and see when I can start. Otherwise, the main thing is finding a job and somewhere to live. I can't afford to stay at this hotel for more than three nights.'

'Good luck with all that. Let me know how it goes. Are you keeping the same phone?'

'For now. I'll get a local one once I have some money and an address.'

'I'll probably give you a call sometime.'

'Please. I'm feeling a bit isolated right at the moment.'

'What did you expect?'

'Point taken. But it would be nice to hear what you're up to sometimes. I'll find an internet café but emails aren't the same as hearing someone.' I brighten. 'You could visit. They have some great deals for city breaks.'

'Let's see how long you stay there first, shall we?'

I know exactly what that tone means. She won't be surprised if I turn up on her doorstep again once my hotel reservation runs out. Honestly, she has so little faith in me. To be fair, she wouldn't gloat if I came back, and neither would she say, 'I told you so'. She would just chuck my cases back into my room and leave me to unpack. I tear my thoughts away from this scenario. I mustn't think too much about our untidy, cosy little flat. I will soon have somewhere of my own and this homesickness will go away.

'My credit's running low. I've got to go.'

'OK, talk to you soon.'

She hangs up without a goodbye or wishing me luck but that's just Becca. Words to her convey facts and meaning and never sentiment. But when she does say something kind, she means it. I wouldn't swap her for a million pounds. Just before I put my phone in my pocket, I remember what day it is and type a text. *Don't forget, dustbins out tonight.* I wait a moment for her to answer, but the screen stays blank.

Chapter Nine

I wake early and slide out from underneath my warm quilt to inspect the day. The sky is white but it doesn't look as though it plans to rain imminently. I am halfway through my shower before I remember they took my bottle of shampoo from me at the airport and I forgot to replace it. I scrabble around with one hand and realise to my horror that there are no little sachets in the shower basket. My hair needs washing, so eventually I rub my head with the tiny bar of soap and resign myself to a day of static madness.

When I emerge onto the street, I realise I am very hungry. I am determined not to go back to McDonald's, however familiar it might be. This is the new me in my new country and I can do better than that. I walk back towards the main train station and across the road. Tivoli has closed for the autumn and I can't see anything much over its tall stone walls. I skirt round it and find myself at the top of Strøget. My guide book informs me that it is the main shopping street in the city so I head down it. Surely there will be a café somewhere. I stick my chilled hands into my pocket and try to feel adventurous. The street opens into a square and I see a likely-looking café across the stones.

The air inside is warm and sugary, with enough caffeine in it to give me a kick even before I order. I survey the pastries for a minute. They appear fresh and crisp and none of them look as though they have ever seen the inside of a plastic wrapper.

'Could I have one of those things with custard?' I point at a Danish pastry. It seems appropriate, considering where I am.

'*Wienerbrød*? Of course. And a drink?'

'Decaf latte, please.'

'We only serve coffee with caffeine.'

'You're kidding.'

The guy laughs. 'No, you'll have to get used to it. You should try it. It gives a much better taste.'

'Go on, then.' I dip into my purse and look hopelessly at the coins before picking out a note and a coin. 'Is that right?'

'Sixty kroner. That is perfect. I can bring over your coffee.'

I sit near the window so I can look outside at the crowds. There don't seem to be that many people yet and those that there are walk quickly down the street. There are bikes everywhere but no cars. The main shops don't open until ten so these must be office workers. When the coffee arrives, I sip it and make plans for the day. First, I need to register for one of these number things that Becca was talking about. She seemed to think they were pretty important. I have a vision of myself being hauled off a tram for questioning and not being able to produce my papers. But this isn't wartime Germany and I'm not Ingrid Bergman. I finish my coffee and start on the pastry and I almost swoon. It is crisp and buttery and melting and the apricot in the centre could have been picked this morning from some sunny orchard. I think without regret of the Danish pastries in the staff canteen, pale and scared-looking under their slices of canned peach. As I stand to leave, I go over to look at the pastries again to memorise their name. I definitely want to have one of these again.

'Can I help you?' The guy is back.

'I just wanted to learn some of the names of these Danish pastries.'

'We don't call them that. We call them *wienerbrød* - Vienna bread.'

'You guys don't want to take credit for them? They're the best I've ever tasted.'

'Maybe we are a modest nation, or maybe we have so much else to take credit for?' He laughs. 'I'm glad you enjoyed it. Come in again sometime.'

'I will.' I wave and head back up Strøget. I feel warmer now, despite the cold wind biting at my exposed hands. Buying gloves and a hat should probably go on my to-do list.

With the help of my guidebook, I find the town hall and spend the morning taking various tickets and waiting in long lines. I emerge triumphantly a couple of hours later, with the promise of my number arriving in a few days. I feel a tiny sense of belonging now that I will be able to get a job, open a bank account, rent an apartment, whatever I like. The fact that none of these things seems any closer than it did yesterday, is immaterial. I have managed to achieve something all by myself and that is something to celebrate. I would love to go back to the café I found this morning and buy lunch, but the prices over here pretty much rule that out so I go into a 7-Eleven and buy bread, cheese triangles and a bottle of water. It is too cold to sit outside so I go back to the hotel and walk quickly through the lobby before the woman can see my carrier bag.

The room has been cleaned and smells of polish and disinfectant. I sit on the bed and eat my lunch while considering my next move. I only realised last week that I don't have Christian's address, although I know from what he has said that he lives somewhere to the North of the city. I tried ringing his mobile but it was a work one and he must have given it back when he left. His email was also a UK work one. I don't know if he has a personal Danish email now he is home. In London, I always contacted him at work or phoned his flat. I feel a little hurt when I think about how totally he has disappeared but I squash the feeling. He told me that it was better if we didn't stay in touch. He must have meant better for me and I smile at how little he knows me. I am far more resilient than he seems to think and could easily have coped with a long-distance relationship with all its uncertainties.

I push myself reluctantly off the bed and collect my guide book. I thought I might wander down and take a look at Christian's office this afternoon, just to get a feel of what his life is like now. It will be a bonus if he happens to come out while I am there but I am definitely not expecting it. I would simply like to see a bit more of the city and get my bearings. The office is in a place called Hellerup so I walk back down to the train station and buy myself a *klippekort*, which is good for ten journeys. I am beginning to feel like an old hand now with this train business. I run down the steps to my platform and wait for one of the red trains to arrive. It is just pulling out of the station when my phone rings. It has to be Becca. No one over here has my number and everyone in London knows I am out of the country. I flick the button without looking at the screen.

'Becca, am I glad to hear from you!'

There is a moment's silence and I glance at the screen. It isn't Becca's number at all. In fact it's a local call. My heart stops momentarily. It's Christian, it has to be. Somehow he must have heard I am over here and he has phoned me right away. He must love me still. My fingers can hardly hold the phone as I wait for him to speak. I never dared to dream it would be this straightforward.

'This is Kate? Kate Merrit?' It is a woman's voice, pleasant and slightly accented.

'Uh huh.' Who on earth can this be? I have my CPR number on the way. Surely they can't have tracked me down already? I know Danes are efficient but this is ridiculous. I remind myself I haven't done anything wrong and wait.

'Good. My name is Ilse Andersen. I work at *D-Zine* and I am a friend of Becca also. She gave me this number. I hope you don't mind?'

'*Becca* did?' This makes no sense. She hasn't mentioned any friends over here.

'Yes, she emailed me a few days ago to tell me a friend of hers was coming to Copenhagen for a while and to ask if I would look out a little for her. Of course I said I would be delighted. Then she called me last night and gave me this number. I have been hoping that it is all right for me to have it.'

I shake myself. I don't know what this woman must think of my non-existent phone manner. 'That's absolutely fine. Thank you for calling.'

'She said it might be a little difficult for you in a new country just at first, not knowing anyone. She didn't tell me why you are over here. I assume it is for work?'

I clear my throat while I think rapidly. Becca clearly hasn't given me away. She has left me to tell whatever story I like and not for the first time I bless the fact that she hasn't an interfering or controlling bone in her body.

I keep my voice as casual yet confident as I can. 'Actually, I just fancied a change. I was in a bit of a dead end job and I decided to try something new.'

'How brave. You are not an architect like Becca?'

I snort at the thought then turn it into a cough. 'No, I've been more in the ... electrical industry. But I'd like a complete break from all that.'

'I see. So, I was wondering if you would like to meet sometime that suits you. You could ask me some questions about Copenhagen if you have any. Where are you at the moment?'

'I'm on the train to Hellerup.'

'But that is where our offices are. How lucky. Do you have time to meet this afternoon?'

'Absolutely.' I am not turning this invitation down. This woman must know Christian. If I am smart enough, I can probably find out some more about his new life without her even noticing.

'Let's see. It is two o'clock now. I take a break at about half past three. There is a supermarket near to our offices with a little café next to it. Will it be convenient to meet there and have a cup of coffee and talk?'

'Perfect. I'll see you then.'

The train is coming in to my stop as I ring off and I run for the door. The last thing I want is to be carried on up the coast and end up in ... Norway or somewhere. I must have a proper look at a map.

I have an hour and a half to spare so I walk away from the station and along the nearest road. My eyes open wide as I look at the houses. They are seriously huge and ornate. I have never seen anything like them. I wonder if all Danes live like this. If so, it must be a very rich country. I turn and walk back towards the station. I don't want to get lost and the map I printed of this area cuts off soon. I only brought the one page. I walk down towards the shops and shiver in the cold breeze that blasts along the high street. In one direction, I can see glimpses of the sea. It is grey and flat and I can't ever imagine wanting to swim in it. I poke around a few of the shops, ignoring the horrendous prices, and eventually walk, a little early, to the supermarket. The café is easy to locate, sitting as it does at the foot of a white tower. I go inside and sit down to wait for Ilse. The afternoon is less cheerful now. Grey clouds are pouring in from the sea but it is warm and cosy in here. Every table has a tiny spray of flowers in a slender vase and a lit candle growing out of a glass of coffee beans. It makes a change from Phil's wine bar, where lopsided candles dribble wax down cheap wine bottles and the flowers are plastic.

'Kate?'

I have been so lost in thoughts of London that I haven't noticed anyone come in. I stand and Ilse shakes my hand firmly. She is tall and slim and has a warm smile.

'How lovely to meet you at last. If you are a friend of Becca, you are my friend too.'

'You knew her well?' I ask as we sit back down.

'Quite well when she was over here. We stay in touch and I see her sometimes when I come over to the London office.'

'I don't remember her mentioning you.'

'That is Becca. She doesn't mention anything that isn't strictly relevant.'

'True, she's not one for chatter.'

'She is an original. She has a good heart and I am very fond of her.'

'Me too.' I feel another pang of homesickness and thrust it away. 'Have you been in London lately?'

'Not for over a year.'

I relax. Becca is hardly likely to have mentioned that her flatmate was seeing a workmate. It wouldn't cross her mind. If I had bought a bookshop, she might have mentioned it, but nothing short of that.

Ilse stands. 'What will you drink?'

'Oh, you don't need to do that. I should buy you a drink.'

'Nonsense, it is to welcome you to Denmark.'

I see her chatting to the woman behind the counter and she returns a minute later with two brimming glasses. 'They do a very nice latte here.'

I sip at it. I am clearly going to have to get used to drinking caffeine at all hours. I wonder if Danes ever sleep. Maybe they don't and that's why they're all so rich. I wipe the foam off my lip. 'I went for a walk round Hellerup just now. The houses were pretty amazing. Does everyone over here live in such enormous houses?'

'Near to the station?'

I nod.

'I think you must mean the houses for the Embassies. Did you not see the flags outside?'

I am a little embarrassed at my lack of observation. 'I thought they were for UN day or something.'

'Now, about practical things. Becca said you do not yet have a place to live?'

I force my mind back to harsh realities. 'No, and I need to find somewhere quickly - probably a flat share. I thought I might go to the university and look at their bulletin boards.'

'That is a good idea. If it is not impolite, I have also looked around our internal advertisements for you. There are two trainees who are looking for a third person. It is a two bedroom apartment in Østerbro. They are together so they have the bigger room but they are advertising the smaller room. It is quite a reasonable rent.'

'Sounds great. Do you have the details?'

She hands me the print out and I study it. 'I'll call them tonight. You don't know of any good jobs around here, do you?'

She smiles. 'Unfortunately not because you are not an architect. If you just want something temporary while you look around, I suggest you try the cafés and restaurants. There are plenty of them in the city.'

'I don't speak Danish.'

'None at all?'

I think for a second. 'None,' I say firmly. She doesn't need to hear my one Danish phrase.

'You will soon pick it up and most people speak good English. If you are just making coffee or cooking, it should not be a problem. You are sure you do not want to look for a job in the electrical industry?'

Caroline's pleading face flashes before my eyes. 'You can't seriously prefer cooking in some crummy café to all this? We've just ordered some crepe makers.'

I shake my head. 'I'd like something casual for now. Later on, I can just ... see.'

She glances at her watch. 'Good luck. My break is almost over. Is there anything else I can help you with first?'

I panic. I need to mention Christian but in a way that won't let her know our history. I don't want her jumping to the wrong conclusion and deciding I am some sort of deranged stalker. It's just not a situation that is very easy to explain to other people and I could see how some people might twist reality to interpret it badly. I choose my words carefully.

'I think that's everything really. You've been very kind.' I feign a sudden remembrance. 'Oh, there *is* actually one other person I know in Copenhagen. I met him at Becca's work Christmas party in London. His name is Christian Sørensen. Have you heard of him?'

'Christian!' Her face lights up in the way everyone's face does whenever he is mentioned. 'What a piece of luck. He is just recently returned to us from the London Office. We were all so pleased to get him back. Do you know him well?'

'He's a very friendly guy,' I temporise. 'I liked him a lot.'

'Who doesn't?' She laughs and pulls a diary out of her bag. 'Let me just check. Yes, I thought so. I am having him and some other friends over to my apartment for dinner on Saturday night. Would you be able to join us?'

I keep my face straight and suppress and urge to leap and whirl around like a dervish. This will be *so* much better than '*accidentally*' bumping into him outside his office.

'I'd love to. That's very kind.'

'You know, I think I won't mention it to Christian. It will be such a nice surprise for him to meet an old friend from London. I'll call you with the details.'

She shakes hands again. I watch her long legs striding across the car park outside the window and smile to myself. She is right about one thing. On Saturday night, Christian is indeed headed for a complete surprise. I just hope he likes it.

Chapter Ten

The next couple of days fly by. When I look back each evening, the day blurs and melts into a haze of exhaustion but things fall into place far more quickly than I ever dared to imagine.

The day after I meet Ilse, I start the rounds of all the cafés and restaurants I can find. Most of the restaurants want Danish speaking waitresses or experienced cooks. After the second morning of shaken heads and polite rejections, I almost decide to bite the bullet and start looking in the department stores at the white goods departments. How hard could it really be to learn the key phrases in Danish? *Fantastic value. New line. Energy efficient.* I might even be an attraction for the store; an exotic foreign sales person who doesn't speak the language.

I stop for a sandwich lunch at a café right down on the waterfront — *Kanelsneglen*. I look in my dictionary — *The Cinnamon Snail*. It seems an odd name for a café but I think it suits the small, round building. While I wait for my food, I look out across the water to Sweden. The day is clear and three tiny towers appear and disappear inside the clouds banked along the far horizon. The waiter brings me a coffee and I reluctantly launch into my prepared speech about needing a job and being very hard-working. To my surprise, he neither shrugs nor shakes his head but calls something in Danish to the elderly woman serving behind the counter. She looks at me sharply and I smooth my hair and try to give her the sort of smile that conveys an impression of reliability and efficiency.

'*Kan du tale dansk?*' she shoots at me and I grimace. It's one of the few phrases I have learned during my week here.

'Not really but I'm hoping to learn to speak it as soon as I get a job and a place to live.'

The waiter asks her another question and she looks at me again. She talks for a while and I hear the words *femogtyve* and *aften*.

He smiles. 'She says she doesn't mind trying you for a couple of weeks, mostly for the evening shifts. About twenty-five hours a week for now. Would that be OK?'

I want to hug him but I restrain myself. 'Fantastic, when can I start?'

'Sunday at lunchtime. We get busy then.'

'Doesn't she speak English? I thought all Danes spoke English?'

'We are not born speaking it. Her generation might not always be so fluent. My generation has had American TV.'

His smile is warm and he seems friendly. He tells me his name is Tomas. I give him my details and arrange to come in a little early to be instructed into the mysteries of coffee making.

Buoyed by the prospect of some actual money coming in, I ring the number Ilse gave me and arrange to meet Jens and his girlfriend at their apartment. It is small but very light and airy.

Best of all, it is at the end of the lakes and so within walking distance to my new work, at least on a fine day. They offer me their second room for an initial period of three months.

'To see how we all get on,' said Jens solemnly and I agree. I would prefer not to tie myself down too far ahead either. I still have no idea exactly where it is that Christian lives although, when I lie awake thinking of him every night, I imagine him in one of those houses I saw in Hellerup. I can just picture him in the one with the largest flag. The only problem with my new rental, is a deposit for the room. I had half thought of asking Becca for a loan if I got desperate. But Lisette, Jens' girlfriend, shakes her head at the suggestion. She is French. They met at the Sorbonne and she moved up here to be with him. She has a wonderful line in shrugs and expressive waves and she lifts her shoulders now when I mention the deposit.

'You do not need to. Ilse at our firm said you were to be trusted and that is good enough for me and Jens.'

In the end we agree that I will pay my rent the minute my first pay cheque comes through. I arrange to move in the next morning. They will both be at work but Jens hands me a key and gives me the door code.

I ring Becca that evening from the hotel. It is my last night here and I am throwing clothes into my case and looking forward to the use of a washing machine again.

'Becca, you're never going to believe this.'

'Sweden has invaded and you're all being force fed meatballs?'

'Right. As well as that, I've got a job *and* somewhere to live.'

'Quick work.' She never sounds particularly impressed but I can live with that.

'Yes, I'm going to be making coffee and sandwiches and washing up at a café right next to the water. It's all glass walls and wooden floors. On a clear day I can even see Sweden.'

'Keep an eye on it, you mean. Good idea, you can be a sort of early warning system for the locals.'

'Then your mate Ilse put me in touch with some people at her office, who need a flat-share partner and I move in tomorrow. And, get this, they don't even mind that I don't have a deposit.'

'Trusting people are they, the Danes?'

'They must be. She's French, though.'

'And how about the elephant in the room?'

'What?' I frown for a moment. 'Oh, you mean Christian?'

'He *is* the reason you're there.'

I hesitate whether or not to tell her the truth. I always hate lying to her but I am not quite ready to tell her that I am gate crashing the dinner party on Saturday night. She might feel I am taking advantage of Ilse.

'I haven't seen him yet but there's plenty of time. I've been busy. Thanks a lot for giving Ilse my number. She's been really nice.'

'You're welcome.'

'What's going on at your end?'

'Just the usual — wild parties every night and police raids. I had a squid and grape pizza last night. Pity you weren't there to try it.'

'I had a burger for the third night running. But I wouldn't trade it for that pizza.'

'It was OK actually. Keep in touch, won't you?'

'Of course. I'll call again over the weekend. Perhaps not Saturday because ... anyway, maybe Sunday night. I start work Sunday lunchtime.'

'Knock 'em dead.' And she rings off.

I wake up on Saturday morning with a sinking feeling. Now that I am about to come face to face with Christian, I am filled with the sort of doubts that I never once felt while I was making plans to see him again. I have been so busy since he left that I haven't had time for any kind of a plan. I lie for a while and picture his face in all its moods and try to figure out which one I would prefer to see if I had the choice. At least none of the moods in my imagination is an angry one. I have never once seen Christian lose his temper. He has such a large tolerance for people and such a wish for those around him to be happy, that he never gets upset with them. Even when I was at my snappiest, after a long day, with Caroline even more over-charged than usual, as though she had plugged herself into one of the appliances she loves so much, Christian would let me rant and then take my hand.

'Why does it upset you so much? She may be a little different but she has not hurt you in any way and her intentions are good.'

I used to argue but it was easier in the end to agree. Otherwise I ran the risk of making myself look bitchy and unpleasant. Christian would never understand why anything could irritate me enough to lose my temper so I learned to control it and say something nice or nothing at all. I expect I was the better person for it. It certainly came in handy once I met Marie and Jeremy. I was always bursting to unpick the evenings we spent with them but had to wait until I got back to the flat, where I could unload the lot on Becca, as she lay on her beanbag and snorted with laughter.

So I am not expecting an outburst of any kind when he sees me. But, in the cold light of day, the thought of landing on Ilse's doorstep and greeting him with a cheery wave, seems daunting to say the least. I also wonder what Ilse will make of it all. Short of ringing her at the last minute and refusing the invitation, I have to go through with it. I look round the room. I am pretty much unpacked now and the bed is made up with clean sheets and quilt cover. I could dive under the quilt and stay there until it is time for me to go to work tomorrow. Jens and Lisette would probably never notice. They were out until late last night and I haven't heard either of them up and about yet. Or I could get up, go for a walk along the sea front to clear my head, remember exactly why I am here and stop being such a spineless wimp. After much deliberation, I decide on the latter course and reach for my wash bag so I can use the bathroom before the other two are up. Once I am clean and dry, I make a sandwich and slip out of the apartment without making any noise.

As usual, I walk as fast as I can through the built-up areas and past the blocks of flats with their ornate, carved exteriors, and make for the water. I have always loved walking by the sea. Having one of my boundaries consist of nothing but air and water, feels wonderfully liberating. I make my way along the edge of the harbour. Sweden is invisible today inside the clouds that pour and swirl across the Øresund. I think of Becca's hordes of marauding Swedes. Perhaps they are after the Danish pastries. Jens told me yesterday that it is less than an hour on the train to Malmö and I feel pleasantly cosmopolitan and well-travelled to have settled in a place where a simple train ride will take me to Sweden, Germany and ... Belgium, perhaps? I still haven't bought that map.

An hour later, I am getting cold. I climb down and huddle in the shelter of the concrete promenade while I unwrap my sandwich. I have discovered *rugbrød*, the chewy, caramelly, yet salty, rye bread that everyone here seems to eat. I must take some back for Becca when I visit. I take a huge bite. Jam is possibly not the best filling for this bread but the picture of lingonberries on the jar was enticing. Once I have been paid, I can push the boat out a bit, although I completely draw the line at the jars of raw fish I have seen on all the shop shelves.

I wander back along the seafront and back through the streets to the apartment. I stop at a stall and look at what flowers the woman still has. When I mentioned I was going out tonight, Jens said I should buy flowers. 'Even if you cannot afford anything else, you must always take a Danish hostess flowers.'

Looking at these prices, I am not sure I will even be able to eat for the rest of the weekend but he was very definite, so I select a large bunch of pink roses and pay for them. I hope there is plenty to eat tonight. I need to stock up for the rest of the week.

Back at the apartment, there are signs of life. Lisette is heating soup in the kitchen.

'Good night last night?' I ask her as I put the flowers on the draining board.

'Oof, it was wild. We went to a club to dance and the floor moved.'

Is that like the earth moving, I wonder, but am too polite to ask. She pushes her hair away from her face.

'The floor moved back and forth and everyone screamed and laughed. Jens loved it but I started to feel sick so we went to a bar to meet some friends — and after that I forget.'

She pulls such a funny face that I laugh. 'Is soup a French hangover cure?'

'It is the end of the month. We need to be paid.'

I thought architects earned the earth but perhaps apprentices don't. I can hardly ask a complete stranger how much she is paid so I just nod. 'I'm out tonight by the way. I've been asked to Ilse's apartment.'

'Jens said so. Will there be anyone else there?'

'No idea,' I lie and disappear through to my bedroom before she can ask anything else.

I am due at Ilse's at seven o'clock and am ready at least an hour beforehand. I sit on the bed to calm my nerves, then check myself one last time in the mirror before leaving. I am wearing my smartest dark jeans and a purple top with a deep V neck. I chose it mainly because this way I can wear the amethyst necklace Christian gave me for my birthday. It won't harm him to be reminded of happier times. I pull on a light jacket and make for the door.

Lisette appears from the kitchen. 'Are you walking?'

'Yes, it's not far.'

'You will freeze, you silly girl. I have a mauve coat you can borrow.' She ignores my protests and goes into her bedroom, emerging with a gorgeous winter coat with a dyed faux fur collar.

She looks at me consideringly. 'It suits you. It came from Paris so they will all be very impressed.'

'Thanks, Lisette. I'll take good care of it.'

She is right, the air outside feels even colder than usual because it's damp. There is a hint of fog rolling in from the sea and I stuff my hands deep inside the coat pockets and walk faster.

Ten minutes later I arrive at Ilse's. Her apartment is on the 2nd floor and I press the buzzer and wait. It reminds me of all those dreadful dinners at Marie's. I half expect Ilse to greet me with a shriek of '*Darling!*' and a demand to know whether Christian is with me. But she just calls '*Hej*' and buzzes me in. I climb the two flights of stairs and wait outside the door to compose myself, before knocking.

Ilse answers the door and beams widely. 'Such lovely flowers. You should not have done so. It is wonderful that you could come tonight — and what a fantastic coat. Shall I hang it up?'

I let her take it and I smooth my hair down nervously, looking around for everyone else. I am exactly on time. Perhaps you are meant to be fashionably late in Denmark. It is just another one of those tiny unknowns that make me feel like a fish out of water.

'Come and meet everyone.'

She holds out a hand and I follow her through the entrance hall and into a side room. There seem to be about eighteen people sitting round in various chairs and staring at me. When the mist in front of my eyes clears, I see there are only four. And I only have eyes for one of them. Sitting on a cream sofa, looking more handsome than ever in an expensive pale green shirt, is Christian, and he is staring at me with an unfathomable expression in his deep, blue eyes.

Chapter Eleven

I break the silence first. I had the advantage of being prepared for this meeting. He hasn't moved from the sofa where, I notice for the first time, he is sitting very close to a willowy brunette.

'Hi.' I lift a hand and only just restrain myself from giving a stupid grin and adding, 'Surprise!'

'Christian, how do you like the surprise?' Ilse is right behind me. I jump in to break the silence before she can say anything else and maybe land me in it.

'Hi, Christian. I didn't expect to see you again so soon.'

'Nor I you.' He stands and holds out his hand for me to shake. He could at least have kissed me on the cheek. 'What brings you to Copenhagen?'

'I'm, er, taking a bit of a break from things. I thought I'd try something new.'

'And why Copenhagen?' He still hasn't smiled and Ilse is now looking at me in puzzlement.

'I heard so many nice things about it. I thought I'd take a look.'

'I see.' He clearly does and I pray that his innate good manners stop him from telling everyone what I have done. At least while I am still here.

'*Aftensmad* – dinner.' announces Ilse. 'Come on through, everybody.'

She sits me opposite Christian and the dark haired girl and next to a man she introduces as Henrik. She sits at one end of the table and her boyfriend, Lars, is at the other end. He pours me a glass of wine and I bury my face in it, not wanting to catch Christian's eye.

We start with soup and I keep my eyes fixed on that and let the chatter swirl around me. Henrik passes me a basket of bread. 'How are you finding Denmark after just a week?'

Out of the corner of my eye, I see Christian's spoon hover in mid-air as he waits for my answer. Now is the time to let him know how much I love the place and how well I would fit in.

'It's been great. Everyone has been so friendly' – I lift my eyes and stare challengingly at him for a second – 'and I love the scenery.'

'It is not so good just now. Wait until the spring and then you will see how pretty Denmark can be.'

Christian breaks in. 'Will you still be here in the spring?'

I meet his eyes more confidently. I have as much right to be here as he does. I never challenged his right to be in London. If he can invade my city, why can't I invade his?

'I don't have any exact plans yet. I'm going with the flow.'

'I hear you are living with Jens and Lisette?' says Henrik.

'That's right. Just round the corner from here. They both seem really nice. Do you work at *D-Zine* too?'

He laughs loudly. 'We all do. It is what you might call a clique here tonight. I think we all work such long hours that we do not have so much time for meeting other people. Ilse and Lars met at work. Christian and Miranda did in a way too.'

My eyes jump up in shock and I see the girl opposite looking back at me. I can't quite read her expression.

'Miranda?' I ask, hoping my voice hasn't gone all squeaky.

'That would be me.' She has a slightly Sloaney drawl and I stare at her.

'You're British.'

'Spot on.' One side of her beautifully-shaped mouth curls up in amusement.

'So you and Christian ...'

She doesn't answer, just lifts one hand and traces his cheek with her finger. He has the grace to look uncomfortable.

'How long have you two been together?' I ask. I am determined to keep my voice under control I spite of the shock. My heart might feel as though it has just splintered into a million pieces but I have some pathetic shreds of dignity to preserve.

'Since he came back home.' She puts a tiny emphasis on the word *home*. 'But time isn't everything, is it? Sometimes you just know.'

'I've always thought so.'

I can't drink any more of my soup. I think about hurling it over Christian's immaculately brushed hair and storming out but Ilse hasn't done anything to deserve that. I am her guest and I need to behave myself. I can throw things later.

Henrik helps collect the bowls. 'Miranda works at your British embassy. Our firm has very good connections there.

Lucky for Christian.' He gives his loud laugh again and I want to hit him.

'Would you mind helping me in the kitchen, Kate?' asks Ilse and I nod automatically and follow her out with the bowls. The chatter breaks out again as we leave and I grind my teeth as I hear it is in Danish this time and that Miranda is obviously fluent. She would be. I dump the bowls on the counter and turn to face Ilse.

'What would you like me to do?'

'Nothing, it is all under control. I thought you might like to take a moment.'

'You know?'

'I didn't but I do now. You have a very expressive face.'

'Do you think the others guessed?'

She shakes her head. 'Lars needs a sledge hammer before he notices anything even slightly romantic and Henrik enjoys his dinner too much to have time for broken hearts.'

'Is it that obvious?'

She takes my hand. I don't pull it away. It's as much as I can do not to break down and howl all over her designer plates.

'I can see that you knew Christian more than slightly.'

'I'm sorry, Ilse. I didn't mean to mess you around when you've been so kind. But I needed to see him again, to try to sort things out. Of course, I needn't have bothered. He hasn't taken long to hook up with someone else.'

'You were together for long?'

'About eight months. But you know the thing that bugs me most about this Miranda character? He told me he was dumping me because he couldn't see me fitting in over here with a foreign culture. But she's British too.'

'It seems a very difficult situation. What would you like to do now? If you would prefer to leave, I will understand.'

I almost accept. I want nothing more than to slide out of a back door, climb down the fire escape, go home and pack. Becca will take me back. But I can't. That would be what the old Kate would do and I'm on a mission to prove I'm not the old Kate. The new Kate will stay and keep her head high and prove that nothing can throw her off course.

'I'm absolutely fine,' I say and smile as best I can. 'I'd love to stay and get to know everyone.' Get to know Christian's friends and Miranda, I think, though I don't say it. Until you size up the enemy, you can't decide how to beat it.

'I am glad you are OK,' she says. 'It can be hard to accept seeing someone you love with a new person but it is always best if we can manage it quickly.'

'I'll be fine.' I don't want her worrying about me. It is no skin off her nose if I don't quite manage that acceptance thing as quickly as she would like. As long as I behave properly and don't embarrass her guests, what is it to her?'

'Will you take these potatoes through for me?' She hands me a dish and I walk back into the dining room.

The conversation switches automatically back into English as I come in. These people are either incredibly polite or they have been talking about me behind my back. Stop it, I tell myself. The situation is bad enough without introducing paranoia into the mix.

'Lovely,' says Henrik, as Ilse follows with a casserole dish and begins to serve people.

'So, Kate,' says Lars when we are all eating, 'if I am to ask you to prepare me a typical English meal, what would the menu be?'

I lay down my fork while I think. 'I don't know. Pasta maybe, or pizza?'

There is a gale of laughter round the table. I recoil in embarrassment but see by their faces that luckily they think I am joking. Miranda doesn't laugh. She is staring at me as though she can't make me out at all. I join in the laughter to show I was being ironic and think quickly. But my brain refuses to slide into gear and help me out. I need to come up with something quickly. Everyone is staring at me curiously.

'I'm not sure really. If you were very posh, then perhaps roast swan or something.' Even I can hear how ridiculous this sounds but they nod, apparently happy to have pigeonholed me and my country's cuisine.

I catch Christian's eye and he is grinning at me. My heart turns over and I am whisked straight back to the hundreds of dinner parties when Marie has said something even more outrageous than usual and we have caught each other's eyes. Not to belittle her or make fun, because Christian would never do that, but in joint appreciation of the absurdity and with a promise of being alone together later. As I remember this, it hits me that I may never be alone with him again and I have to bite the inside of my lip to stop the tears.

'Roast swan?' Miranda leans forward with just that touch of bitchy incredulity in her voice that another woman would hear but would sail straight over a man's head, especially when she is as pretty as Miranda.

Christian nods. 'Of course. I can't tell you bored I became of roast swan before I finished my time in London, especially when they stuffed it with jellied eels.'

I smile at him gratefully and he moves on to recount the time he was given tripe and had no idea what it was. 'But I learned to avoid it after that.' His face is straight but everyone laughs.

The conversation about foods around the world keeps everyone going until the last of the apple and marzipan tart has been demolished.

'Shall we have some coffee in the *stue*?' asks Ilse.

'I'll bring it,' says Lars. 'You others please go through.'

As I push back my chair, Christian takes my arm. I hadn't seen him come round behind me.

'While we wait for the coffee, Kate and I will go outside onto the balcony and chat. No one minds two old friends catching up, do they?'

'Go ahead. You will freeze and die but go ahead.' Henrik sinks into a leather armchair. Miranda doesn't even blink, but moves through to the other room with Lars without breaking her conversation. She's good. I would have been a bit bothered if Christian had gone off with an old girlfriend like this. But maybe she doesn't know I'm an old girlfriend. Even worse, she might not care. She might be perfectly aware of the fact but not see me as any kind of competition. Looking at her long, elegant legs, her shining hair and her Hermes handbag, I can kind of see why.

Christian ushers me outside and closes the window behind us. The bitterly cold wind whipping off the Baltic is the only thing that feels at all different from the wind whipping off the Thames five weeks ago. I fold my arms around myself and lean back into the shelter of the building. He wordlessly offers his jacket but I shake my head. That feels too much like last time and anyway, Miranda is the one who wears his jacket now. Not that I can imagine her doing so. A designer pashmina for every occasion will be more like it.

'It is quite a surprise to see you here.' His tone is surprisingly neutral and I sneak a glance at him. His face is as unruffled as ever. I am not sure whether to be annoyed that I haven't upset him, or relieved.

'You don't mind?' It's a terrible question and puts me straight at a disadvantage. He has no right to mind what I do or don't do. He gave up that right when he watched me crying on Marie's balcony and did nothing about it.

'It isn't for me to dictate what other people do, is it?'

'That's me, is it? *Other people*. That didn't take long.'

'No, of course it is not. But you and I are no longer a couple. What would give me the right to say where you can and cannot live?'

'Damn right.'

'Which is what I said. But what brings you here, Kate?'

It was never going to be a question I could avoid permanently. Try as I might, I haven't been able to come up with an answer that sounds convincing to myself, let alone anyone else.

'I wanted a change. I was very unsettled after we broke up.' That doesn't sound too bad. In fact, it might even soften his heart a little. Just mentioning the break-up makes my throat tighten.

'So you moved to the home city of the man who had broken up with you?'

'Do you mind?'

'Not if it is what you want. But is it? Will it make you happy?'

'Staying in London wasn't making me happy.'

'What are you hoping to achieve?'

Now would be the time to tell him that I love him, that I can't imagine life without him, that I can learn to fit in with his home and his friends and be whatever he wants me to be. But that is a little more difficult now that Miranda is on the scene.

'I thought it might be nice to see you again. It felt as though we had unfinished business.'

'How so?' He slides his hands into his jacket sleeves for warmth.

'It was all so ... sudden. Usually when people break up, it's more of a joint decision. Unless one of them has been cheating or something.' I break off and stare at him, wondering how long exactly he has been seeing Miranda? Maybe she's a man stealing bitch and I could hate her with good reason instead of irrationally and because of her legs. 'You got together with Miranda pretty quickly.' I watch his face but it doesn't change.

'We met the first day I came back. She had just been placed in your embassy and some of us were asked over. Our firm had done some work for them.'

'If you ask me, that was still pretty quick. In fact, most people would say it was on the rebound.'

'They might but I had not come from a messy and painful break-up, just a sensible decision. She was single too, so why should we not have gone out?'

Hearing him refer to himself as single hurts just as badly as his saying our break-up wasn't painful. If that is true, then why did it leave me curled in a tiny ball on the bed, feeling as though little elves were sticking me with red hot needles?

'But she's British.'

It's my second grievance — second only to the fact that he stomped on my heart and breezed off without a second thought.

'So? You are British too. You see that I am wonderfully unprejudiced.'

'Very funny. You told me that you didn't see me fitting into your life here. I sort of thought that was because of the cultural difference. How is it different with her?'

'She is very well-travelled. She speaks the language. Her mother is Danish and her father English. She seems to fit here already.'

'Yeah, whatever. Well, watch this space, you might be surprised.'

'If you say so. You need to take it at your own pace and do what you need to do. One day you will get the closure you need.'

'Oh, will you stop being so flaming reasonable?'

He laughs. 'I will try.'

I am too cold to stay out here any longer and it is clear from his demeanour that I am not going to get the answers I need — at least not tonight. Luckily, time is on my side. This thing will get sorted out but it is going to take a while. I have to ask him one question before I go in.

'Why did you break up with me in front of everyone, Christian? That was beyond cruel. Was it cowardice on your part?'

His face contracts in shock. 'No, how can you say so? I was thinking only of you.'

'You dump me and humiliate me in front of your friends and it's for *my* sake?'

He shrugs in exasperation at my inability to understand. 'Kate, we always knew it was just temporary. I never promised you anything else. You never asked for anything else.'

'I didn't think I needed to. I thought you knew me. I thought you loved me.'

'Of course I did. But it was not to be for the long term and I always made that clear. Maybe you didn't want to listen.'

I pass over this unfairness in the interest of making the point that has bugged me ever since that appalling evening in Marie's flat. 'Granted that you weren't actually breaking any promises to me, why did you have to rip out my heart and stamp on it in front of that lot?'

'That lot? I don't understand. They were my dear friends. They were your dear friends too. I thought about it for a long time and decided that it was a good place to tell you. That way, our friends were there to offer you support and love if you needed it. But you didn't seem to. I wasn't to know that you had drunk too much to listen properly.'

I drag the icy air into my lungs fast enough to stop me speaking immediately. My first urge is to tip him bodily off the balcony. If he could seriously think that those people were my friends, that I did any more than tolerate those awful evenings with them for the sake of spending time with him, then perhaps we understood each other less than I thought. But that isn't possible. It is a simple cultural misunderstanding. I think carefully before speaking.

'I appreciate that you put some thought into this but you got it totally wrong. They were always your friends, Christian, not mine. I liked them about as much as they liked me. And don't tell me they loved me. We'll just have to agree to differ on that one. Anyway, you hurt me badly that night and you ought to know that.'

'I can see that. And I apologise, Kate, really I do. I did what I thought was for the best. The last thing I ever wanted to do – ever will want to do – is to hurt you.'

'Good. Now I'm going in. It's at least fifty below and it's still only November. How do you Danes manage in the winter?'

He shrugs. 'Maybe you won't be here that long. Now that you know about Miranda, might you not be going back to London sooner rather than later?'

I almost nod but something stops me. If I no longer have any links to Christian, then neither do I have to take his suggestions on board. I smile at him.

'Actually, I really like it here. I think I'll be staying for the foreseeable future.'

And I march back into the living room and sit down again next to Ilse.

Chapter Twelve

I arrive at *The Cinnamon Snail* early. I want to make a good first impression and to show how keen I am. That might make up a bit for my total lack of coffee and sandwich making skills. The elderly woman is there and she nods unsmilingly. I hold out my hand.

'Kate.'

'Mette.'

She stares at me for a moment and I wish I had managed to learn just a few words of Danish, something simple and friendly, just to break the ice. '*I am delighted to be a guest in your country and look forward to a long and productive working relationship.*'

'Tomas?' She calls over her shoulder and I am thankful to see the same guy I talked to on Wednesday.

'*Hej.*' He shakes my hand firmly.

'Hi.' It seems a fairly safe and universal greeting.

'I wondered if you would come or if you would have second thoughts.'

'Why would I do that?'

'It seems quite a big thing, taking a job when you don't speak the language. Not everyone would be so brave.'

I feel quite pleased when he says this. Up until now, I have been uneasily aware that people who don't understand the situation might think I am foolhardy rather than brave. Really unkind people might say stupid. It is nice that someone else can see it as an adventure and understand that I do have every right to be here. Even Christian admitted that and, if he doesn't have a problem with it, no one else ought to.

'What will I be doing?' I ask Tomas.

He pushes his fair hair back from his forehead and looks around. 'Taking some of the work off Mette. Our last barista left suddenly the day before you came in and so she had to come back. It is her café you see. But she doesn't want to be doing this. As soon as you are trained, she can leave it all to us again.'

'I'll work as hard as I can,' I say to her. Maybe she understands some English because she smiles and nods. Tomas reaches under the counter.

'First we have some forms for you. Can you sit at the table there and write them for us? You have a CPR number?'

I brandish my plastic card at him. It arrived this morning and I intend to guard it with my life. Everyone I have met over here has told me about the importance of my number.

'And a bank account?'

'Not a Danish one. I needed a CPR number first.'

'Of course.' He seems to take these numbers as seriously as everyone else does.

'I've got the card safely in my purse. I'm awful at remembering numbers.'

He takes the card and looks at it. 'It's easy. I can tell you are twenty-four and a female.'

'I would kind of hope you might have worked out the female for yourself. How about the age?'

'The first six numbers are your birth date. Did you not notice?'

'I didn't really look. And the rest?'

'The other four numbers are personal but males end in an odd number and females in an even. That is how I could tell you are a woman.'

'Hey!'

He laughs. 'It is the only possible clue.'

I put the car back in my purse and look at the rest of the forms while he serves the steady stream of customers. Once I have finished, he gives them to Mette and shows me the kitchenette behind the café.

'Here are the hygiene rules. They are in pictures too, which will help.'

I feel like a three year old when he says this but I nod and study them carefully.

He grins at me. 'For now, the only phrase you need to learn is *"vaske op"*.'

'Even I can figure that one out. I'm a dab hand at washing up. What about making coffee?'

'Not until you have had some lessons. We do not want to poison the customers. So, here is where we put the empty bowls and cups. We have a dishwasher so it is quite easy. You load and unload it. Then we have a sink as well for us to wash by hand. Can you manage?'

'There is *nothing* I don't know about dishwashers,' I tell him loftily. 'Ooh, it's a Miele. Very upmarket. My old workmate would have loved this.'

'OK. The Sunday lunchtime people are beginning to arrive so I have to go. Good luck.'

I unpack the first dishwasher and start to re-load it. Mette comes in and out, stirring the leek and potato soup and loading up the sandwich press with focaccia. I watch her as carefully as possible in between packing and unpacking and she shows me where things are kept, making me repeat what she says in Danish. None of it makes any sense yet but perhaps it will stick eventually. If the awful Miranda can speak the language then so will I, or die trying. Anyway, she cheated. She has a Danish mother. Mine is from Derbyshire so she was never going to be much help.

By about four o'clock, the crowds are dying down. Tomas comes through.

'How are you doing?'

'OK, I think. There are no more plates to wash.'

'So have a break. I will make you a coffee and you can watch what I do.'

'How about a cappuccino?'

'Coming up.'

I watch him scoop and press the coffee into the filter and he shows me how to clip it into place in the machine. He whirls the steam nozzle around in the jug of milk until it froths up, sends a stream of hot milk into the mug and adds the coffee. 'Lots of foam?'

'Sounds good.'

He piles a drift of foam onto the drink and shakes chocolate across it. 'Choose a cake or pastry if you are hungry.'

'Really? But they cost the earth.'

'Only to the customer. And you have earned it.'

I hover for a second over the trays of cakes, suddenly aware of how hungry I am. I worked straight through lunch. I select a strawberry tart and sit down at a table near the counter.

'Do your feet hurt?' he asks.

'They feel like they're on fire.'

'I remember but it passes. By next Sunday you won't even notice.'

The cake is amazing. Underneath the strawberries is a thick swirl of custard and the pastry beneath that has been brushed with chocolate to stay crisp. By the time I have finished my cappuccino, I feel ready for another four hours washing up and I tell him so. He nods.

'We are quiet until about six o'clock. Come and make me a latte for my break.'

I raise an eyebrow at him. 'You're brave.'

I try to remember what he did and I get the espresso trickling through, although it is a bit watery looking. I half fill the jug with milk and turn on the steamer.

'I love this machine. It's so sleek and professional looking and red is one of my favourite colours. Maybe I'll get a coffee maker for the apartment. One of my flatmates is French and I'm sure she's used to really good coffee.'

'You'll need about twenty or thirty thousand kroner if you want one like this.' He laughs at my startled expression.

'Twenty thousand ... oh, right. Well, this one would be too big for us anyway. Our kitchen is tiny. But they must do smaller ones for about ... 200 kroner?'

'Actually they do. We have a Danish word for such things — *kedel*. Your foam is going to run over.' He gestures at the jug.

'Oh, right, sorry.' I pour the milk onto the espresso and scoop some foam on top before handing him the tall glass. He takes a sip.

'It is actually OK. You couldn't sell it but I am not so fussy. You need to use more coffee next time and push it down harder. But not bad. From now on, you will make all the drinks for our breaks until I think we can sell them without us being prosecuted or closed down.'

He takes a croissant and sits down. He leans back and stretches his long legs under the table, while I stay behind the bar and hope desperately that no one tries to speak any Danish to me.

'Have you worked here for long?' I ask him once he has finished his croissant.

'Three years.'

'Full-time?' I am vaguely surprised that anyone would want to stay making coffee in the same place that long. Maybe he's like Caroline and has a total passion for what he does. He may see it as his mission on earth to educate the Danish palate into the mysteries of tea bags and hot milk.

'No, evenings and weekends mostly. I study part-time.'

'Anything interesting?'

'Most of the time. I study law.'

'What d'you want to be?'

'I would like to do environmental law. But to start with, anything that pays enough to live. How about you?'

'I have an English degree and absolutely no idea what I want to do. I've been selling washing machines and stuff for the past two years but I hated it. I didn't know how much until I left.'

'That is a shame. This might not be the best job in the world but I quite enjoy it. I like to meet the customers and the work is not hard.'

'My work wasn't hard either but my manager was totally insane. She thought there could be no higher calling than flogging, er, *selling* useless bits of equipment that no one needed.'

'They could have said no.'

'You'd have to meet her. I swear half of them bought things just to shut her up and then returned them on her day off.'

He laughs. 'I think you like to exaggerate.'

'I'm underselling it. You had to be there.'

'Is she the reason you came here?'

I kick myself. I pretty much walked into that one. I don't want to tangle myself up in a load of lies but I don't want to talk about Christian to a stranger whom I have only just met, however nice he seems.

'It wasn't just the job. I was getting a bit bored with staying in the one place and one day I realised I didn't have to. I'm not married. I don't have a career. I can see the world a little.'

'And where next? When you have seen Denmark, where will you try?'

I have no answer to this. I keep telling people I am seeing the world when, if I am honest, I only want to see Christian, wherever he might be living. I shrug lightly at the question.

'Who knows? I like to take things a day at a time.'

I don't really. I prefer to plan things years at a time, decades even if I get the chance but Christian has pretty much taken that away from me, leaving me floating round in some helpless limbo and trying to plan my next move.

'I think you are very brave,' he says again and comes back round the bar. 'The next customers will be arriving soon. Can you have some more plates and cups ready?'

By nine o'clock, I am ready to drop. The last customers wander off, talking and laughing and Tomas comes through to the kitchen.

'Mette has left at about eight o'clock. You must have impressed her or she would have stayed and watched you.'

'You can't go too far wrong putting plates into a dishwasher and wiping the worktops.'

'But you are a hard worker. She says you have a willing spirit.'

'*Tak*.'

He laughs. 'One evening here and you are nearly fluent.'

'*Tak*.'

'Are you going to learn Danish?'

'I thought I would go to the language school in town but I have to figure out which times of the week I'll be free.'

'Ideally we would like you here from six until closing Monday to Friday and then lunchtime until closing at the weekends. How would that suit you?'

'Sounds great. I really need to earn my way. I have a room in an apartment in Østerbro and on top of that I need money for bills and food. London was such an expensive place to live that I never really saved much.'

This is true. If I am honest, though, I thought I would be living with Becca until I moved in permanently with Christian. I turn pink even thinking about it. Perhaps it wasn't that wise to put all my eggs in one basket. It wasn't that I ever wanted to live off him financially but I was so focussed on the time that we would decide to move in together, or even marry, that I put other things on hold. I thought there would be time enough for a career once everything else had fallen into place. But that has come crashing down around my ears now so maybe I should make it into a positive. Christian clearly needs some time to think so I will give it to him. I can use the time to learn his language, get to know his country and decide what role I would like to play here in the longer term.

Tomas taps my arm. 'Are you going to sleep?'

I shake myself free of my thoughts. Regrets aren't going to get me anywhere. I need to be looking to the future, not the past. I may not have got everything right so far but I have plenty of time to fix that.

'Is it OK if I get going now?' I ask him. 'It's a longer walk than I thought.'

'You do not have a bike?'

'No, should I?'

'You cannot live in Copenhagen and not have a bike.'

'If you say so. Where's the best place to get one?'

'The main train station.'

'What on earth …?'

'It is where most of mine seem to be stolen from.'

I give a crack of laughter. 'I may just go the legal route. Once I get paid of course.'

'At the end of the first week here, providing you have not broken my beautiful coffee machine before then, you will be paid. So hurry up and get a bank account.'

'First thing tomorrow,' I promise.

He locks the door and follows me out. I shiver in the frosty air. It doesn't get like this in London until January or February. He shakes his head at me.

'No hat?'

'I was going to bring things like that over here after Christmas.'

'Gloves, scarf, thick boots?'

'Pay me first.'

'Fair enough but, if you are to become a Dane, then you must learn to dress for our weather.' He looks at his watch. 'It is a long walk. I saw your address on the forms. Why not take a bus? It goes from just over there.' He points and I see several people standing at a bus stop by the main road.

'Good idea. Just until I get a bike. Thanks for helping me so much today, Tomas. See you tomorrow.'

I run across the road and join the huddle of people at the stop, hoping that no one asks me for directions. I have a couple of Danish phrases now, quite apart from my declaration of love, which I am keeping all ready for the time it is eventually needed. But the other phrases, although useful in a café context, won't help me strike up meaningful friendships with people around me. Tomas has crossed the road too and I see him heading up a side street, when I remember something.

'Hey, Tomas!'

He turns to look at me.

'What does that word *kedel* mean?'

His face breaks into a grin. 'Kettle.' With a last wave of his hand, he disappears.

Chapter Thirteen

I start at the language school on Tuesday morning. I am unsure what to pack but I sling a few pens and a ruler into my backpack, along with a pad of paper, and hope for the best. I fill a water bottle and make a packet of sandwiches, before running for the bus. I watch the stops go by and try to choke down a feeling of nervousness. It feels as though I am going back to school and I fight visions of Miss Turner, who smelled of cats and Mr Higson, who always seemed to home in on me during physics lessons, just to humiliate me. This, I remind myself, will be a group of adults, all of whom actually want to be there and who have the same goals. Maybe not entirely the same goals – I doubt that many of the others will be motivated by the thought of sticking it to their ex-boyfriend's snotty new girlfriend – but close enough.

I follow the stream of students down the path and inside. There is obviously a wide range of nationalities represented here. They mill around in the entrance hall, alone or in small groups, chattering in languages I mostly can't identify. Once we have all registered and been allocated classes, I climb the stairs to find my room. There is only one other person there as yet, a young guy, rocking back in his chair and rubbing his eyes.

'Hi,' I say.

'Hi, I'm Stefan.'

'Kate.'

'OK, Kate from the UK.'

'And Stefan from ...?'

'Germany. You have to excuse my tiredness. It was a good last party. I only flew in this morning.'

'Can you speak any Danish yet?' I ask anxiously. It has been my private fear all week that, even in the beginners' class, everyone else will have learned plenty of Danish by now and I will look completely stupid. I am quite aware that my nationality already has me tagged with the label of being unable or unwilling to learn anyone else's language.

'*Nej.*'

'That's no in Danish.'

'*Ja.*'

'So you do speak some?'

He thumps his chair legs down and grins amiably. 'No, only that much. How about you?'

'*Hej* means hi and *tak* means thank you. That's about it apart from café stuff like *vaske op* but I only know that because it's my job.' I am not mentioning my most important phrase – '*Jeg elsker dig*'. He's not that cute.

'I'm not bothered. They say German speakers have no trouble with Danish. We have all the same vowel sounds you see.'

'Great.'

I feel gloomier than ever. I am sure I will be the only in the entire class doomed to repeat the beginners' class over and over. I will probably be here a year from now, still failing to get my vowel sounds correct, until the guardians of the sacred CPR number catch me and deport me for utter uselessness. I can see Christian coming to the airport to wave me off, looking sympathetic, with Miranda clutching his arm and smirking. It is almost enough to make me repack my bag and make a run for it and I am glad when we are interrupted.

'*Goddag!*' Our tutor has arrived without me noticing. 'You are the enthusiastic ones I see. We have about five minutes until we start. I am Peder. Your names are …?'

We give him our names and he asks where we are from and how long we have been over here. Stefan of course has the perfect excuse, having only landed an hour ago. I feel ashamed to admit I have been here more than a week and learned nothing useful.

'How long before I can hold a proper conversation with a Dane?' I ask Peder and he shrugs and grins.

'It depends how good a pupil you are and how hard you work. The Danes will go out of their way to make it difficult for you.'

'Really?'

He nods again. 'Indeed they will. Most Danes speak excellent English and are very happy to have a chance to practise it, especially if they hear you really *are* British. But don't worry. I will give you a phrase to learn before you leave today, that you can use in such situations. Your Danish friends will think they are being helpful but I want you to speak in Danish all the time. Practise is what makes perfect.'

I nod but the thought of speaking Danish all the time is terrifying. So far, it just sounds to me like a long stream of vowels, with no time to draw breath. Even the words I can make out in print, seem to be pronounced completely differently. It is a pity I am not trying to learn English instead. That has always seemed like such an easy language.

While we have been talking, the other students have wandered in. I am thankful to see none of them look intimidating. Most of them are about my age but there are a few in their forties and fifties and one white haired man who looks about eighty. He announces as soon as he takes his chair that he is from Italy, has fallen in love with a *'bella, bella, molto bella'* Danish woman and has moved here to be with her. Listening to his enthusiasm, I relax. If an elderly guy like this can leave his family, exchange a home in the Italian sunshine for the Danish climate and even brave a new language, just to follow his heart, then I can get through my own particular difficulties. And Christian is definitely *bella, bella* too. Or *belli* or *bello* or something. Whichever, he is definitely it, and learning his language is a very small effort when I think of the future reward.

An hour later, I am beginning to change my mind. Peder has drilled us relentlessly in the vowel sounds. I am annoyed and slightly envious that Stefan was right. He makes the vowel sounds effortlessly whereas, no matter how I try to copy the shape of Peder's lips, nothing comes out but a strangulated squeak.

'Flat *A*, Kate,' he keeps saying. 'Your *A* vowel sound is too open. Tighten your mouth.'

I make one last desperate attempt but end up sounding like someone from *EastEnders*. My eyes prickle and I stare at my hands, determined not to succumb to the ultimate humiliation of crying over a stupid language lesson.

'Break time,' announces Peder. He touches my shoulder as I pass and lowers his voice. 'Don't be discouraged only one hour in. Some of these students will find it very easy but you will struggle for a while at getting the vowels just perfect. When it comes to the grammar, you will have very little trouble and poor Kai-Ying will have to work extra hard.'

'Thanks.' I feel grateful that he has noticed my distress and tried to encourage me. Perhaps he's not a Mr Higson, only out to humiliate me.

'You're very keen. That's half the battle.'

'I have a good reason.'

'That helps. You have just time to get some coffee before we tackle the Danish vowels again.'

'I can't wait.'

After a drink and a bag of crisps from the vending machine, I feel ready to face the vowels and do my Albert Square impression again, though *æ*, *ø* and *å* nearly finish me off. We leave at the end of the second hour, loaded with textbooks and a stack of homework, and I catch the bus home, murmuring the vowels over and over to myself until I catch the eye of an elderly lady and stop. As I walk back to the apartment, I look at all the names on the corner shops and try to pronounce them. The apartment is empty when I let myself in and I make a cup of coffee, murmuring, '*kaffe, ka-ffey, ka-ffur, kaffu,*' until it sounds vaguely like the pronunciation in the book. I will try it out on Tomas tonight.

I spend the afternoon repeating the vowel sounds and memorising as much vocabulary as I can. Jens and Lisette come in just after five and I glance at my watch. I will have to walk very fast or else catch a bus again.

'*Hej.*' I wave a hand at them.

'*God aften,*' says Jens.

'It's not afternoon, it's dark.'

'*Aften* means evening.'

'Oh.' I subside. Perhaps I should steer away from trying to teach a Dane his native language, just for now.

Twenty minutes later, I jump off the bus and run across the grass, just in time for my shift. Mette is wiping tables and nods at me. I beam at her. '*God aften.*'

'*God aften.*' Her face breaks into a rare smile and I go into the kitchen quickly before she decides to follow it up with something incomprehensible.

Tomas is reaching down a stack of plates and he looks up as I rush in.

'You came back for more.'

'I had to. You haven't paid me yet.'

'Good point. Seeing that you are here, can you start to prepare some salad? Did Mette show you?'

'Yes.' I start to scrub my hands and he watches me slice tomatoes for a moment then nods and goes back into the café. I finish the salads and load the dishwasher, while Mette makes pancakes and ladles soup into the bowls. She instructs me in everything she is doing and I repeat obediently. '*Pandekager, Suppe.*'

She nods or shakes her head and makes me repeat everything until she is satisfied. I don't mind. I am lucky to have someone who isn't determined to speak English to me.

Tomas comes in half an hour later, to ask if I want to try making him a drink. I put on my most pained and insulted expression and shrug my shoulders at him.

'Lad være at tale engelsk til mig. Jeg vil hellere tale dansk.'

He gives me a round of applause and breaks into a flood of Danish, grinning all the while.

I slap at his arm. 'Stop it. You know that's all I know.'

'You just told me to stop speaking English to you. You would rather speak Danish. I assumed from this that you are now perfectly fluent.'

'Like heck you did. It's a good phrase though, isn't it?'

'Perfect and your accent isn't at all bad. I will give you two more days and then we speak nothing but Danish.'

'It will be very quiet in here.'

We are both still laughing as I go through to make us both a latte. I am just scooping out the coffee when I hear a familiar voice.

'Kate? What on earth are you doing in here?'

It's Christian and my smile of delight as I look up at him, is tempered first by the fact that he clearly didn't expect to see me here, so he hasn't come in specially, and secondly, by the realisation that he has Miranda with him.

'Hi, Christian. Hi, Miranda,' I say.

'Kate, you work here now?' asks Christian when she doesn't bother to respond.

'I started yesterday.'

'I am surprised.'

'Because?' I give him a challenging stare. This is my territory and he is on it. Worse still, he has brought the vile Miranda onto it, which adds insult to injury.

'I thought your stay here was only temporary.'

'I told you on Saturday it wasn't.'

'True.' He smiles and concedes. 'Well, now we are here, may we order a drink? Miranda?'

'Are you making it?' she asks me. Only I hear the tone of her voice. Christian doesn't react.

Tomas has been standing behind me all this time and he answers her. 'No, I am very sorry but I am on duty tonight. Kate makes an excellent cappuccino but we take strict turns so you are stuck with me.'

I silently bless him. Christian nods at Tomas. 'Nice to meet you. I am Christian and this is my friend, Miranda.'

Any wild hope I may have that he really means this and they are simply friends who occasionally socialise together, is dashed when she puts her arm around him and nods at Tomas. He slides the coffee filter out again without them noticing, adds more coffee and tamps it down deftly.

'What can I get you?'

'Black coffee for me,' says Christian. 'How about you, Miranda?'

'I'll have a glass of white wine,' she says and I glower. If that was all she wanted, then why ask if I was making it? She just wanted to make a point and make me look useless and inefficient in front of Christian.

'Kate, can you get that?' asks Tomas.

I reach down and take a bottle of wine from the fridge. She watches me like a hawk, although I am not sure where she thinks I can go wrong with pouring a glass of wine. Perhaps she thinks I might spit in it. I expect someone like her has to be on the watch for that quite often. I hold out the glass but she doesn't take it.

'I'm just going to the ladies. Take it over to my table, will you?'

'I'll bring them both over if you would like to sit down,' interrupts Tomas and Christian nods and makes for a table right over by the window.

'What did you do to *her*?' asked Tomas. He looks amused.

'Stole her boyfriend,' I say flatly. 'Oh, sorry, I mean the other way round.'

'You and he were ...'

'Still would be if she hadn't come on the scene.' My conscience pricks me. 'That's not quite true but she's sure as hell not helping.'

'You want to talk about it?'

'I really don't.'

'OK.'

He makes his way round the counter and I see him put the drinks on Christian's table. Christian says something to him and Tomas nods but doesn't stay to chat. I want to go back and hide in the kitchen but something makes me stay and watch to see what he and Miranda look like together when other people aren't around. She emerges from the entrance lobby and saunters past, giving me another chance to see how much taller and more slender she is than me. She stops next to me.

'How's the Danish going?' Her voice is sweetly patronising and her smile condescending, although I still somehow doubt that Christian will notice. He sees the best in everyone.

Tomas slides himself back behind the counter. 'I was just saying to Kate how impressed I have been at her swift progress. She has a very good ear.' He squeezes my hand under the counter.

She smirks. '*Det er vidunderlig!*'

'I agree,' he answers in English, so I can understand. 'It is wonderful to hear. It is also wonderful that she is feeling so at home here and learning our language. I hope we keep her for a good while.'

She walks over to Christian, moves her chair very close to his and starts running her fingers through his hair and whispering in his ear. I go back through to the kitchen, so as not to be there when they leave. I don't feel as bad as I thought I would. She may be a total bitch and she may have her claws well into Christian but she is clearly not as secure as she likes to pretend — talking to Tomas in her perfect Danish, taking every opportunity to have a jab at me. Even I am not stupid enough to think that someone like her would see me as very much of a threat but she is clearly either jealous enough or uneasy enough to see me as someone who needs keeping firmly in my place. It isn't much of an encouragement but it's a start.

Chapter Fourteen

It is amazing how quickly I settle into my new life. After the first week goes by, I no longer have the excuse of being a total stranger and people stop welcoming me to my new country. For a couple of weeks, I still wake every morning with the feeling that I am an imposter, a stranger playing at having a life in a strange city, and that any minute I will be found out and sent home. But imperceptibly I find myself falling into a routine of language school, work and taking time to explore the city. I find a tiny coffee shop near our apartment which is open until late and where the manager doesn't mind me sitting for hours with my grammar book and practising my increasing number of phrases on him. I even manage to pass my preliminary pronunciation class and am now concentrating on making my way up the various levels at language school. Peder will move up through the classes with us and I couldn't have a better teacher. He is endlessly patient and never cracks a grin even at our most horrendous howlers.

I now recognise some of the regular customers in *The Cinnamon Snail* and the prospect of them greeting me in Danish is less terrifying than it used to be. I make an attempt to understand their orders and, remembering Peder's instructions, don't let them switch into English. Tomas usually comes to my rescue when I become hopelessly entangled in the middle of a sentence and most people seem happy that I am making the effort and are very tolerant. By the fourth week, I agree to let Tomas speak Danish to me during work time, on the condition that we speak English in my breaks.

'Twenty-four hours of non-stop Danish is sending my brain into melt down,' I grumble and he laughs and agrees.

I enjoy our breaks, even though we both have to take them at different times. We take it in turns to man the coffee machine while the other one sits at the table nearest the counter and we chat to each other in between customers. I hear all about Tomas' ex-girlfriend in law school, who left him after their fourth lecture for their Property Law tutor, and about his family in Jylland. He has a younger sister who is horse mad and his parents run a Bed and Breakfast near Legoland.

I tell him bits and pieces about my life. He asks me one evening about my parents and pulls a face when I tell him they are divorced and don't speak to each other, which means in practice that I hardly spend time with either, for fear of the other one getting upset.

'It is not divorce that's the real problem,' he says. 'It is how uncivilised people can be afterwards. It is very unfair on the children.'

'It was after I left for University. I've always thought they stayed together until I was an adult, which was thoughtful in a way.'

'You didn't suspect?'

'Not really. I'm the youngest child. My sister and brother are quite close in age to me and we all spent a lot of time together. You don't notice much when you're young, I suppose.'

'What do your sister and brother do now?'

'My brother is a doctor and my sister is a solicitor, married to a stockbroker. So they're the respectable ones. I've been a bit unfocussed so I doubt my parents boast about me quite as much as they do about the others.'

'You lived in London, I think?'

This is getting dangerously close to the subject of Christian and I am not quite sure how much I want to talk about that. For one thing, we may be back together quite soon and I am not going to feel good if I have criticised him even slightly. For another, on a bad day, even the subject of him makes me want to break down and cry, especially as the weeks have passed and there has been no sign of him coming back in, despite knowing that I am working here most days. I bet Miranda has forbidden him. I can see her insisting on him finding another café near to his work and then checking every day that he has been there and not here. I have bumped into Ilse and Lars a few times but they have always been in a rush, so we haven't talked about Christian at all.

All this means that the topic of Christian is off the table for now but there is no harm talking about Becca, so I fill Tomas in on our life together in the flat and our time at University.

'Even then, she was totally focussed on being an architect. I've never seen anyone work so hard, in a laid back, uncompetitive sort of way. She goes after her own goals but she never measures herself against anyone else or cares how well or badly they do.'

'She sounds a very unusual person. I would like to meet her. Will she come and stay?'

We are edging back towards the subject of Christian here. I am not going to explain that Becca won't come unless I stay here long enough. He might ask me why she thinks I won't and that might lead to her views on my moving country and even to mentions of lobotomies.

'I don't know. She might. I'm going back for Christmas if Mette can give me a few days off. I can't wait. Becca's got one of her deadly pizzas in mind for Christmas day, unless I promise to cook the turkey.'

'It is a pity you will not be here for your first Danish Christmas. You could have come to Jylland with me.'

I stare at him. 'Really? That's very kind but your parents don't know me.'

'Why should that matter? They like everyone.'

'A bit like you then.'

'I like most people, yes,' he concedes. 'But that is only because it is more effort to dislike people and I am lazy.'

I am curious. 'Whom do you dislike?'

'Anyone who hurts a friend of mine.'

I decide to change the subject quickly. It could be a generic statement but he could also conceivably be referring to Christian. I don't really see how he should be but it is better to steer clear. They have only met once and I haven't said anything about our break-up, apart from the fact that it happened. I cheer up when I realise he probably means Miranda. She is the one who has hurt me, not Christian.

'Your turn for a break,' I say, and swallow my last mouthful of soup. Mette is quite happy for me to eat here in the evenings and it saves me having to cook at home. We switch places. I make him his latte and whisk the last froth onto the top with a flourish. He can make leaves and flowers on the foam but I have only just mastered the perfect latte, so I stick to that. Once the evening customers arrive in force, we don't really have a chance to talk further and I cycle home at the end of the evening, exhausted as usual.

The following morning, I am very touched to receive an invitation in the post from Ilse. It is a printed card, decorated with Christmas trees and the beautiful Danish red and white Christmas hearts. It invites me to a party at her apartment in the middle of December and she has scribbled a handwritten message at the bottom of it. *'Do come if you can manage it. Lars and I would love to see you again and catch up on all your news. If you would like to, then you should bring a guest.'*

I wonder if Christian will be there. If so, will he be alone? I am pleased to realise that I would want to go to the party even if I knew he wouldn't be there. I hesitate for a while over the idea of taking a guest, in case Christian gets the wrong idea, but decide in the end to see if Tomas is free. I would like to pay him back a little for some of his kindness. And Christian knows we work together so he won't jump to any conclusions. He doesn't jump to many anyway. He is always very measured and ready to give everyone the benefit of the doubt. And it's none of his business, a little voice whispers. He has a new girlfriend and so would have no reason to object even if I were seeing someone else. But I reject the thought as unworthy. Christian is totally honest and he doesn't play games so neither will I. If we are to get through this, we need to be completely straight with one another.

The party is on a Saturday night and Tomas agrees to join me once the café is shut.

'Mette can't spare us both but, if things are quiet, she will let me sneak off early.'

I give him Ilse's address and arrange to meet him there as soon as possible. I spend far less time planning my outfit than I did the first time I went round there. For one thing, I am more used to the Danish lifestyle now and how casual everything is. It suits me fine. I was never one for dressing up and the memory of that last awful evening at Marie and Jeremy's still haunts me. I have also come to accept that I am never going to win Christian back by sheer glamour. For one thing, I have none, and for another, Miranda has enough for half the female population of Copenhagen. Christian must have fallen for more than my looks. He is so handsome he could have any woman he wants — except Becca it seems. There must have been something about my personality he liked, so I will have to rely on that instead. I pull on my smartest jeans and a cherry red cashmere sweater as it is Christmas. Christian's amethyst necklace won't go with it but it didn't exactly bring me luck the last time I went to Ilse's, so I settle for a silver chain with a red stone instead, collect my flowers from the sink and wine from the fridge and set out for the party.

The apartment is fuller than the last time I was here. Jens and Ilse have pushed back all the furniture to make more space and I am greeted by the smell of *gløgg*, the mulled wine we have been serving in the café all this month. Ilse takes me through to meet a few people and politely ignores my frantic scanning round the room for Christian. I don't have the courage to ask her if she has invited him. Of course she has. Everyone always invites Christian and their faces fall if he can't accept. In fact, I feel vaguely guilty for being here without him, even though we are no longer a couple. I have been conditioned by too many evenings in London, where Milla or Marie's face dropped a fraction when they opened the door to find just me on the doorstep, before they hoicked their cheeks back up into full face-lift mode. After one dreadful evening when Christian phoned to say he was delayed at work but urged me to go anyway — 'They *love* you, Kate' — I resolved never to agree to arrive at any event unless I knew he was either there, or had phoned to tell me he was on his way.

He doesn't appear to be here yet. Perhaps he and Miranda are at some impossibly glamorous dinner with the Ambassador - or she won't let him out of the house in case he meets me.

Ilse introduces me to a group of workmates and we chat for a while. They speak English to me but I am pleased to find, when I hear snippets of other conversations in the room, that I can pick out words and even phrases that I understand. We had a whole session on Christmas customs and vocabulary in Peder's class this week, so now I can wish people *god jul og godt nytår* with the best of them. He also told us about the *nisser*, the naughty Danish Elves, who have to be fed rice pudding to keep them sweet and who leave little gifts for good children during December. They sound more interesting than anything we have back home.

Lars waves a plate of tiny dumplings at us as he passes. 'I will put them on the table. Come and get them.'

'*Æbleskiver?*' I ask my neighbour and he nods.

'You are learning fast. Have you had them ever?'

I shake my head. 'Do I want to?'

'Surely. Come over and take a plate.' He helps me to a heap of the round, golden balls and shows me how to pour melted jam over the pile and sprinkle them with icing sugar. I plunge my fork into one of the balls, drag it through the jam and take a bite. They are delicious, crisp and soft at the same time and I quickly take a second.

'Kate, you are here!'

I spin around at the sound of the familiar voice, to find Christian standing behind me, resplendent in a navy sweater that makes his eyes bluer than ever. For a moment, I am knocked sideways by the rush of love and emotion that sweeps through me and I can't do anything but stare at him. So it takes me a second to register the scornfully amused face next to him. She leans towards me. 'Did you know you have jam on your face?'

I scrub at it furiously with a napkin and feel my face reddening. 'Of course I didn't or I would have rubbed it off.'

'But why? It matches your sweater.' She turns away to greet Ilse and I frown as I see them kiss and greet each other like old friends.

'You look lovely,' says Christian.

'Apart from the jam.'

'Even with the jam.' He smiles and it is as much as I can do not to fling myself into his arms and kiss him.

Miranda turns back to us. 'And ... how ... are ... you ... finding ... things ... here?'

I gape at her and she shakes her head and laughs musically. 'Silly me, I forgot. It's Danish you can't speak, not English.'

I look at Christian. Surely he is going to notice this hostility. But he is laughing.

'Her English is perfect.'

'Of course it is!' I snap. 'She's just trying to make me look stupid.'

'Not at all,' she says. 'I just forgot for a moment exactly what you do and don't understand.'

Her eyes challenge me. Even if Christian is too dim or too besotted to notice, I understand perfectly well what she means. I am fed up of her snideness. She has got Christian. What more does she want? I am simply not letting her get away with these backhanded remarks.

'I'm not stupid, you know,' I fling at her. 'Don't you think I know what you're getting at?'

'Kate?' Christian sounds a little shocked and she reaches for his hand, smiling slightly. 'There is no reason for you to be so ...'

'Kate?' I feel Tomas' arms go round me from behind. He hugs me and I lean back thankfully against his solid warmth.

'Tomas, I'm so glad you're here.'

'Tomas.' Christian holds out his hand and Tomas shakes it, looking round at the three of us.

'Having a good party?'

'Yes'

'No.'

Christian and I answer simultaneously and Tomas grins.

'Well, the *æbleskiver* look good.' He grabs a fork and lifts one off my plate. I hand him the rest.

'Go on, have them all. I'm not hungry anymore.'

'I am sorry you are not enjoying the party, Kate.' Christian's eyes are unfathomable as he puts his arm around Miranda and points her towards the other room, where Henrik is waving at them both. 'Perhaps now that Tomas is here, you will enjoy it better.'

'What?' But he has already turned away. Miranda throws me the tiniest smile as they go. This is awful. He seems to think ... does he think that Tomas and I ...?

I turn back to the table. 'This party's a washout. I knew it was going to be a total failure from the moment I heard about it.'

'So thanks for including me in it.' Tomas laughs at me and I smile reluctantly.

'I didn't mean it exactly like that but first of all Miranda was horrible to me and now it seems as though Christian thinks you and I are an item.'

'Is that so bad?' he interrupts and I frown. Surely he can't mean anything by this. The last thing I need in my life is any extra complications. He smiles at my expression.

'Don't look so horrified. If he thinks you have found someone else, it might make him know his own mind more quickly.'

'Oh. Well, it might do I suppose but he's found someone else who's completely horrible so he doesn't show any signs yet of knowing his own mind.'

'He might know his own mind and just like her for herself.' He sees my face. 'Stupid thought. Of course not.'

'I know you're teasing me but, honestly, can you imagine anyone liking her for anything other than her outward appearance?'

'She is not my type for sure but are you not imagining the worst things into all her behaviour?'

'No.'

He laughs and takes my hand. 'OK, then. She is a monster and he is a fool.'

'He is not.' I pull my hand away and he shrugs.

'What is he then?'

I think for a moment. 'He's confused. Just very, very confused. And she's taking advantage of that.'

'As you will. Shall we go and talk to the others?'

The party doesn't get any better. I talk and laugh and try to understand some of what is being said to me. Christian and Miranda sit together on the far side of the room and I couldn't get near them even if I wanted to. As usual, he is surrounded by a chattering group. At one point, he lifts his eyes to see me staring at him and he gives me a half smile. He doesn't look angry any longer, more understanding. If anything, that is worse. I don't want his understanding. It is only one step away from pity and that is the one thing I couldn't bear from him.

At about 11pm it feels all right to leave without being rude and I find Ilse to thank her for the invitation.

'You had a good time, I hope?'

'Of course, and thank you so much for asking me.'

'I like your friend. He is very pleasant.'

'Tomas? Yes, he's a good friend.'

'Are you and he ...?' She pauses delicately and I shake my head at once. I don't want her or anyone else getting any ideas. She sees Christian all the time and the last thing I need is her telling him her suspicions as fact. Time to knock that one on the head.

'No, he's a good friend. We work together. As for anything else — no way, not ever.'

'Are you ready to go?'

I spin round to find that Tomas is behind me. I had thought he was still in the other room. With all the noise around us, I hope he didn't hear what I said. He probably didn't. His face is impassive and his smile is as friendly as ever as he thanks Ilse, helps me on with my jacket and follows me out into the night.

Chapter Fifteen

Christmas has not so much crept up on me as rocketed up and I feel horribly unprepared when I wake on the 22nd December and realise it is my last day at the café. I am looking forward to going home. Of course I am, but it would have been nice to see my first proper Danish Christmas too. Maybe next year.

I think of Tomas' invitation to his parents' house. He has been so kind these past few months. There have been times when I don't know how I would have got through everything without him. He is always there, always calm and unflustered and ready to see the funny side of any situation. In many ways, he reminds me of Becca, without her fake grumpy side. I have wondered several times over the past few weeks how they would get on together. They could be the perfect match. I hope that she will book a holiday here in the spring or summer and I can introduce them. Assuming of course that she hasn't yet managed to let Jon in IT know how she feels. Maybe she has seized the moment and I will go back to find he has moved in and is sharing her marmalade and bacon pizzas each night. After all, it has been two and a half months. It has flown by for me because I have had so much to do, but for her it might have been quite a long time. I need to be prepared to find things have changed and not selfishly assume that time has stood still for everyone in London while they waited for me to return.

I arrive at work a little early. Mette asked me to come in for the lunchtime rush, as today is many people's last day at the office and they tend to eat out to celebrate that fact. So I put her and Tomas' presents in my bag, strap on my bike helmet and cycle as fast as possible along the sea front because it is so cold. It isn't the lovely crisp cold we have had all week either, with bright blue skies and the sun skimming the tops of the waves and tipping them with gold as I fly past. It is grey and damp with a biting wind and a hint of fog rolling off the sea. Not very Christmassy at all, I think, as I lock the bike and dive inside.

The café is more cheerful. We have strings of lights everywhere and they fill the dark corners with light and the promise of the holiday to come. All the tables have the usual vase of flowers, which bloom cheerfully in the soft pools of light thrown around them by the candles.

Lunchtime is as busy as Mette predicted, but everyone who comes in seems so cheerful that my spirits rise too. I will see Becca again tomorrow and it will be lovely to spend Christmas in London. And I will be back here before I know it and looking forward to the spring. I try not to think about anything else I might look forward to. After the Christmas party, Christian seems further away than ever but I am not giving up yet. He is worth far more than the paltry three months of my life I have so far invested in winning him back.

When the lunchtime crowd has drifted back to its offices where, judging by the glasses of wine and spirits I have poured, I suspect very little work will be done, I work hard to get the kitchen in order ready for the evening. When the last plate has been wiped and put away, Tomas appears in the doorway. 'You were due a break half an hour ago. You must be hungry.'

I follow him through to the café. 'Not really. It's all been such a rush I haven't had time to think about it. But I will have one of these fruit tarts. It will be the last decent pastry I get for a week.'

'London does not have such good ones?'

'Probably Harrods or somewhere like that does but the baker round the corner from us sells awful buns with pink icing and bits of coconut – and big, white meringues with fake cream and hundreds and thousands.'

'So there is something at least to bring you back here?'

'What do you mean? There are a million things to bring me back here. The pastries are just a bonus.'

'I wondered — that is all.'

'You're kidding?' I scan his face to see whether he is making one of his usual jokes but he looks very serious as he pours steaming milk into my glass. 'Tomas, I love it here. I love the apartment. I love my job. It will be great to see Becca again but I'm already looking forward to coming back.'

'I think you have a bigger reason than your apartment and job,' he says quietly and I am annoyed at how quickly my face heats up.

'You know?'

'Of course. I have met him, don't forget.'

'And his girlfriend,' I remind him, trying to keep my voice uncaring and failing miserably.

'I don't think she makes much difference to how you feel, does she?'

'Not really.'

I take the glass he hands me and sit down. I suppose that I dislike Miranda so much that I can't see her and Christian staying together. He's not stupid. He must see through her at some point. I remember Marie and wonder if I am right. She seemed so shallow to me, even making a play for my boyfriend with me in the room, but Christian never seemed to see through her. I reassure myself that he is just so kind that he probably saw through her faults to the person beneath and tolerated her many stupidities because he could see she had a beautiful soul. *Quite* a nice soul, I amend in my head as I remember her more clearly. Perhaps he also sees through Miranda's bitchy, condescending exterior, to the loveliness beneath. It's a worrying thought but it doesn't take long to shrug it off. There is no loveliness beneath. She has just thrown him temporarily with her long legs and her annoying ability to speak Danish. They quite obviously have nothing in common. They don't seem to share the laughs that he and I did and she clearly has no sense of humour. I don't need to worry that it will last. And, when his eyes are opened and he gets rid of her, I will be right here, making a life, learning his language, mixing happily with his friends. It won't take long for him to realise what he has lost.

'I am still here.' Tomas is staring at me and I have the uncomfortable feeling he has read my thoughts pretty directly. He doesn't ask any more questions so I don't have to pursue the subject.

'Sorry, Tomas, I was day dreaming. I've got a lot going on. I fly at lunchtime tomorrow and I'm sure there's a load of things I've forgotten.'

'The turkey?'

I burst out laughing. 'I'm not flying with a turkey, you idiot, or on one. Becca will have got that. At least, I hope she will. Otherwise it will be a hungry Christmas.'

'I have something for you.' He reaches behind the counter and hands me a wrapped parcel.

'Thank you so much. Can I open it?'

'If you like.'

'Open yours too.' I go round the counter and open my bag. 'There you go.' I toss a wrapped box over to him and he laughs.

'I hope it is not breakable.'

'You'll have to find out.'

I rip through the paper on my gift, smiling at the little *nisser* dancing across a snowy background, and pull out something soft and teal coloured. It is a beautiful wool scarf and I find a matching hat and gloves wrapped inside it. I don't speak for a moment as I slide their soft warmth through my fingers.

'Tomas, they're lovely,' I say at last.

'I am glad you like them.' He delves into his package and emerges with a state of the art kettle. I got Caroline to post it to me, which made her year. His face breaks into a grin. 'Perfect. How well you know me.'

'I'd have got something nicer if I'd known what you were getting me. How did you know this was my favourite colour?'

'I guessed. I couldn't stand seeing you come in every day with blue fingers and a red nose.'

'I was waiting to go home and pick up my winter things, but they're not even a tenth as nice as these, so I think I'll leave them for Becca if she wants them.' I wind the scarf round my neck and pull on the gloves and hat. 'I'm wearing them this evening.'

'In the café? You will boil like my kettle.'

'I don't care. I'm keeping them on — except for the gloves because I have to wash up.' I march into the kitchen, leaving him laughing.

I am just bringing out the clean milk jugs for him, when the door opens, letting in a flurry of cold air. I look up and Christian is standing there. He is wearing his cashmere coat and tiny ice flakes sparkle and dance against the charcoal grey, before vanishing.

'*God aften*,' I greet him and his face breaks into a beam.

'*God aften. En kaffe latte og en kanelsnegl.*'

He watches me as I set up the coffee maker and reach for the pastries. I like the little cinnamon snails too. It feels like a small link between us.

'You are doing so well with the language, Kate.'

'*Tak.*'

He reaches for his wallet and pays. 'I don't suppose you have a minute?'

'Actually, I've just had my ...'

Tomas intervenes. 'You are just about due for a break, aren't you? I have finished mine.'

'Thanks, Tomas.'

I pull off my apron and follow Christian to the same table in the window where he sat with Miranda. I feel a little uncomfortable at the thought but brush it away. He is the one who ought to feel uncomfortable, not me.

'You're all alone tonight?' I ask as I pull out a chair and sit down. I refuse to mention Miranda's name. It will only make her more real and there is always the chance that they are not together any longer. In which case, why remind him of her?

'Yes, I am alone. Miranda has an Embassy do.'

I try not to pull a face when he says her name. I need to show him how mature I can be. Obviously her nasty behaviour at the party didn't register. Men can be so slow sometimes, even Christian.

'You weren't invited?'

'I was but it sounded very dull and I have been wishing for a while to come back here and see you.'

I don't dare think about the implications of this. On the face of it, there is no reason why someone as gregarious as Christian wouldn't drop in and chat to an old friend. He must now know by now that any pet rabbits he may have acquired since his return, are safe from me. But I am not just any old friend and he knows exactly why I am here in Copenhagen, so stopping by just for a gossip might be more unusual. He doesn't mess people around and he never plays games. At worst, he must still care about me and be checking how I am. At best ... but I don't let myself finish this thought, just give him the most relaxed smile I can manage.

'It must be an incredibly boring party if you turned down an invite. You love parties.'

'There were to be speeches by economists, Kate, and nameless things in pastry.' His face breaks into a smile and I can't help laughing with him, even though I am determined not to show any emotion apart from a casual friendliness before he does.

'I admit that I would take a *kanelsnegl* over an economic *vol-au-vent* any day. How's the coffee?'

He sips it and nods. 'I am impressed. You have learned a lot since you came here.'

'I can make pancakes too.'

'It's not what I meant. I would like you to know that even though things have not been so ... happy between us, I was wrong about how well you would cope in a strange city.'

I hold my breath. Does that mean he could see things working between us again? He doesn't pursue the subject and I can't think of a way to do so, so we sit and chat idly about his return home and his work here. He asks me about the apartment and I tell him about the bike I have bought, with flowers woven around the basket.

'You are practically a native now.' His eyes are warm with laughter.

'Nowhere near I'm afraid, but I'm getting there.' I hold his gaze as long as I dare when I say this.

'I like your scarf and hat.' He gestures to my head and my hand flies up to touch them. I am slightly embarrassed by his noticing them.

'I'm just trying them on.' I don't know why I don't mention they were a gift from Tomas.

'Your favourite colour too.'

'You remember.'

'Of course.'

I hope he isn't remembering the teal dress I bought for his farewell party and what a fool I made of myself. I have changed a lot since then. I hope he can see it too.

He drains his glass and pushes his chair back. 'You look like you are busy in here tonight and I have to collect Miranda from the party soon. But I just wanted to wish you a very Happy Christmas. It was good to see you again.' He kisses my cheek and makes for the door, waving at Tomas as he passes him. '*Godnat, Tomas.*'

Tomas raises a hand and, once Christian has gone, comes round the counter to me.

'Are you OK?'

'Fine, I'm fine. Why wouldn't I be?'

'You are a little flushed.'

'It's hot in here. It was nice of Christian to come by and see how I'm doing, don't you think?'

'For sure. Is that all he wanted?'

'What else? We split up, remember?'

'I remember. If you are sure you are OK, shall we clear some tables?'

'Great.'

I deliberately start at the opposite end of the café to Tomas, to avoid any further questions and to sort out in my mind what just happened. I stack dishes and wipe tables automatically as I remember the light in Christian's eyes when he smiled at me. It was as though nothing had ever changed between us. Surely he doesn't look at Miranda like that too? Or does he in fact look at everyone like that, just because he likes people so much, and I always misinterpreted it as something special just for me?

Ten minutes later, I have given up thinking. I am not going to solve this particular puzzle and my head hurts. I have to stick to the fact that Christian clearly still cares about me enough to come in and see how I am. I don't buy him blowing off a party just because it sounded boring. He finds something or someone interesting at any gathering. Anyway, wouldn't most people want to go along and support their new girlfriend, however horrible she might be? I stop myself mid-thought and remember that it is entirely possible that Christian doesn't find her quite as vile as I do. Anyway, he chose me over her tonight. He let her go off alone so he could see me without her hanging around being snippy and showing off her legs and her Danish. I wonder if he has told her who she was dropped for tonight. My elation subsides as I realise he will definitely have told her. He won't have seen any need to keep his visit to me a secret. I am an old friend. He is scrupulous about maintaining contact with everyone he has been friendly with. I am sure he keeps in regular contact with Marie and Jeremy and Milla and Rupe. I imagine scented envelopes arriving each week from Marie, covered in cherry red lipstick kisses.

I am carrying the pile of plates over to the kitchen, when it occurs to me that he never kept in touch with me. He cut all contact and didn't even give me an address or a number where he could be reached. For a second, I am totally crushed to find myself so far down the pecking order, below Marie and Milla. In fact, below probably half the people he worked with. A wave of anger sweeps me and then disappears as swiftly as it came. There must surely be a reason why he behaved like that. He is always so polite, so caring towards everyone and yet he cut me adrift even when he knew how much I was hurt. The longer I think about it, the more it seems to me that that it is entirely possible the decision to break up with me was harder than he realised it would be and the only way he could manage it was to sever all contact. Even if he felt at the time that he had good and sufficient reasons why we should part, my heart leaps at the thought that maybe, just maybe, it was as difficult for him as it was for me.

Tomas is unpacking the dishwasher as I come in. 'That took a while.'

'Sorry, I'm a bit tired I think. Let me finish that.'

'As long as you are OK?'

I look into his friendly, slightly anxious green eyes and nod.

'I'm really fine. Thanks for looking out for me but there's no need. All in all, I think this has been a pretty good evening.'

He nods and jingles the bunch of keys. 'Out with you, then. Have a wonderful holiday.'

'You too.' I hug him tightly and kiss his cheek. '*God jul.*'

His face relaxes as he kisses me back. '*God jul, Kate, og godt nytår.*'

Godt nytår? I think of the New Year to come and smile happily as I unlock my bike. Against all previous odds, there seems every chance that it will be a good one after all.

Chapter Sixteen

When the plane touches down on the tarmac the following afternoon, I feel a rush of excitement. As we flew in over London and I looked down at the patchwork green fields, crisscrossed with tiny roads, I felt a sense of belonging that I haven't felt in the past three months, despite having enjoyed myself. It will come, I remind myself as I unbuckle and stretch my stiff legs. I am still such a stranger over there and I have lived here all my life. I follow the other passengers through the concourse and wave my passport cheerfully at the immigration official.

'You look pleased about something,' he says as he inspects my truly awful photo.

'I've been away for a few months.' I snatch it from his hand as soon as decently possible in the hope he won't remember the madwoman with her hair sticking out on one side and the earnest expression.

'Always nice to be home, isn't it? Have a good Christmas.'

'You too.'

I collect my nearly empty suitcase from the carousel and make for the exit. As I emerge, a babble of chatter and laughter hits me. Family members are screaming and hugging grown-up children arriving home for Christmas, and men in peaked hats stand around, holding cardboard signs scrawled with the names of passengers.

'Are you going to walk right past me?'

I jump and look round to see Becca leaning against a barrier. She looks exactly the same as ever, scruffily dressed, slightly rumpled and sardonic and I promptly burst into tears at the sight of her. She doesn't seem surprised or fazed as she leads me to the nearest table and sits me down.

'Sorry, Becca. I didn't mean to start the weeping as soon as I saw you,' I hiccup.

'It's OK. I actually get that a lot. Shall we have a coffee?'

I nod and she joins a nearby line. Nothing changes, I reflect. I have a crisis, she stays calm, we both drink cappuccino and I find that whatever it was that has brought my entire world crashing around me, isn't actually that important. A great wave of contentment sweeps me and I lean back and wait for her.

'Cappuccino, extra chocolate?' she calls over to me. 'Or are you on the akvavit now?'

'Not before 3pm.'

She comes across with a tray and I take my drink. 'It really is great to see you. I didn't expect you.'

'If you'd flown into Stansted you'd definitely have been on your own.'

'I've got a job now. I thought I'd splash out and come into Heathrow. So how *are* you? You look well.'

'It's been just under ten weeks. I haven't had enough time to go into a decline.'

The Cinnamon Snail

It's nice that she counted the weeks.

'How's Jon?' I ask and she shrugs.

'He's fine as far as I can tell. He has a new boyfriend.'

'He's gay?' I gasp and she grins at my shocked face.

'Exactly, how very *dare* he?'

'When did you find out?'

'My first clue was when a nice-looking young man came to pick him up one day and they left holding hands. After that, I began to have a very slight suspicion. But then I saw him reading Homes and Gardens one day.' She spreads her hands and pulls a face. 'After that little debacle, I knew for sure.'

'Are you OK?'

'Despite our long and passionate history of buying coffee from the same vending machine and saying hi, you mean? Yeah, I think I'll survive.'

'I wish I'd been here. I could have ...'

'I'm all agog. What?'

'Bought you a book token or something,' I say lamely and she laughs. I perk up when I remember Tomas.

'I've actually met someone who'd be perfect for you. He's really nice, really kind and he's even ...'

'... a transvestite?' she finishes. 'No, I'll make my own mistakes, thank you. Talking of your mistake, how is he?'

'He's fine. And he's not a mistake,' I add hurriedly, kicking myself for not pretending not to know to whom she was referring.

'Has he changed his mind yet?'

'Not yet. I think he might be softening but he's being hampered by this awful woman he's met.'

She drains her cup. 'Poor thing. And even that hasn't dampened your ardour?'

'No, so it must be love, don't you think?'

'There's a coach leaving in five minutes if you've finished.'

I accept her change of subject and we board the coach, where I fill her in about everything that has happened since I left. I have sent her loads of emails but her answers all tend to be one-liners and not very informative, so I haven't told her anything more than the facts about my job and apartment and my impressions of life in Copenhagen.

'Sounds like you've had more fun than I expected,' she says as we climb off the coach and wait for a bus home.

'I've had more than I expected,' I agree.

'How long will you stay?'

'Depends. If things go well when I get back, then maybe permanently.'

'And if they don't?'

'They will.'

I remember the look in Christian's eyes as he said goodbye in the café. It was almost like old times. In fact, had it not been for stupid Miranda, I am pretty sure he would have asked me to get back together right then. I sigh as I think how perfect that would have been. My first Christmas in Denmark with the man I love — candles and Christmas hearts and all our friends around us. It will just have to wait until next Christmas instead. It will still be special.

'This is our stop.' She nudges me and we lug the case down the steps and onto the pavement.

The flat is just the same as ever, untidy and friendly and smelling faintly of Chinese food.

'I haven't got any groceries,' she says. 'I thought we could go and do that tomorrow. It's Christmas Eve and the office shuts at lunchtime.'

'Great. I've got all my presents. The shopping is wonderful there, especially this time of year. The main shopping street has lights everywhere and stalls with people selling roasted chestnuts and gorgeous almonds in burnt sugar. Tomas and I went into town one day and we shared a bag of them.'

I think back to that afternoon. It was before he gave me my gloves, so my hands were numb and chapped and he bought me the almonds to warm my fingers. The frosted air was scented with vanilla and caramel.

'What's he like then, this Tomas?'

I jump as she brings me sharply back to London. 'Oh, he's great. He's funny and kind and friendly and he never says anything critical about anyone. He's very like Christian I suppose. I hadn't thought of that before.'

'I thought you said he was funny.'

'So is Christian. He can be very funny.'

'If you say so. What about dinner?'

'Shall we go to Phil's? Is he still doing food?'

'It has been described as such.'

'Come on then, I'll pay. You came to meet me.'

'OK.' She shrugs on her coat. 'I like your hat and scarf.'

I display them proudly. 'Tomas gave them to me. Gloves too. The trouble is, it isn't nearly as cold over here. Denmark has snow forecast for tomorrow.'

'We've got rain and fog coming in tonight. Is nothing ever good enough for you?'

'I should have asked Tomas to buy me an umbrella instead.'

Grape To See You looks exactly the same. It is half empty and I notice a light bulb has blown in the corner fitting.

'He'll never get any customers if he doesn't try a bit harder,' I whisper to Becca as we enter.

'Give him some professional tips,' she says. I am not sure if she is serious.

A booming voice emerges from the darkness behind the bar, followed by Phil. 'I know you two! Long time no see.'

I wave at him. 'I've been away, remember? But you must have seen Becca?'

'I don't think so. I thought you'd both gone away.'

'It wouldn't have done my reputation any good to be seen alone in a bar as a single woman,' she says primly.

'It's all looking the same,' I say, glancing round again. 'How's business?'

'It's slow but it'll pick up. Christmas isn't a good time for places like this.'

If he can't get customers into a wine bar at Christmas, he never will, but I don't say anything. It's up to him how he wants to run his business.

'Good luck with it,' I say and raise my glass.

'It always takes a while to build up a clientele,' he says. 'And if the best customers keep going away for months, what are you going to do?'

'We'll drink you dry this week,' I promise him and his face lights up.

We sip our glasses of wine in comfortable silence. It's the thing I appreciate most about Becca. She doesn't feel the need to fill every silence with chatter. If she has something to say, she says it and doesn't waffle. Otherwise, she is quite happy with silence. I lean back and let the past few months drain from me. It is nice being back at Phil's, even if it isn't the smartest bar I have ever visited. He grins at us over the counter as we chat, and even manages to make us some very edible toasted sandwiches. A few people drift in during the evening and he greets them cheerfully. Perhaps he will make a success of this place eventually. He seems quite relaxed about the whole thing, so I decide to stop worrying on his behalf and concentrate on my own life. It certainly needs concentrating on. Christian and I broke up in September and it is now almost Christmas. I don't want to let things drag on for too long, or he might start to get used to us being apart. Once Christmas is over and I am back in Copenhagen, I need to step up my efforts to see him more regularly and let him see how well things could work between us. Miranda is a slight problem but I push her image to one side. Someone as nice as Christian isn't going to put up with her for much longer.

I sleep like a log when we get home. It is so nice to be back in my own familiar bed and not to wake in the morning to sleet or threatening snow clouds. In fact, it is about ten degrees and sunny when I poke my head out of the front door the next morning, just after the postman has come. I take the pile of letters through to the kitchen, to find Becca slumped in her usual chair, scratching her head and yawning.

'Morning,' I say. 'These look like bills mostly. Oh, and a postcard. Who's sending you postcards at this time of year?'

'Not Jon, that's for sure.' She yawns and holds out a hand. 'Shove it over here.'

I pass it across and fill the kettle. She waves the card at me. 'Unless I changed my name to Kate after all those cocktails last night, which is perfectly possible, then this is for you. Didn't you see the Danish stamp?'

I turn the card over, my heart beating faster, and scan to the end for the signature. Becca is watching me with interest. I shrug in disappointment.

'No, it's from Tomas, not Christian.'

'Why is he sending you postcards already?'

'He must have sent it before I left.' I turn over the card. It is one that the café gives out free for advertising purposes and I show her the photograph of the café looking out over the water. I read the card out loud. *Just to remind you of what you have left behind. The Miele is very much looking forward to seeing you again. Have a great holiday and say hi to your friend. Yours, Tomas.*

'He's keen,' she says.

'You've got the wrong end of that particular stick,' I say, dropping the card back onto the table. 'He's a good friend. He's my best friend over there actually – apart from Christian of course.'

'Of course, apart from Christian.'

She piles butter on her toast and I stare at her, more than a little nettled. She doesn't seem to miss an opportunity to dismiss or belittle Christian, even if just by her tone. It isn't like Becca. She is normally so fair-minded, even if plain spoken. I need to have it out with her before this ruins the holiday, so I sit opposite her and take the plunge.

'Becca, if you've got something to say about Christian, for goodness sake say it. All these sarcastic comments and shrugs don't really do it for me.'

She holds out her hand. 'Pass the jam. I've got no problem talking about Christian. I just thought you didn't want to.'

'I didn't but you have clearly got some feelings about this whole ... situation. So, let's hear them.'

'OK. How long have you been there now?'

'You already told me, about ten weeks.'

'And how many times have you seen Christian?'

'Ilse's dinner party, her Christmas party and, let's see, twice at the café.'

'How many times without his girlfriend?'

'Once.'

'And you're basing your whole future on the fact that you've seen Christian on his own once and he hasn't been too awful to you. Doesn't that strike you as a tiny bit ...'

'What?'

'Desperate.'

For a moment after she says this, I am at a loss for words. This is spectacularly unfair. I may not have seen him often but it took a while for us to break the ice and she didn't see his face the evening he came in to wish me Happy Christmas. But there is no use trying to explain it all to her. She has clearly made up her mind and long experience tells me that she won't change it.

'OK, you've said your piece and I disagree. Shall we drop it?'

'Suits me. We'd better get ready if we're going to the supermarket. They had queues out of the door yesterday. Goodness knows why. It's open again on Boxing Day. No one is exactly going to starve in twenty-four hours.'

Half an hour later, we leave the house and wander down the street. It is actually a bit too warm for my gloves, scarf and hat, but I keep them on anyway. They remind me of what I am coming to think of as my other home. The supermarket, as Becca predicted, is a zoo. Red-faced men are struggling along behind their partners, pushing trolleys piled high with food and drink. When we reach the freezer counter, all the turkeys have gone. The harassed employee piling nearby shelves, tells us when we ask, that all the fresh ones sold out this morning.

'You've left it terribly late, haven't you?'

'Have you got any chickens?' asks Becca.

'Not whole ones. We've probably got some breasts left if you hurry.'

We snatch the last of the chicken breasts and drop them into the basket.

'What else ought we to eat for Christmas?' I ask and Becca frowns and shakes her head.

'I've been thinking. Why should we eat anything we don't want to? I hate sprouts and I never liked Christmas pudding, even as a child. Why don't we buy all the things we really love and never get round to having?'

It takes me a second to get used to the thought of not having a traditional Christmas meal but, the more I think about it, the more I like it.

'Can we have hot dogs?'

'Hell, yes. Let me dump this basket and get a trolley. Then we can really spread ourselves.'

She throws the chicken breasts back into the chilled section, where they are snatched up thankfully by a young mother with three small children in tow. Once Becca has wheeled a trolley through the crowds, we set to work in earnest. I throw in two cans of hot dog sausages.

'Don't you want rolls for them?' she asks.

'No, I always throw most of them away. I only like the sausages. But I do want some of that bright yellow mustard in a squeezy bottle.'

'And I'll have a tin of macaroni cheese. That stuff got me through finals.'

We wander round the shop, dumping in everything that takes our fancy — popcorn, Twiglets, frozen blackberries, a large piece of brie, some brightly coloured cereal with tiny marshmallows, a bottle of Baileys and a pack of lurid looking alcopops. We pause by the ice cream cabinet and spend a while debating the merits of Rocky Road and Tutti Frutti.

'You make a good case,' she announces after five minutes of increasingly heated discussion. 'We clearly need both.'

'And I can get some butterscotch Angel Delight as a topping.'

'I'm not eating that stuff.'

'I wasn't offering you any.'

We arrive at the checkout with a full trolley. I look at the liquorice bootlaces balanced on top of the cheese and bacon balls and nod. It's going to be a good meal. Becca reaches for a Lion Bar as we start to unload the things onto the belt.

'Just an *amuse-bouche*,' she explains.

'I'd better have something nourishing too then. Here we are.' I scoop up a large bar of Dairy Milk and add it to the collection. 'We don't get Cadbury's in Denmark.'

'Philistines.'

She insists on paying for everything. 'You've paid to fly over here.'

'I wanted to. I didn't want to miss Christmas with you.'

'And gourmands around the world would agree with you. But this is on me.'

We cart it all home and unpack it.

'No eating any of it until Christmas Day,' she warns me. 'I'll be checking.'

'What about tonight?'

'They still deliver pizza on Christmas Eve. I checked that out weeks ago.'

'Perfect, but I'll pick my own toppings.'

'Killjoy. OK, you phone up and I'll get the movie ready.'

'*It's a Wonderful Life*. That's perfect. Christmas Eve is never right without it.'

I order the pizza and we settle down in front of the TV. I look round at the flat, at everything I have left behind and at Becca's serious face as she inspects the crayfish on her pizza, before gingerly tasting it. For the first time since I rushed off into the unknown, I wonder if I really do know what I am doing. This is all so familiar, so friendly and cosy. What do I really expect from my new life that could be so much better than the old one? I decide not to think about it until after Christmas Day. Becca glances over at me.

'Are you going to start this film any time soon or do I have to act it out for you?'

'Here we go. Happy Christmas, Becca.'

I open my box of pizza, hit the button on the remote and settle back into my favourite armchair.

Chapter Seventeen

I am woken at what feels like dawn by Becca singing carols in the kitchen. Her voice is not particularly tuneful but is very determined. I pull the quilt over my head in an effort to drown out the more raucous parts of *Oh Come All Ye Faithful* but it's no use. I give in to the inevitable, pull a sweater over my pyjamas and join her in the kitchen.

'No chance of Silent Night instead?' I ask, as I accept the coffee she pushes into my hands.

'Not a hope.' She breaks into a chorus of *Good King Wenceslas* and I fling up a hand.

'Let me get some caffeine into my bloodstream first, for pity's sake. Denmark's got me hooked.'

She subsides to a hum and reaches into the cupboard behind her. 'I bought Stollen.'

'Fantastic. I had some of that one day at the café. But I thought you didn't want a traditional Christmas. I was expecting cocoa pops and tomato juice for breakfast.'

She switches on the gas ring. 'It really won't seem all that traditional with fried bacon.'

'Stollen straight up for me, I think. Happy Christmas, Becca.'

She leans across and kisses my cheek. It's an astoundingly rare gesture for her.

'Happy Christmas. I'm glad you came back.'

I feel the strongest pang of guilt yet at leaving her and going off to Copenhagen. I wonder what her Christmas would have been like if I had given in to temptation and stayed there over the holidays in the hope of seeing Christian. But she does have a large and equally haphazard family whom she could have visited. She and I went there for Christmas once when we were at University. Even though she was two years above me, we got along from day one and she always looked out for me. My parents were mid-divorce at the time and seemed to see the three of us children as a Christmas prize to wave at the other one. Dan went to Dad's, Megan to Mum's and I refused to have anything to do with the whole stupid thing and decided to stay in Hall for the holidays. Becca wasn't having any of that and I found myself on a train to Oxfordshire without being quite sure how it came about. Her family live in a massive house in a village just outside Oxford and didn't bat an eyelid when we turned up. We had the most fantastic Christmas, eating bizarre meals at very odd times, staying up late and getting up at all hours. I lost count of the number of people who visited or stayed over on various nights, but they never seemed to faze Becca's large and good natured parents.

'Didn't you want to go home this Christmas?' I ask her and she shakes her head.

'They've gone to India for Christmas. They asked me along of course but it didn't seem very ... Christmassy.'

'As opposed to macaroni cheese? Got it.' I nod solemnly and she grins.

'I've got some people dropping in this evening. Mostly people from work who don't have families. Hope that's OK?'

That's typical Becca. She never seems to notice what's going on around her but she has the kindest heart.

'Great. Anyone I know?'

'You may have met a couple of them at work things.'

'I only really met Christian at your work dos.'

'That's right. Time to broaden your horizons.'

I don't like the implication but I am not getting into this again on Christmas Day so I nod vaguely.

Once we have finished breakfast and cleared up, we decide to go for a walk before lunch. But first, I go into my bedroom and open my case. Inside is a hand embroidered stocking, covered with snowflakes and hearts. I bring it out and hand it to her. She turns pink.

'Kate, I don't know what to say.'

'Don't bother. Just open it, it's nothing much.'

She switches on the gas fire in the living room and we perch next to it as she pulls out the tiny parcels one at a time. The day we went into the city together, Tomas helped me choose several Danish Christmas gifts and I wrapped them carefully in different coloured papers. She lifts them out now and unwraps them without tearing the paper — a bag of frosted ginger cookies, another of sugared almonds, a tiny music box with figures skating and spinning across the mirrored ice, a miniature book giving the history of Copenhagen, a T shirt with The Little Mermaid on the front and an amber necklace.

'I haven't had a stocking since I was about eight,' she says.

'About time you had another. Glad you like it.'

I think back to the day we bought them. Tomas' face was serious and thoughtful as we went into every single shop in Strøget, or so it seemed, in a bid to find the perfect gifts, and all for someone he hadn't even met. We stopped in a café for cookies and *gløgg*, inspected our haul and argued over a Little Mermaid or a Viking ship T shirt. It was a day of laughter and I have a pang of homesickness when I think of everyone in Copenhagen enjoying their Christmas without me. I don't know what's wrong with me. When I landed yesterday, I felt as though I was coming home and now I'm pining for Denmark. I'm just being contrary.

'Penny for them?' She looks curious but I shake my head. She shrugs. 'It's not as good as this but you'd better have yours now.'

She disappears and returns with a parcel, which she tosses onto my lap. I rip off the paper and pull out a pair of theatre tickets for Monday night.

'Becca, that's fantastic.' I hug her warmly. 'I've wanted to see *The Mouse Trap* forever. And you didn't even have the fun of going into a bookshop for it.'

'Yeah, I did. I went in afterwards.' She smooths her wrapping paper into a flat pile and throws my crumpled piece into the bin.

It is colder out today. The threatened rain hasn't arrived yet but the clouds are piling swiftly and high across the horizon and I shiver as we stride along the embankment. Hardly anyone else is around. Looking at the dark shop fronts we pass, it is hard to feel as though it really is Christmas Day. Maybe you need to have a family – a family that gets along, I correct myself – really to enjoy Christmas, or at least the Disney version of it.

When we are too cold to walk further, we take the tube back to our stop and run the rest of the way, just beating the first drops of rain. It spits and hisses on the pavement as we fling ourselves in at the front door.

'Hungry yet?' asks Becca and I nod.

'Starving.'

We unpack yesterday's groceries and I imagine Tomas' quizzical face if he saw them. I can also imagine Christian's raised eyebrows. Of course he wouldn't say anything but I have the feeling that he might not be all that impressed. I spread brie and pickle onto my favourite water biscuits. This is my meal, not his. Next year might be a different story.

We eat until we can't move, watch the Queen's speech and doze by the fire. It seems to me that this is a pretty typical British Christmas really, even without the turkey. I wonder what everyone in Copenhagen is doing, then remember that they have their celebration on the night of the 24th. I have an impulse to ring Tomas and ask what the weather is like and how his Christmas in Jylland went but I suppress it. I definitely wouldn't dare ring Christian's number, even if I had it. I need to play it very carefully now that he seems to be thawing slightly. He hates to be pressured. I just need to feel a connection to the people in my new life, to know that it didn't disappear just because I flew elsewhere for a week. I do feel at home here with Becca, but I also felt at home in Denmark. It is a weird and disturbing feeling. Surely both can't be true at the same time. I could equally say that I don't feel quite at home in either country, knowing that the other one exists and that I have a sort of place there too. I shrug off the feeling of displacement and sit up. The disconnect is probably just because I don't know exactly what my future holds and I have always liked to know. When I left London to follow Christian, it was terrifying because so much hung on my success or failure but it was also exciting because, for the first time in my life, I felt that the future lay in my own hands, if I could only get it right. As the weeks have gone by, my goal has remained just the same but I have met new people and woven unexpected and interesting strands into my life and the desperation seems to have gone out of it all. Christian is still my future as well as my past but it no longer feels so urgent that he realises that immediately. Next week, next month, it all feels appropriate. I can wait.

Becca stirs. 'Wossa time?'

'It's about four thirty. What time are they coming?'

She stretches and yawns. 'Don't know, I just said evening.'

'That could mean anything from 5pm to 10pm.'

'Keep your hair on. So what? We're not doing anything special, are we? They can just, sort of, join in.'

'But they're not going to want to eat Angel Delight and sleep on the sofa. Do we have anything real to feed them?'

'Erm, let's go and see.'

I follow her through to the kitchen and survey the wreck of the groceries. We didn't eat anything in any particular order, just broke into whatever looked good. I start throwing wrappers and boxes into the recycling bin.

'We've got bits of loads of things but it depends on how many people turn up. Will they bring food?'

'Shouldn't think so. I didn't ask them to.'

'So it's Baileys, cheese sauce and Tutti Frutti ice cream all round?'

'Sounds OK to me.'

'No, it doesn't. Is there anywhere open where we could get groceries?'

'Probably, but why bother? No one will be hungry. I don't want to eat again until the New Year and I expect they'll be the same.'

I fidget about the kitchen, thinking hard. 'Phil's! Is he open tonight?'

'Knowing Phil, no. Knowing Phil, he probably closes for the whole of December in case he makes a profit.'

'Let's go and check.'

I fling on a fleece and my hat and gloves and she follows me down the road, grumbling gently. I ignore her. There are no lights in Phil's and the door is locked. I aim a kick at it in frustration.

'Hey, what are you doing?' Phil leans out of the upstairs flat and peers down at us. I wave.

'Phil, Happy Christmas. Are you opening tonight?'

'I wasn't going to.'

'Now you are. We're having friends over and we want to bring them here. Can you handle that?'

He scratches his head and doesn't speak. Becca steps forward. 'The answer is yes, you most certainly can. People might want a snack so make sure that's sorted and we'll be in later, OK?'

She walks away, leaving him staring down at us. I catch her up. 'You don't think that was a bit harsh of us?'

'I know he has a sort of allergic reaction to anything that might make him a bit of money but he'll thank us in the end.'

'Is that your philosophy? Tell people what to do and they'll thank you later.'

She brushes the rain out of her eyes as she fumbles for her key. 'When did I ever tell you what to do?'

She's right. She didn't make any objection to my going to Copenhagen, even though I knew what she was thinking underneath. She still doesn't seem that enthusiastic but she hasn't actually said anything negative since I got back. She couldn't find much to say anyway. It's all going brilliantly. I have a life over there and Christian is obviously getting used to the idea of me being around. If she had made any serious objections, she would surely have to eat her words now.

We clean up the flat to a basic standard, which means pushing most of the clutter into both of our bedrooms and spraying air freshener around the living room.

At six o'clock there is a knock at the door. A bedraggled woman is standing outside and Becca ushers her into the hall. 'Hi, Janine. Had a good Christmas?'

The woman sneezes. 'Crap. Ted didn't turn up.'

'Ted?'

'Fourth floor, red hair. We've been going out off and on since the summer. I invited him over and he said he would be there but I had a text this morning to say he'd got back with his old girlfriend last night so he wouldn't be there. On Christmas Day, of all days.' She sneezes again and wipes her eyes.

'Bastard.' Becca helps her out of her soaking jacket and ushers her into the living room.

I pour the last of the crisps into little bowls and arrange the alcopops in order of colour around them. By seven o'clock the flat is full. There must be fifteen people here, perched on the furniture and sitting on the floor, swigging the drinks and telling their various tales of woe.

'How many did you invite?' I whisper to Becca and she lifts her shoulders.

'It was a general invitation. I put it out on the system. It just said any losers were welcome at mine on Christmas Evening.'

I look round at the people jammed into our flat. They arrived in dribs and drabs, most of them looking depressed and some of them nearly suicidal. Now they are laughing and talking, basking in the warmth of more than Becca's electric fire. She really has a gift for this sort of thing. She's a sort of conduit of happiness. She sees people's needs and does something about them, although in the most unobtrusive way possible. I hope she gets some happiness of her own soon. No one deserves it more. She claps her hands. 'Who's hungry?'

'Me!' There comes a great roar and everyone laughs.

'OK, we're going round to *Grape To See You*. The owner is a friend of ours so be nice to him and spend all your money.'

Everyone surges to the door and we all troop round the corner. Phil has the lights on and there is an inflatable Santa in the window. He has made a real effort inside. The broken light bulbs have been replaced and he has strung paper chains across the ceiling.

Everyone makes for the bar and Phil is kept busy for the next fifteen minutes, pouring drinks and taking orders for snacks. We pull several tables together and he lights some candles, which remind me of *The Cinnamon Snail*. We sit and talk for hours and I learn more about the firm than I ever have from Becca. She tells them I have recently moved to Copenhagen and I am besieged with questions about the city. One girl asks if I know Christian Sørensen and blushes madly when everyone laughs at her.

'Yeah, I see him occasionally,' I say. The question doesn't hurt as it would have done only three months ago. People start to exchange reminiscences about him and his time in London. I relax when I realise none of them seem to know anything about me, although that seems a little strange, given how long we were going out.

As the evening goes on, several more people come in.

'We didn't think there was anywhere round here open today,' says one man. 'Great idea though. Families are all very well in small doses, but ...'

The party finally breaks up around midnight and everyone says goodbye to a beaming Phil. I noticed several of the younger guys clustered around him earlier, telling him exactly what they want from a wine bar like this and he was nodding and scribbling notes. Becca and I say our final goodbyes and start for home.

'I enjoyed that,' she says. 'I don't know why we didn't think of Phil's before. We'll have to make it a yearly event.'

I look back at the groups of people laughing and singing their way back down the street. 'It certainly isn't the Christmas I hoped for a few months ago, but it's been one of the best I've ever had. That's all down to you, Becca.'

'It was pretty good, wasn't it? A day to remember when you go back.'

Go back? I was just starting to feel rooted here again and the thought of going back in a couple of days is quite a jolt. All this back and forth stuff can be fun for a while but it is fairly unsettling too. I decide that my New Year's resolution has got to be getting my future settled once and for all. I might well be over here again next Christmas and spending the evening at Phil's again, but this time it will be with Christian. I will be back in Denmark in three days and I need to focus more than ever on just what I want for my future, and how exactly I plan to make it happen.

Chapter Eighteen

It is hard to say goodbye to Becca. I agreed to be back at work over New Year and I'm quite looking forward to that but I've had such a good time in London that I don't really want to leave. We went to see *The Mouse Trap* and I finally know who did it. Becca took me to dinner beforehand in Covent Garden, where we had the best tiramisu I have ever tasted. When we left, she asked for two more portions in a doggy bag, which were only partially spoiled when I sat on the bag in the theatre. We spent hours just lounging around in the flat and talking. I didn't bring up the subject of Christian but we talked about everything else. She seemed extremely interested in Tomas and I tried to persuade her to come and visit once the weather warms up.

'You can share my room. Jens and Lisette won't mind.'

She agreed to look at her work calendar and think about it. After her earlier reaction, I don't press the subject of Tomas. If it happens, it happens.

I don't let her come to the airport. 'I'll only cry again and embarrass you.'

She agrees to say goodbye at the flat and I hug her when she leaves for work. 'See you in a few months.' I don't mention the fact that I hope to be back with Christian by then. I don't want one of her sardonic looks to be the last thing I remember about leaving her.

I arrive at the airport in plenty of time. I brought my suitcase home almost empty so that I could fill it with things to take back, now that I know I am staying. But when I looked through my things, there was very little I had really missed, very little that seemed to translate to my new life. In the end, I threw in some summer clothes, just in case the sun ever reappears. The triumph of hope over experience I think, as I dump my case onto the scales for weighing.

'You travel light,' says the woman as she clips on the tag.

'I travel faster that way,' I tell her.

As we come down through the clouds into Copenhagen, it doesn't take the announcement from the cockpit to let us know it is snowing. It is whitening the windows as we descend and I can't see the ground. The wheels skim along the runway and flurries of white flakes spin up and away from us. I pull my hat closer over my ears as I disembark and line up at customs, before emerging into the arrivals hall. At least this time I know where the train station is and I start to wheel my case towards the ramp.

'*Velkommen til Danmark!*' Tomas is in my path and he is waving a paper Danish flag.

'You came to meet me. That was so nice of you.'

'Mette sent me. She wanted to make sure you were back in time for work.'

'She did not.'

He takes my case. 'She didn't say it but it was written on her face.' He lifts the case up and down. 'How is this? I thought you were going to bring back all your things?'

'I was but they didn't seem to fit here so I left them behind.'

'I understand.'

I glance at him. I am not sure exactly what it is he thinks he understands. We run down the ramp and clip our cards.

The journey back passes quickly. He tells me about his Christmas in Jylland and his sister's new pony. He doubles up with laughter when I describe our Christmas lunch. I tell him about the evening at Phil's and how Becca scooped up all the waifs and strays.

'She really is the best. I know you'll like her.'

'Is she coming out?'

'She says she will — maybe in the spring. I can't wait for you two to meet.'

He carries my case back to the apartment but won't come in. 'Things to do. See you at work tonight?'

'I'll be there.'

As I expected, the apartment is empty. Lisette went back to France for Christmas and Jens stayed here to work. She will be back for the New Year and they will be spending it with his family. I am not sure yet what I will be doing. I unpack my few things and spend the rest of the afternoon with my language books. The school opens again on January 2nd and I haven't even thought about Danish grammar over Christmas.

I am just revising my past tense verbs for the tenth time, when I hear the lock click and I go into the hall to find Jens arriving home.

'Coffee?' I ask and he nods. I start the percolator and we sit at the kitchen table and exchange news of our Christmases.

'I am glad to have caught you,' he says at last. 'I met someone last night who is looking for someone exactly like you.'

I wonder for a moment if he means a blind date and open my mouth to give a firm refusal. I haven't told him and Lisette about Christian but I am fairly sure they must know something is going on.

'It is a family who will move to England in the spring because of work. They have three children who have not learned much English yet and they are looking to find a tutor for them so they can go to an English school. I thought of you.'

'I don't have any qualifications,' I say automatically.

'You do not speak English as a first language?' He is laughing at me.

'Well, yes but I don't really know the grammar. Not enough to teach it.'

'I think they are looking for the children to have some practise at speaking. You could easily do that. They would pay of course.'

The idea of some extra pay sounds good, especially after Christmas, which has totally cleaned me out. I don't want to tell Jens that I find children intimidating en masse. After all, three of them is hardly *en masse*. I imagine them dressed in curtains, skipping behind me through the streets of Copenhagen and singing.

'I suppose I could talk to the parents,' I say uncertainly.

'Of course you could. I have written their number. They don't live far.'

He reaches into his pocket and hands me a crumpled slip of paper. I put it into my bag.

'OK, I'll call. Thanks for that. I have to get to work now but I'll call them tomorrow.'

I cycle off into the freezing dark. The snow is coming down harder. The cycle path has been gritted but it is still slightly slippery and I am relieved to arrive safely at the café.

Mette is here. Once I learned to make coffees and prepare the food, she stopped coming in so often but she must have been back in these past few days to cover for me. She shakes hands and thanks me for my Christmas present. It was a bit like coals to Newcastle but I gave her a candle in a glass holder and she seems pleased. She already gave Tomas and me a Christmas bonus, which was unexpected but very welcome.

She says she is off home and I am left completely in charge for the first time. My half-forgotten Danish is definitely not up to this tonight, not unless people speak to me entirely using past tense verbs. Luckily, Tomas comes in before I can do any serious damage to our trade. I tell him about Jens' idea and he is enthusiastic. 'I can see you doing that.'

'I'm not so sure. I almost went into teaching after I graduated but then I saw the children walking to school round our way and had second thoughts.'

'You are joking, right?'

'Not totally. They're all twice my size and they look scary.'

'Chicken! Go on and give it a try. They can't do anything so very bad to you. Don't always be looking too far ahead for trouble.'

'OK, I'll give the parents a ring and see what it involves. It would be right after school so it shouldn't get in the way of my work here.'

'Go for it.'

We have very few customers this evening. The snow is getting heavier and I don't blame people for staying indoors. As soon as we close, I say goodbye and make a dash for the door. My bike saddle is an inch deep in snow and I shiver as I brush it off with a gloved hand. Tomas comes out after me. 'You are not cycling home in this?'

'Why not?'

'It's three degrees below, the snow is coming faster and it's completely dark. Get a bus.'

'What about my bike?'

'Get it tomorrow if the weather is better.'

'It will get stolen.'

'Then the thief will break his neck and it will serve him right. Seriously, Kate, I do not want to see you try to cycle in this weather.'

'What is it to you?' I kick the snow off the pedals as I consider my options.

'Do you really want to know?'

His tone is unmistakeable and I am caught off guard. I don't know what to say. I don't want to hurt him by bringing up the subject of Christian again. I decide it is better to avoid the subject, as he has given me the opportunity to do so.

'OK, I'll get a bus, just this once.'

'Good. I will walk across with you.'

We pick our way across the grass and he steadies me when I slip on the pavement. I am glad to see that the bus is just pulling up, which saves any potential embarrassment. I wave a gloved hand.

'See you tomorrow. If my bike has gone, I'll sue.'

'OK.'

He waves cheerfully and I watch him through the bus window, picking his way up the snowy street. He looks quite happy so I probably read more into that little exchange than was strictly necessary. He knows the score with Christian and he can't seriously be expecting anything to happen between us. I am glad now that I didn't pick him up on his comment. That could have been embarrassing.

It snows right through the night and I wake to bright light forcing its way into the bedroom. I hop out and open the blind. It is amazing. The street below is completely white. A few intrepid cars are moving in very slow motion towards the city but the snow muffles the sound they make. The sky above is a deep turquoise and the sun is shining brightly, although even from indoors I can tell it is well below freezing. I have the briefest of showers and shiver into my clothes, adding two sweaters for good effect. I pull on my down-filled jacket and push my feet into trainers before running down the stairs.

The snow throws a dazzling light across the whole street and I squint in the unaccustomed sunshine. It is so beautiful. I kick my way up the street, ruffling clouds of snow into the air and standing entranced to watch it puff and swirl in the light breeze. I wander on down the street, with the words to *Winter Wonderland* singing in my ears. I only wake up to the fact that my feet are sodden and freezing after about ten minutes. I look ruefully at my trainers. The snow has pushed down into the gap between them and my ankles and icy water is trickling down and soaking my socks. On an impulse, I jump on a bus heading towards the city and sit and nurse my frozen feet. I get off at Nørreport and walk as quickly as I can past the Round Tower and down towards Strøget. I stop at the first likely looking shoe shop and collapse onto a chair inside.

'Kan jeg hjælpe dig?'

A pleasant-faced, older lady comes through from the back and I point to my feet and explain in a mixture of Danish and English that yes, she can help me get these wet trainers off. She gets the point. After we have both tugged at them for a while, they come free. I peel off my soggy socks and she shakes her head at them. She brings me several pairs of snow boots to try and I choose a black pair with a spray of brightly-coloured flowers embroidered down the outside. I try not to look too hard at the price. If it is going to get any colder than this, they will be worth it and it is about the amount of my bonus. I select a pair of thick socks and pay for everything. She puts my trainers and wet socks in a bag and hands them back to me.

I smile at her. *'Tak for hjælpen.'*

'Selv tak,' she says politely.

Once outside again, I give an experimental skip and beam. My toes stay completely warm. I scoop up a handful of snow and toss it at the nearest building. The snow soaks through the wool of my gloves and I decide to stop while I am ahead. There is a *konditori* on the way back to the bus stop and I push through the door into the warm, sweet interior. I am just sitting down at one of spindly legged tables with my hot chocolate and éclair, when I remember the English tutoring. I take a bite of the cake, pull out my mobile and dial. A woman answers.

'Hallo, det er Anna.'

'Hi,' I say cautiously. Surely, if I am a potential English teacher, it is acceptable to speak English. 'My name is Kate Merrit. I was given your number by Jens.'

'Oh, I know. Thank you for ringing back to us so quickly.' She has a strong accent but her English sounds fine.

'He mentioned that you need someone to tutor your children. I hope you don't mind me asking, but your English sounds very good. Couldn't you do it yourself?'

She laughs. 'We will both do what we can but we work until six o'clock most days and there is so much to do after that. The children must eat and do some homework and get to bed. So we thought, if we could find someone who will collect them from their school and spend maybe two hours talking to them most days until we leave in May, it would be a good idea. Would you be interested?'

'To be honest, I'm not quite sure. I haven't had any experience. How about giving it a week's trial?'

'It sounds very good.' She gives me their address and I arrange to go over to meet them on Saturday morning before work.

I sit for a while longer and finish my hot chocolate. Even I can probably manage a week with these children. If I don't like it after that, I can say so. There must be plenty of other English speakers in Copenhagen who would be glad of the job. I will try to remember what Tomas said, stop worrying about the distant future and take it one day at a time.

Chapter Nineteen

I arrive at Anna's house early on Saturday morning. Most of the snow has melted and I pick my way through the piles of slush, thankful for my snow boots. I glance down at the flowers. It is so typical of the Danes to have added some extra design to the plain utility of my boots — just like the flowers that edge my bicycle basket. I knock at the front door and it is opened by a harassed looking man. He has a friendly smile and shakes my hand when I introduce myself.

'Jørgen,' he says and beckons me to come inside. The hall is a chaotic jumble of snow boots and toys. 'Excuse us, please. The children have been sledging all morning in the garden.'

'But it's almost melted now,' I say in surprise.

'Yes, but they wished to make the most of it. So they have been half sliding, half swimming round the garden and now they are all frozen and must take a bath. Anna is upstairs watching them.'

'You have three children?' I ask, listening to the shrieks and screams of laughter floating down the stairwell.

'We have. We expected two but the second one turned out to be *tvillinger* – twins. Here they come.'

A series of thumps announces the arrival of the first child, a girl of about eleven. She has dark shoulder-length hair and stares at me without speaking. I decide I had better introduce myself.

'*Hej, jeg hedder Kate,*' I say. She doesn't respond.

'Josefina, say hello,' says Jørgen.

She raises a hand. '*Hej.*'

He shakes his head at her. 'Josefina speaks a little English. She is old enough to be doing it at school. She will warm up and talk to you soon.'

Two more thumps and two blonde children with identical short curly hair come to a skidding halt at the foot of the stairs and stare at me, giggling and poking each other.

'Rasmus and Rebecca,' says their father.

'*Hej,*' I say.

'*Hej,* I spik English,' says the girl and collapses in hysterical laughter on her brother's shoulder.

'Good. What else can you say?'

She stares at me blankly. Her brother waves his arms at me. 'David Beckham. Wayne Rooney. Manchester United.' He nudges her and they scoot away into the lounge.

'They are nine and they don't know so much yet,' says Jørgen. 'I hope you will be able to teach them the basic vocabulary they need for an English school.'

My mind flicks back to the children who paraded daily past our flat and pushed me out of the way at the bus stop and I mentally compile a list of useful phrases - *Oy*, *Get lost* and *I'm calling your parole officer*. I shrug these thoughts off. Just because groups of school children make me nervous, doesn't mean there is essentially anything wrong with them.

'Where are you moving to?'

'Surrey. I am to work in London and we will rent a house in Godalming.'

In which case, I think they will be OK.

'Shall we go and meet them properly?' he asks and I follow him through the living room to the kitchen. Anna must have come down the back stairs because she is already there, handing out *pebernødder*. She smiles when she sees me and offers me the plate. I like these little ginger puffs with a light frosting. They taste of Christmas. I take one and sit down next to the twins.

'*Kan du tale engelsk?*' I ask Rebecca. Even with my English accent, she must surely understand me asking if she speaks English. But she shrugs and pretends not to understand.

'*Kan du tale dansk?*' she says and snickers to herself.

'That's enough,' says her father sharply in Danish. He turns to me. 'Your Danish is actually very good. She just thinks she is being funny.' He says something else to her that I don't catch and she turns red and goes to stand behind her mother.

'She can know some words,' says Rasmus and I turn to him thankfully. Things were looking sticky there just for a moment.

'What can you say?' I ask him and he grins.

'Football.'

'OK, then we can find some football stories to read together. How about Rebecca?'

'Rebecca likes football too,' says Jørgen.

'And what about Josefina?'

She hears her name and looks up from her *pebernødder*. 'I like to cook.'

Anna nods. 'It is true. She is very good at cooking.'

'I'm not very good,' I tell Josefina. 'Will you teach me?'

Her mother translates and she nods. 'OK.'

'Great. It's about time I learned to make cookies at least. I can make sandwiches and soup and pancakes at the café but that's about it.'

We arrange my hours and I agree to pick the three of them up from school each day after I finish at the language school and bring them back here for a couple of hours before I go to work. I walk back to the bus stop, feeling exhausted in anticipation. Maybe this is why I am not getting edgy about Christian any more. Two paying jobs, language school every day and all my homework, should keep me pretty busy for the foreseeable future.

I don't stop long at the flat because I have arranged to meet Ilse this afternoon. Lars is in Hong Kong for two weeks so I am going to buy her lunch. I haven't had a chance to thank her properly for helping me settle in when I arrived and for inviting me to dinner and to her Christmas party. I take a bus into town and walk down to the Round Tower. I haven't been up it yet. As I am still quite early, I pay and make my way up the spiral path. It is a long hike to the top and involves some undignified scrambling up the last few steps but the view, when I finally make it up there, is magnificent. I wander right round, admiring the city from a whole new angle, amazed at how narrow some of the buildings are and how many of them seem to lean towards each other.

When I have circled the whole tower, feeling like a bird perched among the rooftops, I glance at my watch. I run down and land, panting, at the bottom before walking as quickly as I can down towards Strøget and the corner where I have arranged

The Cinnamon Snail

to meet Ilse. She is admiring the flower display in Illum and laughs when I skid to a halt beside her.

'You need not rush. I am quite happy window shopping.'

'Aren't you cold?'

'Not particularly.' She shows me her fur-lined boots. 'But they are not as pretty as your boots. You look very Danish.'

I point to my hat and scarf and she nods approvingly. 'And a coat filled with feathers. I must admit you looked very chilly when I first met you.'

'It's a fair bit colder here than it is in London. Tomas bought me the hat and scarf.'

'He is very thoughtful.' She leads the way back up towards a small side street I haven't explored yet. It opens out into a square and she points to a restaurant.

'If it is all right with you, I think this is a nice place to eat. I come here quite often with Lars. But you have to be this shape to eat there.' She gestures crookedly with her arms and I look at her in bemusement. She laughs. 'You will see.'

And I do see once she climbs the steps and pushes through the door. The wooden floors and the walls aren't perpendicular but join at a crazy angle. We follow the waiter uphill to our table and sit by a window looking out on the square. I am amused to see that the bottle of wine he brings has little lines on it, marking out the number of glasses drunk.

'You pay by the glass?' I ask.

'It makes sense. People without so much money can have a glass of wine without paying for their companion's wine too.'

I imagine Marie's face if she were to be presented with one of these bottles, and laugh. Ilse looks at me enquiringly.

'Sorry. I was just thinking of some friends in London - friends of Christian's really - who seem to drink wine by the bucket full. One in particular would be very put out if anyone tried to ration her like that.'

'You miss London?' She is skimming the menu so I don't have to catch her eye.

'Only when I'm there. I spent Christmas with Becca and we had a great time. To be honest, it was a bit of a wrench to leave. But as soon as we touched down here, it felt like coming home. It's all a bit puzzling.'

'One home is more than some people have. Maybe you should just think of yourself as being twice lucky.'

'I do really. But I don't totally belong to either place. I suppose at some point I will have to choose.'

'You have to choose your food first.' She greets the waiter and breaks into a flood of Danish. I laboriously order my fish and salad and he writes down the order and leaves.

'You have been progressing fast. I had no idea.' She looks impressed.

'Not as fast as I'd like. I have to make everyone speak very slowly but it's getting easier.'

'You know, I think Christian should be very flattered. Whatever happens, not all people would be as committed as you are.'

'Becca thinks I ought to be committed.' I pull a rueful face. As she looks politely puzzled, I shrug and stand. 'Don't worry about it. Just a stupid joke. I'll get some salad.'

I fill my salad plate and wonder how the conversation has turned, as always, so swiftly to Christian, even when he isn't here. I sit down and our fish arrives, swimming lazily through a buttery sauce.

'Looks good.' I spear a piece and chew happily.

'How is everything else going?' she asks.

'Everything else apart from Christian, you mean?'

'I suppose so. Your work is fun?'

'Yes, I love it.'

'But it must be temporary. I think you said you were previously in the electrical industry.'

I choke at the remembrance and take a gulp of wine before bursting out laughing.

'I'm sorry, Ilse. It seems that I wasn't quite straight with you about anything when we first met. It was awful of me but I wasn't ready to tell anyone '

'We all have our secrets.' She doesn't seem remotely put out.

'You caught on to my biggest lie when I came over for dinner.'

'Christian Sørensen.' I feel disapproval wafting across the table from her when she says his entire name.

'Yes. The other thing was that I used to sell white goods in a department store. Nothing as upmarket as Illum and Magasin, I'm afraid. Just a dingy old department store in a back street, that needs knocking down and rebuilding. I know Becca would volunteer to light the fuse, given half the chance.'

'Do you have other qualifications?'

'An English degree. It hasn't come in particularly useful until now but I am just about to start tutoring three children for a couple of hours a day.'

'Good for you. Will it be fun?'

'Amazingly, I think it will be. I thought they'd eat me alive but I've met them now and they seem funny and sweet and I think I'll get quite a kick out of hearing them learn new words.'

'And you are working as many hours at the café?'

'Oh, yes. I need the money and it's a great place to work. You'd love Tomas. Of course, you met him at your apartment. Do you remember?'

'I certainly do and I liked him very much. He's very different from Christian.'

'Why should that matter to me? I'm not in love with Tomas.'

'And you are still in love with Christian? It's been a while.'

'Always.' I lay down my cutlery and slowly finish my wine. There is nothing more to say. It has always been Christian. It always will be.

'Always is a long time.'

I decide to put the ball in her court. 'How long will you be in love with Lars?'

'Always, I hope.' She leans back and smiles at me.

'There you go then.'

'I am in a relationship with him. Isn't that a difference?'

'This isn't some guy I've seen in a movie sometime. We went out together for eight months. We had something really special. OK, things went a bit pear-shaped when your stupid company decided to bring him back here but I think we're slowly getting back to normal.'

'And Miranda?'

'Come on, Ilse. She's not right for him. She was just the easy option because he thought she fitted in with his life here. I'm not worried about Miranda at all.'

'You may be right.'

'I know I'm right. So, what's been going on with you?'

She accepts my change of subject and we spend a happy hour exchanging gossip and finishing the bottle of wine.

'It's kinder if we make it easy for the waiter,' I say. 'Just in case he isn't good at maths.'

'You're very thoughtful.'

'That's me — thoughtful.'

'Before I forget, our office always has a party on New Year's Eve. Lars will be away so I thought you might like to come with me as my guest. We have a great view of the fireworks at midnight.'

'Tomorrow? I'd love to. That's very kind of you.'

'Would you like to bring your friend?'

'Tomas?'

'Yes. He seemed so nice and I hardly got a chance to talk to him.'

'I'll think about it.'

I don't think I will. It was disastrous having him at her Christmas Party, giving people the possible impression that we were together. If he turns up with me at New Year too, Christian will never believe we are not a couple.

'Hands off Tomas by the way,' I add. 'I've got him earmarked for Becca.'

'Really? I wouldn't have thought ...'

'They'd be perfect. They're exactly like each other. She's coming out here in the spring.'

She brightens. 'Wonderful. If you have no room, she can stay with me and Lars.'

'Thanks but her pyjamas might scare him. I'll dump her in a corner somewhere.'

'I can imagine. And now I must thank you for lunch and go. I am having some work colleagues over tonight for us to enjoy some food and do some necessary work. I have nothing prepared yet thanks to you and this lunch.'

I wonder uneasily if these work colleagues include Christian. I can't ask without sounding horribly insecure and she doesn't elaborate. If she sees him, maybe she will mention our lunch and how well I am doing. I hope she doesn't mention Tomas. Things are precarious enough without anyone throwing extra spanners in the works. I pay and she hugs me goodbye. I watch her picking her way swiftly through the slush and ice and wonder whether, if Christian is one of the colleagues she mentioned, Miranda will be invited too. If she is, I hope she is completely in the way and Christian sees her for the liability she undoubtedly is. I trudge back up the street towards the bus stop a little less enthusiastically than I raced down it. Some days, it is harder than others to keep faith and to focus on my future with Christian and this is clearly one of them. It will pass. I just need to see him as often as possible and the work party tomorrow will be a great start. After that, New Year is just round the corner, with its promise of new beginnings and hope. I decide to take that as a symbol of things to come.

Chapter Twenty

We close the café the following evening and prepare for the celebrations. When the subject of New Year came up on Saturday night, I didn't invite Tomas to Ilse's party and then promptly felt guilty because he asked me to join a group of his friends to watch the fireworks down by the harbour. But he wouldn't want to come to a stuffy office party when he has the chance to spend the evening with friends. To be honest, neither would I if there hadn't been the chance of meeting Christian. From now on, I have to snatch at every opportunity that comes my way. Not that I told Tomas any of this. I suspect he would be no more supportive of my aim to get back with Christian than Becca has been. At least he hasn't given any further indication that he is interested in me as anything other than a friend. Either that was just a passing idea or, more likely, I misinterpreted him.

'Won't you freeze down by the water?' I asked him and he shook his head.

'We go every year. We wear all the clothes we own and meet at a restaurant that stays open late. After dinner, we join the crowds round the harbour and watch the fireworks go off at midnight. It is great fun.'

'It sounds it,' I said and I meant it. I am generally not fond of parties and office parties are the worst of all. But I comfort myself with the fact that I first met Christian at an office party. Maybe that is a good omen.

Once we have locked up, Tomas wishes me a Happy New Year. I want to stop and talk but he is in a hurry. When I realise it is minus five outside, I decide to get home as soon as possible. I ride home along the frozen cycle path. The air sears and burns with each breath I drag into my lungs and not even Tomas' gloves are enough to prevent my fingers from growing numb. I jump off the bike, lock it up and run upstairs. Jens and Lisette are just about to leave and they offer to wait for me. Knowing they are waiting stops me spending an age staring at myself in the mirror and comparing myself to Miranda, which has to be a good thing. It isn't a contest I am ever going to win. I choose a clean top and then bundle my sweater, jacket and boots back on, throwing a smarter pair of shoes into my bag for later. We walk as quickly as possible through the streets to the station and catch a train that will stop near the office.

The huge glass building is lit from top to bottom and throws a shining path across the Øresund. Jens and Lisette show their security passes and the guard nods us through.

'*Godt nytår*,' I say as I pass him and he nods. My spirits are rising fast in the warmth and light. I follow Jens and Lisette up an escalator, which rises steeply in the middle of the building. It has glass sides and I hold the rail tightly, trying not to look down. We step off into the middle of a noisy, laughing crowd. I recognise a few faces as we push through to the makeshift bar in the centre and a couple of people wave at me. After a moment, I remember to look around for Christian. I spot him on the far side of the room. He is standing with his arm thrown loosely around Miranda's shoulders, chatting to an older man. I dart a quick look at Miranda. She is wearing a simple black shift dress that shows off her figure. She is also snuggled up as close as possible to Christian.

'Kate?' It's Lisette and she is looking at me curiously. 'I've asked you three times what you wish to drink. What is so interesting over there?'

'Just looking at the view.'

'It is so lit up in here that you can't see out,' she says and then her gaze fixes on Christian. She looks quickly at me and away again and I see that she knows. I am tempted to ask her how but decide not to. I refuse to be ashamed of my feelings for him.

'I'll have a red wine please.'

I wander in the general direction of Christian, not daring to get too close. Miranda hasn't seen me yet but I am pretty sure Christian has. His eyes slide in my direction and away again. I hover near the window and try to peer out past the reflected lights inside. I can just make out the water below.

'Kate?' Ilse has come up behind me while I have been sidling nearer to Christian. Miranda still has her back to me so it has been like playing *'What's the time, Mr Wolf?'* I freeze as Ilse greets me. Then I turn and nod as though I have been considering a new job as a window designer and am just checking out the competition.

'Are you hoping to speak to Christian?' she asks directly and I smile awkwardly.

'Not while he's with the Black Widow.'

'Are you not being a little childish?' Her eyes are uncomfortably direct and I can't even meet them because, in my heart of hearts, I know she is right.

'OK, that wasn't a very funny joke. But there's no reason why I shouldn't talk to Christian at a party, is there? He's an old friend and it's a free country.'

'He's an old boyfriend with a new girlfriend,' she adds to my expurgated version of events.

'If she's sure he's happy with her, she's got nothing to worry about, has she? And if he's not happy with her, why should he be tied to her forever?'

'Is not that his decision — and Miranda's? Let me put it differently. How would you have felt when you two were together if Miranda had followed him to your country and then pursued him?'

It hits like a sledge hammer and I can't speak for a moment. All of a sudden I remember Marie, hanging on Christian's every word, making little digs about me that he never got but that I did, wearing her lowest-cut blouses and leaning all over him whenever she got the chance. I hated it. She started out as a comic figure but gradually I grew to dislike her more and more. Is it possible that what Ilse is saying is true? Am I nothing more than a quieter, less shrieking version of Marie? It is true that I can put another and kinder interpretation on most of what I have done. He ended our relationship without consulting me and then disappeared so that I had no chance to straighten things out or put my point of view. It is entirely reasonable that I shouldn't have wanted to leave things in the messy state they were in. But I didn't just get his phone number and call him, I moved to a different country. Even when I found he had met someone new, that didn't stop me. I have spent the past four months plotting and scheming to find ways to break up the pair of them. Now that it hits me just how I have behaved, I feel more humiliated than I can ever remember. I am glad that the lights in here are dim as I feel my face flaming red. It is beyond me how anyone over here is still speaking to me, let alone being so kind and inviting me to parties and dinners, when they must have seen exactly what I have been doing.

'I have upset you,' she says directly.

'You've told me the truth,' I say and put my glass down on the window will. 'Ilse, I don't know what I've been doing. I'd like you to believe that this isn't me. I've never done anything remotely like this before. I must have been mad.'

'I think that in matters of love none of us behave like ourselves and sometimes not appropriately,' she says.

'Not appropriately is a kind way of describing it. Becca's right, I ought to be locked up.'

'She didn't say such a thing?' She looks shocked.

'No, but she's been thinking it. Or she should have been. I can't stay here tonight.'

'Are you sure? You could come and join the group I am with.'

I shake my head. 'I don't want to be rude but I won't, thanks. I need to do some serious thinking and I don't need to be anywhere near Christian when I do it.'

'Shall I call a taxi for you?'

'Give me a moment, will you?'

'Kate, what a nice surprise to see you here.' Christian has joined us without me noticing. I automatically put out a hand and he shakes it, smiling ironically at the formal gesture. 'Are you OK? You look a little distracted.'

'I'm fine but I'm not staying. I just popped in for a while to wish Ilse a Happy New Year.'

'Not me?' His eyes are teasing and I would give anything to throw myself into his arms.

'Yes, you too — and Miranda of course.' She has followed him over and is staring at me with undisguised hostility, for which I don't blame her. I look directly at her. 'Happy New Year, Miranda.'

I seem to have caught her off balance. She doesn't speak for a moment but eyes me as though I have a rattlesnake up my sleeve. I smile at them again. 'Enjoy the party. I have to rush but it was nice to see you both.'

'Are you sure you will not stay?' asks Christian. 'It would be good to catch up with you and to hear about your Christmas with Becca.'

'I'm sure I can't. See you all next year. Bye, Ilse.'

She leans over to hug me and whispers so he doesn't hear. 'You will be OK?'

I give her a quick nod, wave at Lisette and Jens and head for the escalator. I ride down to the ground floor without looking at anyone. In the lobby I pull on my jacket and, on an impulse, pull out my mobile and dial. Tomas answers almost immediately.

'Kate, is everything OK?'

'Fine, everything's fine. I was wondering if I might take you up on that invitation.'

'Of course.' His voice is muffled by the crowd of voices around him. 'Hang on a minute while I find somewhere quieter. What happened with your party?'

'It was pretty boring. I was never good at parties. Your plans sounded much more fun.'

'Are you still there? I will be with you in thirty minutes.'

'No, I'll come and find you.'

'Not in this crowd you won't. Stay there. I can be on the train in two minutes.'

He rings off, leaving me torn between pleasure that he is coming over and guilt that I have taken him away from his friends — and in this weather too. I sit in the lobby and try not to catch the eye of the security guard. A few people are still arriving and I huddle in the corner in case I see anyone I know. I glance at my watch. Nearly 10 p.m.

The door bursts open in a flurry of snowflakes and icy air and Tomas enters. He is reassuringly large and cheerful. I glance at the security guard as if this was my plan all along and I am on a party-hopping circuit, having been invited too many parties to fit them all in.

'I am very glad you called. Now you can see New Year as it is meant to be seen, not in some corporate offices.' Tomas glances round at the beautifully matched decorations with a disdainful eye and I wonder how much of his dislike is because Christian works here. He has been polite but fairly reserved on the occasions they have met.

'Shall we go?'

He holds out a hand and we step out onto the icy street. The air frosts the inside of my lungs and makes me gasp.

'You didn't need to come all the way back here just to get me. You must be frozen.'

'I wanted to. It was no trouble.'

We run to the station and climb onto the first train into town, which is filled with noisy revellers. I stamp my feet to warm them up and he asks again about the party.

'It was pretty boring,' I say. It is a half-truth at least.

'Christian wasn't there?' he asks directly and I grimace.

'Yes, he was. I suppose you're another one who thinks I've been an idiot.'

'Not at all.'

'You should. I do. I've realised a few things tonight. One is that it's pretty insane to chase someone halfway across the world when they've made it clear they don't want you.'

'Love is like that.'

'I suppose.' I think of the girlfriend who dumped him for his law tutor and wonder if he is still carrying a torch for her. Even if he is, I am willing to bet he wouldn't do anything half as stupid as I have done.

'Our stop.'

He jumps me off the step and I relax. I can beat myself up some other time. It would be a shame to waste my first New Year in Denmark, with thoughts of Christian. I have just got to find a way to put it all behind me. I will think about the mess I have got myself into later.

We run across the town hall square and down Strøget to Nyhavn. By the time we reach it, I am completely breathless but I have warmed up. We wander through the crowds to look for his friends and stop to share a sausage and a coffee from the *pølser* stand.

'There they are.' He points at a group of people laughing and kicking snow around. We walk over to join them and he gestures vaguely at them. 'These are my friends. Everyone, this is Kate. She speaks very good Danish but, this late at night, I think you should be kind and speak English to her.'

They crowd round us, shaking hands and greeting me. I lose track of whom I have met and after a while I just smile and nod. We make our way down to the water and sit at a café, where Tomas orders *gløgg* for us both. The others are drinking coffee and akvavit and I am surprised to see it is nearly midnight. The crowds start the countdown in a huge roar of sound and Tomas leans down so his mouth is nearly touching my ear. 'You have never seen anything like this, I promise you.'

The clocks strike twelve and the waterfront breaks into cheers one second before the whole city erupts in a blaze of light, bangs and crashes. I gasp and for one moment clutch at Tomas' sleeve, before realising it is only fireworks. But this isn't like any firework display I have ever seen. The entire world is consumed by coloured lights, flying across the water and off buildings and sliding back down the clouds. We are drowned in a pool of colour. It is all around us, above and below and it goes on and on. I turn my head to watch a shower of golden rain and catch Tomas' eye. We sit for a moment, our gaze locked, and my heart starts to thump in time with the rockets still launching off all around the waterfront.

'Tomas!'

Another group of revellers have fought their way across to us and are exchanging excited greetings. The girl who called to Tomas is small and fair and he spins around in recognition.

'Tomas!' She throws her arms around him.

'Susanne!' He hugs her delightedly. '*Godt nytår!*'

'*Godt nytår.*'

She pulls his head down and kisses him fondly. He emerges at long last and turns to me, still holding her hand.

'Kate, this is Susanne. I told you about her.'

'The law student?' I ask, feeling slightly dizzy at the speed with which events have overtaken me.

'He told you much about me, I expect,' she says to me.

'Not much. Just that you and he ... you and your tutor ...'

She laughs at this. She is disastrously pretty when she laughs.

'Oh, that is over now for some weeks. I am single again and now, on this night of all others, I meet with Tomas. What a piece of luck for us both.'

Chapter Twenty-One

It is almost 3 a.m. when I get home and into bed. The fireworks went on for two full hours. I hadn't realised there was that much gunpowder in the world. I forgot the cold as I watched them erupt and spin and dance and light up the water in front of us. Once Susanne arrived, I was particularly glad to have the excuse of watching the fireworks. She stayed with our group until we left to go home, and spent most of the time talking and laughing with Tomas, who looked delighted to see her. After the first shock had worn off, I decided it was a very good thing she had turned up. If they are going to get back together then how much better if it happens without any mess and complications. Tomas and I were possibly on the edge of a very big mistake, fuelled by the adrenaline of the party atmosphere and my disappointment about the office party. The last thing I need in my life is any more turmoil. I need to think through my relationship with Christian very carefully. If it is finally time to let go, I have to figure out a way to do that with dignity and without my heart being torn into pieces.

I sleep badly and am quite glad when my alarm wakes me, even though I have a stress headache thumping behind my eyes and I suspect it is only going to get worse before the day is out. Headache or not, I have to work today, so I pull on some warm clothes and decide to go out for a walk to clear my thoughts. There is no sign that Lisette or Jens is awake as I tiptoe out of the flat as quietly as possible and head down towards the lakes. It is cloudy and a fraction warmer than last night but still below freezing and a chilly mist swirls across the ice. There is also a sour smell which, after a moment's thought, I identify as gunpowder. There are empty firework wrappers and casings everywhere and they symbolise my current mood. The lights and fireworks of the past few months have gone out and I am left facing nothing but cold and emptiness until spring. I shake my head. This may be an ending of sorts but there is always hope. I just need to find it. I need to plan a better year than the last.

At this moment, I seem to be the only person awake — apart from the swans sitting in icy splendour in the middle of the lake. I break into a run and reach the end of the first lake before a burning pain in my side forces me to stop. I would kill for a hot cup of coffee but nowhere seems to be open so I walk more slowly back along the other side of the lake and through the streets to my apartment, thinking more positively about the year ahead. Lisette is sitting in a huddle, watching the slow drip of the percolator.

'Great. Is there enough for me?'

My voice must be louder than I thought because she winces. 'Only if you whisper.'

'Bad head?'

'A little. Jens is worse. They opened champagne at midnight and he drank almost a whole bottle to himself.'

'It sounds like a good party.'

She shakes her head. 'It was OK. What happened to you?'

I hesitate for a moment, picking over possible lies only to discard them. My life has recently been too full of prevarication and half-truths. I owe it to myself to face facts.

'I decided I didn't want to spend New Year's Eve in the same room as Christian. It's not doing me any good.'

'Oh, I did wonder.' She pours me a mug of coffee and I press my chilled fingers around it and look into the sludgy depths.

'Yes, I expect you both did. I haven't been behaving too intelligently since I arrived. But that's all over. I've got lots of New Year's resolutions.'

'Are they to do with never drinking again?' Jens walks unsteadily into the kitchen and slumps down next to Lisette.

'No, not particularly.'

'Mine are. I am to be teetotal until at least ... let me see ...'

'Tonight,' says Lisette. 'We have dinner with your family. Remember?'

'That gives you about eight hours to detox,' I say with a grin.

'Why are you so cheerful?' he asks and accepts the mug she hands him.

'First, I only had one glass of *gløgg*. Secondly, I've put this past year behind me and I've been making plans for the coming year and that's quite a cheerful thing to do.'

It's true. I usually don't keep my resolutions much beyond the first week of January but I have always loved that feeling of washing away the past, looking forward and not back, seeing the year ahead as a sheet of paper not yet written on, filled with possibilities for great changes and new directions.

'You are too good to be true. Go away.' He gulps at his coffee and gives me a half smile.

'I'm off to work. Hope you enjoy dinner with your parents.' I wave at them and leave them sitting with their coffee. I sing in the shower and decide to wear my cherry red sweater to work instead of my usual black or grey, in honour of the new me.

Tomas is opening up when I arrive. '*Godt nytår.* How's it going?'

I don't meet his eye. 'Yeah, *godt* whatever. Everything's great, thanks. How was your head this morning?'

'It is actually OK. I have a very strong head.' He opens the door for me and follows me inside.

'Thanks for last night.'

'It was my pleasure. Everyone was very pleased to meet you.'

Everyone? I want to ask if that includes Susanne but she isn't really any of my business. Per, one of Tomas' friends, was taking the train back to my station last night and offered to accompany me so I have no idea when or with whom Tomas went home. He doesn't volunteer anything else and we stack glasses and plates in silence.

'We may be quite busy tonight,' he warns. 'People who couldn't face lunch will suddenly find they are hungry this evening. Also, people who have had enough of their families for one holiday week.'

'Jens and Lisette are having dinner with his family. I hope his head is better. Apparently he drank half the champagne in

Europe at their party last night. I should have bought futures in French vineyards.'

'I would have had to drink a lot too if I was stuck in some office party. I am glad you escaped.'

'Me too. Your party was far more fun.'

I don't add that the ending was somewhat confusing. That is for him to mention if he wants to.

'Susanne is coming in tonight,' he says and I glance sharply at him to see if he looks self-conscious. He doesn't.

'That's nice.' I fumble around for a question that might give me some information, without sounding unduly curious about something which is very definitely nothing to do with me.

'She is looking for some part-time work,' he adds.

'You mean here?'

'Possibly. I know Mette would be happy to find someone.'

'Wouldn't that be uncomfortable for you?'

'For me? Why so?'

'Having your ...' I hesitate for a moment over what to call her. I assume she is still an ex-girlfriend, but who knows? She was certainly friendly enough when she met him last night and he didn't seem to be holding any grudges. He has probably been waiting for her to come to her senses ever since she went off with their tutor. Much like me waiting for Christian, I suppose. But I have to admit he has taken a far more dignified approach to the whole thing.

'Having my what?'

'Well, having someone you have a history with working with you.' That keeps my options open as to what exactly she is now.

'Kate, she was a good friend. She still is. She needs a job now she and Benjamin have broken up.'

'I suppose so. Did she move in with him?'

'Yes, but her sister has a spare room so it was no difficulty to go there when things went bad.'

'Wasn't it a bit weird her even going out with him? I didn't think you were meant to do that if you were a tutor.'

'Maybe it was a bit unusual but she switched classes so they didn't meet professionally. We are all adults and it is the twenty-first century.'

I feel slightly rebuked when he says this. It is as though he thinks I am too immature to understand adult relationships. But I don't say anything. He may have a point. I have hardly been demonstrating a mature understanding of how to handle a break-up. I am still curious about him and Susanne.

'What went wrong with her and Benjamin?'

He shrugs. 'Things didn't work out. It happens.'

'I suppose so. Were you very hurt when she left you for him?'

He switches on the coffee maker and thinks for a moment. 'I thought the world had come to an end.'

'She meant that much to you?'

'We had been together for two years. It is a long time.'

That isn't exactly an answer but I can't see how to prise any more information out of him without being intrusive. If she doesn't mean anything to him any longer then he would surely say so. For now, I have to assume that he, like me, has unfinished business. I pick up a stack of dishes and pause before taking them through to the kitchen. 'For what it's worth, I think she was a fool to leave you for him.'

'How can you say that? You haven't met him.'

'No, but he must have known you were together and he went ahead anyway.'

I don't mention that Susanne knew they were together and she went ahead anyway too. And just because I haven't met the guy doesn't stop me thinking that it is extremely unlikely that he is nicer, kinder or funnier than Tomas. Maybe Susanne saw that quite quickly. Maybe, unlike me with Christian, she is lucky enough not to have burned her boats and there is a happier ending ahead for her and Tomas than seems likely for me.

'You look tired, Kate.'

I smile as brightly as possible. 'Late night. I'll be fine by tomorrow. I have all sorts of New Year's resolutions.'

'Are you going to tell me?'

'No, then they won't come true.'

Actually, I would love to talk to him about the conclusions I reached last night and how I might move forward this year. But I don't feel comfortable doing that while I am not sure where he stands. He might be back in his old relationship and I don't want to risk sharing everything with a complete stranger too, however nice she seemed.

Business picks up fairly quickly. He seems to be right about people wanting to avoid their families. People drift in alone or in pairs, with none of the large groups we were serving over the run up to Christmas. We close at nine tonight and Susanne hasn't appeared by eight. Perhaps she isn't coming in. She may have found herself a job already, or even decided that she was too quick in breaking up with her tutor. She may be moving her things back in to his apartment at this moment, laughing with him at the foolish decision that followed too quickly from what was probably a simple misunderstanding. I hope she tells Tomas soon if she has changed her mind. I know how hard it is either to hold on to or to let go of hope, when all the signals are mixed.

I scrub busily at the bowls and rinse and dry them as I ponder this. Tomas' voice makes me jump.

'Kate? We need some glasses.'

'Coming.'

I load a tray and go through. It is almost a surprise to find Susanne standing there, watching Tomas froth milk for her latte. I had just ensconced her nicely in a penthouse next to the harbour, with beautiful views across to Sweden. I recollect how much a tutor is likely to be paid, move the pair of them down two floors and change the view to a main road.

'*Hej, Kate.*'

She waves a gloved hand at me, and in spite of myself, I smile back. She has a very short crop, which suits her elfin features and very white teeth when she smiles, which she does easily, showing two large dimples. She is shorter than me and far slimmer. If she wasn't so alive, I would almost think of her as fragile, a word I don't believe could ever be ascribed to me.

'Hi, Susanne. How are you?'

'I am good, thanks. Did you enjoy the fireworks?'

'They were amazing. I've never seen anything quite like it.'

'Aren't they wonderful? Tomas and I went to the harbour each year. That is how I knew where to find him last night.'

'You were looking for him? I thought you said it was luck.'

'Yes, I was looking. I was to spend the evening with Benjamin and his family but it didn't work out. So I thought it would be nicest to be with a friend. But finding him was the luck, don't you think?'

'As long as he wanted to be found.' I wonder if I have gone too far but she doesn't seem annoyed.

'Of course. He will always be a friend, I hope.'

She laughs up at him and I am annoyed to see the easy smile he gives her. He doesn't seem annoyed in the slightest that she left him, broke his heart, walked off with someone he trusted. He seems to think it is quite natural that she should come back when it didn't work out, that she should turn to her old boyfriend. Perhaps he has always known they belong together, has never believed any force would keep them apart for long, has known that any difficulties they encounter along their journey together will ultimately only bring them closer together. Like me and Christian. Or like me and Christian before New Year and the creeping doubts it brought that we could ever return our relationship to what it was. Tomas' face shows no such doubts. Either he has more faith than I do, or their relationship is just better than mine was with Christian. Either way, I feel a complete failure. I nod at her politely and wave towards the kitchen.

'I have to go and do some work. Nice to see you.'

'See you again.'

She turns to Tomas and I hear them resume a rapid-fire conversation in Danish. I can't pick out more than one word in ten and I feel frustrated that I am still so much of a foreigner here, so isolated and alone in the middle of people I thought of as friends but whom I see now are just kind strangers. I don't belong here. Probably Christian was right that I never will. He moved to my country and so he knows what it was like having to adjust. It is probably the reason that he came back here, even at the expense of saying goodbye to friends and breaking off our relationship. The draw of being with his own people, speaking his own language and understanding his own country's customs, must have been stronger than his feelings for me. For the first time since he left, I don't blame him. I had no understanding of what it would really mean to pursue him here. I behaved like a two-year-old and snatched at what I wanted, not counting the cost to me or to anyone, rushing away from one life without really thinking about what I was leaving and not pausing to think what the change would bring.

Christian feels more lost to me than ever and it is all my fault. If I could turn back the clock five months, I would never again do what I have done. And now I am stuck as a stranger among strangers, in a country in which I can barely communicate and without the love of my life. The tears begin to slip down my face and into the soapy water. I wipe my eyes hopelessly on my sleeve but I know I have no one to blame but myself. I got myself into this mess. Somehow, I need to find a way to get myself out of it.

Chapter Twenty-Two

By the end of February, I still haven't seen Christian. After the non-event of New Year's Eve at his office party, I decided to leave well alone and let him choose for himself what he wants. If his future is to include Miranda, I have to accept that. For myself, I can't look too far ahead. I have no job to go back to in London and I do have one here. I also promised to tutor the children until they leave in May and I have no intention of going back on my word. For the rest of the year, I have no plans. Becca is coming out in May, which gives me something to look forward to. It would be a shame not to see something of Denmark in the better weather. I expect I will stay here for the summer and then make plans to go home in the autumn after a year away. Becca hasn't moved anyone else into the flat so I should at least have a place to stay.

Things have been a little strained between me and Tomas these past two months, mostly on my side, as he has been as friendly as ever. He hasn't mentioned Susanne, apart from saying that she has a part-time job at her sister's firm and, like him, is combining it with part-time study. So he must be seeing her at university again. I suppose I feel a little hurt that he isn't being open about what is going on with the pair of them. It is none of my business but he isn't usually secretive. I decide that the fact I have never told him much about Christian is irrelevant. He knows that we were a couple, that I only came to Copenhagen because of Christian and that his relationship with Miranda is making me unhappy. I know nothing about Susanne. For all I know, they may have moved back in together. I find the thought quite difficult to deal with, probably because I know how much she hurt him, as Christian did me. So if they *have* moved in together, in my mind's eye I move her apartment down several more floors and give them two rooms in a basement, with no view of any kind.

Tomas comes into the kitchen one day just as I am finishing up.

'Hey, I was wondering if you have skated yet.'

'Skated? You mean on ice?'

'I do. It is very Danish to skate outside and the rink will be closing soon for the spring.'

'I can't really skate.'

'It isn't important. Don't those children of yours skate?'

'All the time but they belong to a club. They have lessons. I've taken them down there a few times and watched them. They're extremely good. I used to roller-skate with my brother in the local park but that was hundreds of years ago.'

'You don't show your extreme age.'

'Very funny. I was about ten I think.'

If I am honest, in many ways it does feel like hundreds of years. I have been so depressed this past couple of months that I haven't felt like doing anything fun. The weather has lost its novelty and day after day of snow, slush or grey clouds and icy rain, has lowered my mood even further.

'It's about time you tried again, isn't it? I have a class cancelled on Wednesday afternoon. What are your plans?'

'Is Susanne coming?' It sounds a bit abrupt but I don't care.

'Susanne?' He laughs and shakes his head. 'She has classes in the afternoons like me.'

That doesn't exactly answer the question of whether or not she would be coming if she were free. I cast around for a better way to phrase it.

'Do you see her still?'

'I see her very often.'

'Oh.'

He is either stupidly oblivious to what I want to know or he assumes I must realise they are back together, so isn't bothering to spell it out. Or he thinks it is none of my business.

'So, are you free?' he presses me.

'Not on Wednesday. I pick the children up at two o'clock and I promised I would stay with them until it's time for me to come here.'

'Great, we'll take them along too. Then we can bring them here for a snack and their mother or father can pick them up when they are ready.'

'I expect that would work.'

He ignores the ungraciousness in my tone and puts an arm round me and gives me a half hug.

'You haven't been yourself for weeks now, Kate. Is everything all right?'

'Yes, I suppose so. It's been horribly depressing weather and I'm just realising I don't have anything planned for next year.'

'Do you like to plan ahead so much? I thought it was very spontaneous of you coming out here.'

'It wasn't like me at all. I was just ... desperate, I suppose.'

'Do you still see him?' He has dropped his arm and is wiping the milk nozzle hard with a cloth until it shines.

'I haven't seen him since New Year's Eve.' It sounds even worse when I say it out loud.

'Do you still hope to?'

'I don't know what I hope any more, Tomas, and that's the truth. If he's been happy to stay away from me for more than five months, half of me thinks he doesn't care at all and I'm well shot of him. The other half knows that he's the only man I've ever loved and he's worth waiting for, at least a little longer.'

'OK.' He doesn't look as though he thinks I am entirely insane, which is a relief. 'So, Wednesday it is? Shall we meet at the rink?'

'I'll get the children and we'll be there about half past two. Bring some crutches, just in case.'

'I have a feeling you will be a natural.' He walks off to clear some tables, laughing.

On Wednesday afternoon, the four of us arrive a little early at the rink. Tomas isn't here yet. The children delve into their bags and strap on their skates. I pay for us all and hire some skates for myself.

'Can you skate good?' asks Josefina, standing up and pulling on her hat and gloves.

'I haven't ice skated before. Ever.'

'Will I help you?'

'Please.'

She waits for me to finish lacing my boots. I have become very fond of Josefina over these past couple of months. She is quiet and serious and determined to succeed at whatever she does, including learning English. The twins are entirely the opposite, noisy and outgoing and only learning any English because their parents and I are speaking it to them relentlessly and because they are both very bright, not because they are putting any effort into it. I laugh at them both now, zooming round the ice, dodging each other and anyone else in their path. Rasmus has a nasty trick of flying up behind people very fast and skidding to a sideways stop, sending a cloud of ice flying up around his victim. Rebecca copies him, as she copies everything that he does.

'Sorry I'm late.' Tomas' voice behind me, just as I am attempting to balance on what I now realise is a stupidly thin blade of metal, nearly sends me flying. He steadies me and grins at my terrified expression. 'All ready to enjoy yourself?'

'All ready to break something, more like. I could just sit and watch you all instead.'

'Not a hope. Are these the twins?'

Rasmus and Rebecca have spotted him and come pelting across the rink. Rasmus sends a graceful arc of ice around Tomas' head and Rebecca tries to do the same. They stare at Tomas for a moment and then break into a flood of Danish to each other. I only manage to pick out the word *kæreste* and I break in at once.

'Not my boyfriend, you horrible children. Tomas, can you explain who you are?'

He turns to the three of them and introduces himself. They all shake hands with him. Rasmus and Rebecca are still looking first at Tomas and then at me and giggling. I decide to ignore them.

'OK, we all need to speak English this afternoon. Come on, Josefina. You said you would help me.'

She puts her arm under my elbow and guides me onto the ice, where my feet promptly shoot out from under me and I collapse in a painful heap.

'I am more your height. Maybe I should help?' Tomas glides onto the ice and takes my hand. Rasmus and Rebecca break into fresh gales of laughter at this but I don't care. Anything that keeps me upright and off this wet, gritty ice is fine with me. I take a few tottering steps, until I feel sure that he isn't going to let me go, and then strike out more firmly.

'Look at you. I said you would be a natural.' Tomas relaxes his grip and I shriek. 'OK, I'll hold on for a while.'

'It's harder than it looks. I'm all right, Josefina.'

She has been circling us warily, making sure Tomas is able to support me. She nods, waves and flies away, her thick, dark hair streaming out from under her cap.

'Wasn't this a good idea?' he says, as we finish our first lap.

'It's a nice day at least. I thought the sun had given up on Denmark for good.'

'It has been quite a cold winter. But these days make up for it.'

He is right. The air is bitterly cold but the sky is a dazzling turquoise and the sun is warm enough to make me feel that spring might be on its reluctant way. We circle the rink for another hour before I make for the side.

'My legs aren't used to this. They're not going to hold up any longer. You go on and have a turn, Tomas. I've been holding you back.'

'Just a short go.' He sees me safely off the ice and then turns and chases after Rasmus. He is an excellent skater, graceful and quick and I laugh as I see Rasmus catch sight of Tomas and race away. I tug off my skates and watch the two of them darting and dodging. Josefina has joined me on the bench.

'Don't get cold, Josefina.'

She pulls off her cap and laughs. 'Skating is hot.'

'True, but the air is cold. We'll leave in a short while.'

Tomas has caught Rasmus and is towing him, struggling and laughing to the side, where he dumps him and leaves him to unlace his skates while he goes off after Rebecca. Once she has been caught too, we all pack our bags and the children follow us down to the bus stop.

'We need ice cream,' announces Rebecca and Rasmus nods.

'Rebecca - you should not be so ... so ...' Josefina fumbles for the word she wants.

'Hungry,' supplies Rasmus and I aim a fake slap at him.

'We have nice water at the café. And dry bread.'

All three of their faces fall until Tomas and I laugh at them.

'Maybe some cake,' I relent.

'And ice cream?' shrieks Rebecca.

'Perhaps.'

We jump off at the bus stop and the children run across the frozen grass to the café. We follow on behind.

'Nice kids,' says Tomas.

'They really are. If I thought all children were like them, I might have gone into teaching after university.'

'It's not too late.'

'I don't know. Everything feels too late right at the moment. I just need to get a grip.'

'And stop being so hard on yourself.' He opens the door and motions me through.

We sit the children down and Tomas makes them all hot chocolate while I bring over a plate of cookies. Mette doesn't let me pay, although I try. She waves at us all and leaves. Tomas sits with the children while I make coffees and teas for the few customers that drift in. He has obviously forgotten my rule of speaking English with the children because I hear snatches of Danish drifting across amid gales of laughter. My spirits lift slightly as I watch them. Tomas is right, nothing is too late. I just need time and space to think a little.

'*En kop kaffe?*'

Why didn't I see Christian come in?

'You move so quietly,' I accuse him. 'You gave me a shock.'

'A nice one, I hope.' He doesn't wait for an answer but pulls off his coat and hangs it up. I hand him his cup of coffee and give him his change.

'It has been a long time,' he says, leaning against the counter and watching Tomas.

'New Year's Eve.' I don't add anything because the remembrance of that evening still makes me feel hot with shame.

'I wish you would have stayed longer. I hoped to get a chance to talk with you.'

'I had another party to go to.' It isn't entirely true but it's close enough and hopefully will stop him wondering exactly why I was so keen to leave. It's not a conversation I intend to have with him.

'Was the party with Tomas?'

'Yes.' I nod to where he is sitting with the children, building a cookie tower. Christian's gaze is inscrutable.

'Can I be introduced?'

'To Tomas? You've met him several times.'

'To his children.'

'They aren't his. How on earth could you think that? He would have had to be about sixteen when he started. They're mine.'

'Yours?' He lifts an eyebrow comically and I can't help smiling back at him.

'Only in one sense. They're moving to England soon and I'm tutoring them.'

'Good for you. Is Tomas tutoring them too?'

'No, but we all just went skating and now he's taking a well-earned break. He had to stop me falling over for the best part of an hour.'

'I see.' He watches the children laughing and flicking cookie crumbs onto a target that Tomas has drawn on the serviette. 'Kate, it is probably not my right to ask but are you and Tomas together?'

I stare at him. His voice is casual but he his look is curiously intent. I feel the blood rise in my cheeks as I consider the possible implications of his question.

'No,' I say slowly. 'He's a really good friend and I love him but we're not together.'

'Thank you for your honesty.'

He seems to be waiting for me to say something, maybe ask about him and Miranda, but I am determined not to. I made a decision not to interfere any more in their relationship. In an odd way, I am even thankful that I didn't manage to sabotage it. Even if I couldn't see it in the first furious heat of our break-up, I can see now what a terrible foundation that would have been on which to build anything new together. So, if he is waiting for me to ask or make any comment about his new relationship, he can forget it. He has to be responsible for his choices and actions just as I have to be for mine.

'I can see this is not a good time to talk,' he says, gesturing to Tomas and the children. 'You are working and you have other responsibilities. I am leaving for Hong Kong this evening.'

'Business?' It is as near as I dare get to asking if he is going alone. I think he picks up the undertone because he laughs.

'Business. Four weeks of non-stop meetings. But then I am back and I would very much like to have some coffee with you and talk. Am I asking too much?'

My heart is thumping but I keep my voice casual. 'Coffee isn't that big of a deal. I think I could manage that.'

'I will phone you.'

'You don't have my number.'

'True. Then I will phone you if you will be so kind as to give me your number.'

I scribble it on a serviette and hand it to him. I see Tomas looking over at us as I do so. I look away. It's just a phone number, for goodness sake. He has it too.

Christian hands me his cup. 'So long, Kate. I will see you in four weeks. I very much look forward to it.'

'Me too.' I wave at him cheerfully and take the cup through to the kitchen. I am determined not even to think about him for the next month. This meeting could be about anything. There is no reason to think it has anything to do with us getting back together. He might be about to announce his engagement and want to tell me first. He might have a new job in Istanbul and want to say goodbye. He might even want me to know that he has been spending time with Jon in IT and is starting a whole new chapter of his life. Well, good for him, whatever it is. I have a life of my own and a future to plan, so I won't have time to speculate and hope. If he is lucky enough to find me still here after another month, all well and good. I put the cup into the dishwasher and go back out to the café, where Anna has arrived to collect the children.

'Thank you so much. Say goodbye and thank you to Kate and to Tomas,' she instructs them.

'Thank you.'

'Thank you.'

'*Er det din kæreste?*' Rasmus is pointing towards the door through which Christian has just left. Tomas glances at me to see what I am going to answer. I poke Rasmus in the ribs.

'You are my favourite. You can be my *kæreste*.'

I laugh at his horrified expression and wave at the four of them as they pick up their bags and jostle each other across the café and out into the snow.

Chapter Twenty-Three

March is an odd month. It passes in a series of quick jumps, interspersed with days that crawl by at snail speed. I try as much as possible not to speculate about what it is that Christian wants to discuss. There is no point in running imaginary conversations through my head about things that might never happen. The weeks pass in a kind of limbo. In any case, most of the time I am too busy to worry very much. I reach the end of the first stage of language school and have to give a talk on a subject of my tutor's choice, which turns out to be Danish customs. I revise frantically and Tomas listens to me practise every evening during my break and corrects my pronunciation and some of my wilder statements. The rest of the time is taken up with tutoring the children, as Josefina instructs me in the fine art of making chocolate chip cookies and the twins volunteer as testers. I am still working evenings and weekends at the café, so it is really only at night that I have time to lie and wonder what the end of this month will bring. One thing I know for sure, this time it is going to be decisive. Things can't go on as they have done. Whichever way I finally obtain closure, I almost don't care. This has been the oddest year of my life and I need to move on.

By the middle of the month, the last of the snow has melted and there is a change in the weather. It is still very cold and I need my hat and gloves but there is a softness to the air as I cycle to and from work. It is exhilarating after such a long winter. When the first blossom peeps out on the trees, I almost cry. Tomas comes into the kitchen one evening after his break.

'I have just checked the weather forecast for the first weekend in April and it's good. Mette has her daughter staying and I have asked her to let us both have Saturday off.'

'What for?'

'For one thing, neither of us has had a proper day off in months. For another, we are going to *Sverige* – Sweden to you.'

'Says who?'

'You won't come?'

'I might,' I say suspiciously. 'Why Sweden?'

'Because you haven't been and because there is a little café there I want you to see. I think you might like it. I have been waiting for better weather and now it is here. Will you come?'

I think for a moment and then nod. I may not be here for much longer and I have been promising myself that I will see some more of Denmark before I leave. It will be nice to see a tiny bit of Sweden and I can't think of anyone I would rather go with. If it *is* just the two of us, of course. I ask him this.

'Unless you want to ask Mette along?'

'I was more thinking of Susanne.'

'Why is that?'

'You know why, Tomas. I have no idea if you and she are still seeing each other so I never know whether or not to mention her.'

'I see. How long have you thought this?'

'Since New Year. I just assumed that she ... that you ...'

'No. Is this why you have been a little different with me?'

'I didn't think I was being different. I've had a lot on my mind these past few weeks. But I did think you might have put me in the picture. It's always easier when friends do that.'

'There was nothing to say. We were always good friends and we still are. I was happy to see her again but that is all. We were over when she and Benjamin got together. She knows that.'

'But they split up. You might both have realised you made a mistake.'

'I doubt it. We split up for a reason. There is never any going back from that.'

I wonder for a second if he is trying to make a point but he looks as placid as ever. I can see his point. I just hope he can see mine. Christian and I didn't split up for any good reason — that's the difference. He was due back last week and I haven't heard from him yet so maybe whatever he wants to discuss wasn't that important. But I am still keeping my options open. I don't want to get into any kind of argument with Tomas so I nod and change the subject.

'Where are we going in Sweden?'

'Helsingborg. It's just across from Helsingør. We can take a ferry.'

'Sounds good.'

'As I say, there is a little café there that I always visit and I want you to see.'

'You don't think that's a bit of a busman's holiday?'

'No, it is too far for a bus. I will meet you at your train station at eight if that's OK.'

'Suits me.' It is nice to know that some of the finer points of English idiom are lost on him. I usually feel horribly inferior, hearing his superb grasp of my language, while I still stumble and trip along in his.

I arrive at the café on Friday evening for my shift and Tomas is already there. 'Are you ready for tomorrow?'

'I'm looking forward to it. It'll be fantastic having a day off if nothing else.'

'Even if you have to spend it with me?'

I laugh. 'I can think of worse things.'

'You're very kind.' He reaches down a bottle of white wine and puts it in the fridge.

Just before it is time for my break, my phone bleeps and I check the text. It's Christian. *Are you free tonight or tomorrow?*

I think for a moment before texting back. *Out all day tomorrow. I have a break in ten minutes.*

He doesn't reply but I watch the door and sure enough he arrives right on time.

'*Hej, Christian.*' If Tomas is surprised to see him, he doesn't show it.

'*Hej.*' Christian seems a little out of breath and I smile to myself. It is a nice change to have him running round after me. I come round to his side of the counter and he kisses my cheek.

'Tomas, is it OK if I take a break?'

'For sure. Can I get you both a drink?'

'Cappuccino with ...'

'... extra chocolate. I know the drill.'

'I will have the same please,' says Christian and I follow him through the café to the table in the window where we sat just before Christmas. That is obviously on his mind too.

'It is a long time since we talked,' he says and I nod. There is nothing obvious to say to that. It wasn't my choice. I suppose I did choose to withdraw from him and Miranda but it wasn't the way I wanted things to be.

'How was Hong Kong?' I ask politely and he waves a hand to brush the subject away.

'Fine, busy — the same as usual. Kate, I have come to talk to you of more serious things. First of all, you should know that Miranda and I are no longer together.'

'You're joking. When did this happen?'

'Just after New Year.'

I stare at him, dismayed, remembering her territorial behaviour at the party, for which I now don't blame her one bit. I had no right to be there.

'It wasn't because of me, was it?' I am genuinely relieved when he shakes his head.

'Not even a little bit. She met someone at your embassy. In fact, she was seeing him for a little while before she told me it was over with me.'

'You're joking,' I say again, trying to suppress a slight feeling of schadenfreude. Now he knows what it is like to be dumped for someone else. At least he didn't two-time me. That has to hurt. 'Are you OK?'

'I am fine. To be honest, it wasn't that much of a surprise. Things had been a little shaky for a while. I had almost expected her to say something but I think that while you were around, she ...'

'Dug her claws in deeper?'

He grins. 'Not how I would have put it.'

'I don't blame her. I'd have been exactly the same. My behaviour was inexcusable and I'd like to apologise for that. I wish I could apologise to Miranda too.'

'I don't think you need to. You left the party early, didn't you? I think she understood. Was that because of me?'

'Yes, Ilse made me see what a complete jerk I was being and I realised I needed to leave you alone.'

'I was disappointed not to be able to talk to you that night. But, when you left, it made me see how much you had changed. And it made me realise too for the first time how much I must have hurt you.'

I trace a pattern on the glass table in front of me so I don't have to look at him. 'You didn't realise that already?'

'Not properly. I was a little upset with you for coming over here and perhaps I focussed mostly on that.'

'I can understand that.' It is true. I can. I am a little surprised, knowing me so well, that he hadn't picked up on my total devastation in London when we broke up, but maybe he was too concerned about what crazy thing I might do next, properly to appreciate the depths of my heartbreak.

'What does the next year hold for you, Kate?'

It is a question I have no way of answering without knowing what is going on in his mind, and I refuse even to try. I may be to blame for some of what has gone on since he came back here but I have at least recognised my part in that and tried as far as possible to put it right. The ball is in his court now, so I shrug and sit and wait for him to speak.

'OK, maybe that isn't a fair question. I should go first. I have spent some time thinking about this. If you are not with someone else, I think we should spend some time together as friends for a little while. I would like to see if we can rebuild some of what we had. Then we should just see where it takes us next. How do you feel about this?'

I ought to feel overjoyed and, somewhere deep inside, I probably do. But I am so battered by the last few months, the uncertainties and the ups and downs, that I feel very little apart from weariness, as at the end of a very long day. I am able to sit and consider his idea coolly while he watches me. In the end I nod.

'I think that's a good idea. We should take things slowly and see where it goes.'

'Then it's a deal.' He stands and shakes my hand, smiling down at me. I am suddenly exhausted. It has been a long six months. I feel as though I could go to bed and sleep for days.

Christian gives me a tiny wave and leaves and I wander back to the counter in a daze. Tomas doesn't say anything but I see him glancing at me curiously as the evening goes on. I am glad when it is time to lock up. We stand together for a moment outside the door and he hesitates.

'Are we still on for tomorrow?'

'Of course. Why wouldn't we be? Don't say you've got cold feet?'

'No, but I thought you might have.'

'You'd be wrong then, wouldn't you? I'll see you at the station tomorrow bright and early. Don't be late.'

'So you and he are not ...'

'Back together? As a matter of fact we're not.'

It is the exact truth and I don't want to bore him with the details of our on-again, off-again relationship. Even now, it might not go anywhere. It is best not discussed yet, even with such a good friend as Tomas.

'Sorry if I upset you.'

'I'm not upset. But I don't want to talk about Christian. I would rather look forward to our day out. See you at eight o'clock.'

He looks less uncertain now. 'OK, it's a date.'

And he strides off across the grass, whistling cheerfully.

Chapter Twenty-Four

It is still cold when I leave the flat and I am glad of my warm jacket and scarf. I look down at my gloves and remember how woefully unprepared I was for Denmark when I first arrived. In fact, I can hardly believe that I just took off like that, leaving my old life and rushing over here. Looking back, it wasn't a very mature thing to do but it has had the effect of making me grow up, so I am at a loss now to know whether or not I ought to regret it. For now, my impulsive dash to a new country can go into the part of my brain where I keep all my past experiences, good and bad, and I can take it out years from now and decide.

Tomas is already at the station and he is holding two cups of coffee. I pull off my gloves and take the one he offers.

'You're such a star. Always one step ahead. Why didn't I think of this? I pass that little café on the way.'

'You can think about breakfast when we get to the ferry. I would bet that you have not yet had any.'

'How well you know me. My stomach doesn't wake up until about ten o'clock and there's no chance you'll ever change its mind.'

'Here it comes.' He waves at the grey train sliding like a caterpillar along the platform.

He waves a *klippekort* at me. 'You can get us breakfast and then we will be even.'

We find ourselves seats and lean back. I am increasingly excited about seeing something different. So far, I have spent all my time in Denmark here in Copenhagen, and almost all of that in winter weather. It is time I broadened my horizons a little. I watch the sea slide by on one side and the trees and houses on the other, as we head north. The houses become more sparsely scattered. Many of them are thatched and painted in pastel colours like a clutch of Easter eggs in the spring grass. The train finally draws to a stop at the ferry terminal and we clamber out and walk across the concrete to buy our tickets. The ferry isn't due to leave for fifteen minutes so I stand with my nose pressed to the glass wall and look across the sparkling waves to the country on the other side. It feels so strange to be almost within spitting distance of Sweden. Tomas doesn't seem to have noticed anything exciting about it so I keep my thoughts to myself and try to maintain an aura of cool until the ferry has nosed itself into the port, where it bobs squatly on the waves as people unload themselves and walk down the tunnel towards us.

When we have boarded, we make for the café and Tomas decides on chips. I laugh.

'For breakfast?'

'Why not? Have you never eaten eggs or toast for dinner?'

'You have a point.'

We share the chips as the boat rumbles across the water and finally docks in Helsingborg. It is a beautiful little town, sitting right on the water and looking back across to Helsingør. We wander along the quay and through the streets that climb away from the town. Tomas drags me up to the top of a steep hill, where we find a sheltered spot in a garden near the foot of a tower, out of the chilly wind. I hug my knees as I look back across the water. 'It's a beautiful part of the world.'

'So is the UK, is it not?'

'I suppose it is.' I feel a little surprised that I even have to think about it. 'Yes, there are lots of gorgeous places but I live there so I hardly ever visit them.'

'I have only been to London.'

'You tourist,' I tease him.

'Isn't that where you lived?'

'Yes, for the past few years but I wasn't brought up there. My family lives in Dorset, in a little village near Dorchester. Thomas Hardy country.'

'Who?'

'*Tess of the d'Urbervilles*?'

'OK.' I can't tell if he has heard of it or is just not breaking the flow.

'It really is gorgeous down there — rolling countryside for miles, beautiful coastline. Just talking about it makes me homesick.'

I half laugh when I say this but it's true. I have been feeling so disconnected over these past few months that just the thought of something as stable as a childhood home is very attractive, however many bad memories may be attached to it in more recent years.

'Will you go back?'

'To Dorset? I don't expect so. There isn't so much work there.'

'Back to London, I meant.'

'It's possible one day. I mean, I don't belong anywhere else and at least I have a room waiting for me there if I need it.'

'You have a room in Copenhagen.'

'I do for now. I'll just see how it goes.'

I still can't bring myself to mention the subject of Christian and his visit to the café yesterday. I lay awake late into the night, trying to fathom out what he is thinking, and came to the eventual conclusion that, as always with Christian, the facts are as straightforward as his words. He just wants to see how it goes. It's a simple concept and one with which I would have been delighted six months ago. I still think it is the right course for us but I don't seem to be able to recapture the sparkle and excitement of our relationship in London. Too much water has gone under that particular bridge. But I reasoned last night, as I lay awake and stared at the ceiling, that our relationship in London was possibly less permanent and more ephemeral than I recognised at the time. It was rooted in the excitement of Christian's being a stranger, only on loan to us all, and not in the more solid ground of us both knowing more about each other, our backgrounds and our cultures. What we aim to build now might be less frothy and exciting but hopefully will be more realistic and will stand the test of time. He has already had one other relationship and thankfully he doesn't seem too bothered that it has fizzled out. He and I have both had a useful break and time to step back and think. The fact that we both still want to move forward together is encouraging. But I don't seem to be able to put any of this into words for Tomas because I can't trust that he will understand or share my point of view.

For now, I need to keep my plans to myself and not tell him my thoughts until I have something concrete to share.

It occurs to me that this is no different from Tomas not telling me what, if anything, was going on with him and Susanne, but I can't help that. He had nothing to share, so it wouldn't have harmed him to be a bit clearer. I have something to share but it is still so vague and nebulous that it won't do either of us any good to talk about it — and maybe disagree. I stand and pull my hat more closely around my ears. 'I'm cold. Can we see a bit of the town now and maybe have some lunch.'

'You only just had breakfast.'

'You ate most of those chips and you know it. Anyway, I'm hungry. Come on.'

I pull him to his feet and we run across the grass and down the hill towards the main part of the town. The buildings are old and incredibly quaint and he gestures towards a pub, where a sign in English proclaims, *No Mothers-in-Law*.

'I'll bear it in mind if I ever get one,' I say and press my nose against the glass window of the cheese shop on the other side of the pavement. Cheeses of every size colour and shape jostle for position and a savoury aroma drifts out every time someone pushes through the door.

'Still hungry?' asks Tomas and I nod enthusiastically.

'So, we will go to a little café I discovered some years ago. It is a *konditori* and their cakes are even better than ours.'

'Not possible. But it might be interesting to do several taste tests and compare.'

'So much devotion to duty,' he murmurs as we arrive at the *konditori*. I take a quick glance in the window and am suddenly starving. We decide to start with open rolls filled with prawn and egg. With no more than a hopeful glance at the handmade chocolates, I carry my plate through to the room at the back.

'We need a dead body,' I say and he raises his eyebrows in surprise. I look round at the small tables, the genteel chairs and the mural on the wall. 'It's right out of Agatha Christie. Miss Marple would have coffee here and solve mysteries.'

'OK, I have no idea what you are talking about but I'm glad you like it. Shall we try it without the dead body for now?'

'Killjoy.' I seat myself in one of the more comfortable chairs. While we eat our rolls, I look more carefully at the mural. It is a scene of an old market. Women in long dresses are shopping with baskets over their arms. It covers the whole of the wall next to us. Life looks as though it might have been a lot simpler back then.

'You have finished?' asks Tomas.

'Yes and I'm ready for the serious taste-testing.'

We go back through to the *konditori* and he pours us each another cup of coffee. I choose an enormous mixed-fruit tart and he nods.

'Good choice. I shall have a *gåsebryst*.'

'Which is?'

'A goose breast of course. They are delicious. We can share.'

Back at our table he solemnly divides both our cakes in half and we both dive in. The goose breast is delicious — whipped cream encased in sponge and a fine layer of marzipan. The fruit tart is almost as good and I push my last piece over to him with considerable reluctance once I am full.

'What's wrong? On a diet?' He scoops the whole chunk into his mouth in one go.

'I may have to be after too many goose breasts.' I grin at a sudden memory and tell him of a little restaurant Becca and I used to visit when we were at university.

'They called all the dishes stupid names, after Hollywood stars and movies. I always wanted *The Dolly Parton* but I was too embarrassed to order it so I just had to watch Becca eat hers. She refused to order for me as well. She told me to grow up.'

'*The Dolly Parton*? Don't tell me ...'

'*Luscious, tender breasts, lovingly enrobed in pastry*,' I quote from memory as he starts to laugh. 'The thought of ordering that was just too humiliating so I always ended up with *Black Pork Down*.'

'You are very original,' he says and I stop laughing.

'I don't think so. If you ever meet Becca, you'll know what a true original is, but me? There's nothing interesting about me. When Christian left me, all I could think of was that I was lucky to have lasted eight months without him noticing that I wasn't as interesting as most of the women he met.'

I stop abruptly. I hadn't intended even to mention Christian's name today but his face is always there, pushing at the edges of my consciousness, and it takes very little for my mind to drift towards him.

'If he couldn't see that he was one of the luckiest people on earth, he didn't deserve even eight months of you.' Tomas face is serious as he reaches across the table and takes my hand.

'Tomas, please ...' I want to stop him saying whatever he is planning on saying next but it is too late.

'I waited until now because I knew it would take a while for you to get over Christian,' he says. 'But now I need to tell you how I feel before you meet someone else.'

'Tomas!' I pull my hand away and he looks startled. 'Before you say anything else, you should know that Christian and Miranda have split up. He told me yesterday when he came in.'

'Yesterday?'

I can't read the expression in his eyes but I plough on. Now more than ever, it seems only fair to put him in the picture and stop him making plans that can never happen. No matter what happens with me and Christian over the next few months, I can't ever imagine not loving him. I need to make that clear to Tomas in the interests of our friendship.

'He said that he wants to spend some time with me, to see how it goes, in case we can make our relationship work better this time around.'

He doesn't look directly at me so I can't see if his eyes hold disappointment or even hostility. I wait for a long moment and he doesn't speak so I press on.

'I think we have a better shot at it this time. The break has actually been good for me. I feel as though I've grown up a bit. Anyway, that's what's happening. If it doesn't work out, then I really will go home. And actually stay there this time.' I try for a bit of humour at the end.

'Kate, what is he thinking? He was with you for nearly a year and he has seen you on and off since then. How does he not know already exactly what it is that he has got? He let you go once. Amazingly, you have given him another chance. I can't understand what the man is playing at.'

I feel the need to defend Christian as he isn't here. 'I know you don't like him very much. And maybe you're a bit biased, seeing as ... anyway, I think it was a very sensible suggestion. It shows that our relationship has survived quite a bit of turmoil but it recognises that we've both changed since we were together. How would it be better to fall into each other's arms without even seeing if we've changed in different ways?'

'Love isn't a checklist. I really wonder what you are thinking. I thought I knew you, Kate.'

'Perhaps you didn't.' I am feeling more than a little nettled now.

'Yes, I did. I still do.' His eyes soften. He reaches over and takes my hand again and this time I don't stop him. He only has my interests at heart and I have made it clear to him that he and I have no future.

'There is no point in us arguing any more. I am more sorry than I can say that there is no chance for us but I can see that I would only ever be second-best and that wouldn't make either of us happy. So we will stay friends, I hope?'

I wipe my eyes on a serviette and try to smile at him. 'You'll always be my friend, Tomas. I'm sorry how things have worked out but there's no point in me pretending.'

'Would there have been a chance for me if he had stayed with Miranda?'

'How should I know? He didn't. I can see I'd have had a lot less heartbreak if I'd fallen for you instead of him. But I didn't meet you until I was already in love with him and then it was too late. And now we're going to try again and I *have* to see it through. You must see that I do. I can't come this far just to quit right at the end. It isn't me.'

'I know. It's why I love you.' He drops my hand and my eyes fill again.

'Will we still be able to work together?'

'I don't see why not. We both need the money. And I will be able to bully you and push you around just to get my revenge.'

'Try it once. You won't try it twice.'

'OK, I have been warned.' He glances at his watch and stands. 'We have just enough time to see the rest of the town before we should get the ferry. Shall we forget emotion and romance and enjoy ourselves instead?'

'Suits me.'

If it hadn't been for Christian and my need to follow my dreams, it could have been very different. I think Tomas is possibly the nicest man I have ever met. But it is too late for thoughts like that now. I have chosen my path. Luckily, Becca is coming out next month. Maybe she will take his mind off things.

Chapter Twenty-Five

Becca arrives at the beginning of May and I decide to skip a Danish class and take the train to the airport to meet her. Spring here is truly lovely. There is a golden light in the afternoons that I have never seen anywhere else I have travelled. When I rush into the terminal, I see her plane has already landed and it isn't long before she wanders through, lugging an enormous suitcase.

I fold her into an enormous hug. 'Becca! What's with the suitcase? Are you moving here permanently?'

'Be prepared, that's my motto. Where's my flag, then? When I came here last time, they all waved Danish and English paper flags at me and said welcoming things. And not one of them complained about my suitcase.'

'I didn't have time to buy any flags but you know exactly how welcome you are. I've been counting down the days. I'll show you the calendar with the little red crosses when we get back to the apartment.'

'I'll believe it when I see it. You can buy me a coffee now I'm here. I haven't had time to get any Danish money yet.'

We sit in a nearby café and exchange news. I don't mention my day in Sweden and my conversation with Tomas. It doesn't seem fair and I am still hoping they might hit it off. But I tell her about tutoring the children and how much they have improved and about passing my second language exam.

'How much more do you plan on learning?' she asks and I shake my head.

'I don't know. If I stay here permanently, I'll keep at it. I'm nowhere near fluent yet.'

'How's Mr Wonderful?' She knows about my arrangement with Christian but so far hasn't commented. I don't want to start the visit on a bad note so I keep my cool but I need her to know this is entirely my and Christian's business. It is not up for discussion or negotiation.

'Christian's fine. I see him about twice a week for coffee or a walk or something. We're taking our time until we're sure.'

'Which one of you still isn't sure?' She gives me one of her disconcertingly direct looks.

'It's not that. We both just want to take it slowly.'

It's true. I haven't been in any rush to move things on. So much has happened since I left the UK that I want to be very sure about any next steps.

'How's Jon?' I ask, just to tease her and take her mind of the vexed subject of Christian.

'Not so good. His boyfriend left him for someone else. I heard all about it at the vending machine.'

'So there's still hope for you?'

'I wouldn't go that far but I've booked a facial for next week, just in case.'

She follows me down the ramp to the station and I relax. If we can just stay off the subject of Christian this week, we should be fine. I told him that I would be quite busy because Becca was coming over and he seemed to accept it.

'I'll miss you,' he said.

For the first time since we started seeing each other again, I felt something of what I used to feel in the early days. Most of the time when I meet him, I feel almost numb, so even that one flash of familiar emotion was encouraging. This year may have battered me a little but I think I am resilient enough to bounce back eventually.

Becca admires the apartment when we arrive and I show her the sofa we have allocated for her stay.

'If you don't get on with it, you can have my bed and I'll take the sofa. I slept there for a couple of nights when Lisette's mother came over and it was pretty comfortable.'

'If I don't get on with it, I'll find a hotel.' She slings her case out of the way in my room.

'Tell the woman there that you've only got 100 kroner to spend and see where she sends you to eat.'

I have the night off work but I have decided that the café is the easiest place for dinner. In any case, I want her to meet Tomas as soon as possible, so we walk down together in the spring sunshine.

'Mette, this is my friend Becca,' I say as we walk in. They shake hands while I look around for Tomas. He is outside clearing tables and I look at him through the window, wondering what first impressions he and Becca will get of each other. She is looking very nice tonight, wearing a red jacket with a matching red beret perched on her curls. He hasn't seen us yet so I can take a good look at him and try to imagine what she will think. Surely there is nothing for her to object to on first glance. She is looking annoyingly incurious, examining the menu, which is in both Danish and English. Tomas pushes the door and comes in with a tray piled high with plates and cups. He looks surprised to see me.

'You have an evening off and still you come to see us. Now, why are you not in town doing something interesting with your friend?'

I point across at Becca. 'She's here. We thought it would easiest to eat here tonight and sort out something better tomorrow. I mean something different.'

I see him laughing at me. 'For you, double price. It's my best offer.'

She wanders over and I wave a hand at Tomas. 'This is my friend, Tomas. Tomas, I've told you all about Becca.'

I watch as they shake hands and appraise each other. I am hoping for some obvious spark but they are neither of them the type to wear their heart on their sleeve so I decide to give them both time and see what happens.

'What can I get you both from our extensive menu?' he asks as he waves us to a table.

'I'd like some of your pancakes,' says Becca, 'with chicken and bacon.'

'Good choice. And for you, Kate?'

'I'll have the soup, please and one of those brown rolls. Could you make us a couple of cappuccinos as well?'

'Coming up.'

I see Becca looking at him as he walks away.

'He's nice, isn't he?' I murmur under cover of the hiss of steam.

'This is the guy you told me about at Christmas?'

'Yes.'

'The one you've been saving specially for me?'

'I haven't. Well, maybe a bit ...' I catch her eye and flush. 'Anyway, what do you think?'

'I still think you should get that lobotomy.'

'You're hopeless,' I hiss at her. 'You're never going to get anyone if you don't put any effort into it.'

'I'm not looking for anyone. I'm perfectly happy as I am.'

'Well, yes, I know that. But after you spent all that time on Jon for nothing, I thought you'd be grateful that I've done the work for you this time. He really is lovely. You could do worse.'

'So could you.'

'But I'm spoken for and you're not.'

'I don't hear much speaking for going on.'

'I think something will happen very soon. But I don't want to talk about Christian.'

'That's one thing we can agree on.'

I don't take her up on this. This time round with Christian, there have been none of the fireworks and mad infatuation that marked our first attempt at a relationship. Things feel calm and somehow inevitable now, which is why I am not worrying anymore and am content to let myself go with the flow. Becca will understand much better once she sees us back together. This week is for her, not me, and I would like to focus on that.

We finish our meal and say goodnight to Tomas and Mette. We walk back down towards the apartment in companionable silence. Becca is yawning. The air is chilling as dusk approaches. I let us into the apartment. Jens and Lisette are still out so we make up Becca's bed in the living room and she heads for the bathroom, emerging in her Winnie the Pooh pyjamas. I wonder if Tomas would like them. She climbs under her quilt and waves a sleepy hand at me. 'See you tomorrow.'

I fold the ends of the quilt under her and smile at the familiar sight of her face, all ready for sleep, her curls flopping over her eyes. I have the strongest pang of homesickness yet and turn away from her, dragging my thoughts resolutely to the present. This is where I belong now, not in London but here with Christian and my new friends.

I wake early and stare at the window for a while, wondering why I feel so happy, before remembering Becca's arrival. It is such a relief to have someone here with whom I have a history. With her, there is never anything to explain or make excuses for and I realise what an immense strain this past year has been. I have made a new life and new friends but I have been constantly on my guard, watching, listening and learning. Now that Becca is here, I can relax and take a week's break away from fending for myself, confident that someone else has got my back. It would all have been so different if I had come here with Christian as I always planned. His friends would have been my friends and everything would have been made easy for me. He would have helped me find a job and learn Danish and I would have had somewhere to stay. It strikes me that I have never even seen his apartment over here. Anyway, nothing has worked out as I planned. I have had to do everything by myself and he hasn't been there to help. Looking back, it may have been a good thing. It has certainly been difficult but I feel that I have changed. I am more confident and happier in my own skin for having fended for myself. I am not sure I would change anything. I am glad I didn't know up front how stressful it would all be. But, now I am through the worst of it, I can look forward with more confidence to my new life here with

Christian. I must ask Becca sometime if she sees a difference in me.

She is still asleep when I pad through to switch the coffee maker on. I nudge her as I pass and on my return she is sitting up, pushing her tousled hair out of her face and yawning.

'Morning, Becca. Did you sleep OK?'

'Like a log. I always do.'

'You're lucky. I never do in a new place. I keep waking up and not being able to figure out where I am.'

'Too weird.' She sips the coffee I hand her. 'What's on the programme for today?'

'I thought I could take you on a tour of the city. We can pick up a few leaflets and see if there's anywhere you'd like to visit.'

She stretches. 'There isn't really. I did all the touristy stuff last time I was here. It isn't me, to be honest, but my kind workmates insisted I got the full treatment every weekend. If you don't mind, I'll skip the crown jewels and the castles and museums this time.'

'OK, that cuts my list down considerably. Did you go on a boat round the canals?'

'In January? What do you think?'

'Great. Why don't we get ready, have some breakfast and go into town? We can have lunch and go on a boat trip. You have to see the Little Mermaid.'

'Suits me.'

She pulls a towel from her bag and wanders off towards the bathroom. On an impulse, I reach for the phone and dial Tomas' number. If he is free, he might like to come along. That way, he and Becca could get to know each other a bit better.

The Cinnamon Snail

When she finally emerges from the bathroom, I wave the phone at her.

'I hope you don't mind but I just called Tomas to see if he's free. He's busy this morning but he'll meet us at Nyhavn for the boat trip.'

'Suits me,' she says again and rummages through her bag for some clothes.

'There's an iron in my room if you need it,' I offer, looking at the crumpled shirt she is about to put on.

'Since when did you see me and an iron in the same room? I'm fine, thanks.'

I am longing to suggest she puts on something a little more flattering but I don't. Anything I suggest will be a reason for her to dig her heels in further and things will only work if Tomas likes her just as she is. It certainly never did me any good, dressing up smartly just to fit in with Christian. I remember the teal wrap dress and I cringe. I put it in a bin bag and dumped it outside a charity shop before I left the UK. I hope it brings someone else a bit more luck than it brought me.

We make some toast and go downstairs to wait for a bus, munching as we go.

'You know your way round the place pretty well now?' she asks through a mouthful of crust.

'It's an easy city to live in. If in doubt, head for the lakes and remember that we live at the far end of them.'

We climb on the bus and I clip my card for both of us. She stares approvingly at the ornate apartments as we drive along the lakes. We finally jump off and walk towards Strøget.

'I know you're not one for shops but you ought to walk down here just once,' I say.

'I already have. Isn't the harbour at the other end?'

'Yes, but we've got a fair walk first.'

We wander down the street and she stops at a gift shop to buy a plastic Viking helmet. 'For Jon. He needs a confidence boost.'

I am not sure that Viking horns would be a great boost to me after being dumped but she knows him better than me. We stop at the same café I found on my first day and we sit outside to talk. We carry on, heavily freighted with pastries, down to Illum and strike off up some side streets I haven't yet explored. By lunchtime, I am exhausted and I see we are near the restaurant where I had lunch with Ilse so I drag Becca across the square as fast as I can, battling her urge to stop and admire the buildings every second step.

'Aren't they something?' she breathes and I tug at her sleeve.

'This restaurant is really something too. You'll love it. It's all sloping. When you go down to the toilets in the basement, the walls are cut out of the rock beneath.'

I finally get her seated and she agrees vaguely that I can order us both fish and salad.

'I had it when I was here before. It's gorgeous.' I wave at the waitress and order in the most accurate Danish I can manage.

'You really have changed, haven't you?' she says, finally turning her attention away from the brickwork next to her and staring at me as though she hasn't seen me properly since she arrived.

'Good change or bad change?' I screw my fingernails uncomfortably into my palm as I wait for her to answer. Not that it should matter. Everyone is entitled to their opinion but somehow Becca's opinion has always been important to me. She is the only person I know beside Christian who is totally and utterly honest. She never allows herself to be swayed by what anyone else thinks and she is completely unfazed by the idea of anyone else's good opinion. I wish I could be more like her but I never will be. She is one in a million and I am lucky to have her.

She looks at me across the table for a long moment while she thinks. 'You're still you but you're not. The Kate I knew in London wasn't so confident and she cared way too much about what everyone else thought. It's a good change. I never once thought you would manage to make it work over here and that's a fact.'

'Is that why you called Ilse in to rescue me?'

'That's an exaggeration. I said I had a friend coming over here and maybe she could give you a call but I didn't tell her anything about why you were coming here or who it was ...'

She breaks off and I laugh. '... that I was stalking? Believe me, I was grateful for that. As it turned out, I managed to blow my own cover pretty spectacularly by the end of the first week. But I'm glad you left it to me to screw up and didn't interfere.'

'As if.' She slices a mouthful of fish and chews thoughtfully. 'I still thought you'd be back within a week. I kept your bed made up and everything.'

'There were several times I almost came back. I don't know what kept me going at times.'

'Love?' She says it neutrally and her face gives no clue as to her thoughts so I decide not to challenge her.

'You're probably right. And it did get me through. It got me through the first awful weeks here, finding out about Miranda and then all through the winter. And you see I was right in the end. Christian was worth following. It's all worked out for the best.'

'Maybe.'

'Maybe? Becca, you can see me here now. You said yourself I had changed for the better. I'm surviving in a new country and Christian and I will be back together any day. Do you remember the night before I left, when you made that toast at Phil's? You drank to me finding my way. Well, I've found it so now you ought to swallow your pride and make a less grudging toast.'

I finish in a rush and wonder if I have offended her. But that is one of the wonderful things about Becca. She is almost impossible to offend. She stares at her wine glass for a moment as she considers what I have just said, then nods and lifts her glass.

'You're right, I do have a better one this time round. *To Love!*'

She drinks without catching my eye and I think happily of Christian and drink with her.

Chapter Twenty-Six

We meet Tomas at Nyhavn and board a canal boat for a tour of the city. I am pleased to see Tomas and Becca getting on so well. He is always friendly and natural but, on the very rare occasions that Becca takes a dislike to anyone, she is not good at hiding it. She clearly hasn't found anything to dislike in Tomas because they laugh and chat together as the boat edges out past the strip of coloured houses and the guide shouts out that this was Hans Christian Andersen's house. We all look left obediently.

'You know many of his stories?' asks Tomas.

Becca nods. 'I like the Little Match Girl. She always reminds me of me.'

'She was an architect?' he asks with a straight face.

'Probably not but she was terribly overlooked and didn't ever get the credit she deserved.'

'OK, I will take your word for that.' He is grinning as he turns to me. 'How about you, Kate?'

'Ugly Duckling,' I say immediately and he frowns.

'You downplay yourself always.'

'She doesn't mean it,' Becca chips in. 'She really sees herself as the next Kate Moss.'

'How about you, Tomas?' I ask.

'You know, I never really got around to reading them.'

Our laughter is drowned out by the guide's voice, telling us we are about to moor near to the Little Mermaid.

'Where is she?' Becca cranes over the edge of the boat and peers across the water.

Tomas points wordlessly and we both watch her face fall.

'Isn't she ...'

'... small?' he finishes and nods. 'Every single person who sees her for the first time says that. She is very tiny but perfectly formed.'

'Much like Kate,' says Becca and I poke her with my elbow.

'I don't see me as the Little Mermaid. The Little Barmaid, perhaps. I'd better get a photo of her for you now that we're here.'

I wait until there is a break in the crowds around her and take a photo. Several Japanese tourists have clambered across the stones by the harbour front and are posing for photos in front of the statue. Two lads in Manchester United strip have climbed up behind her and are grinning and shouting to the crowds. I am pleased to see one of them lose his footing and slip with a splash into the shallow water below.

The boat backs round and moves off and we wave at the mermaid as she recedes into the distance. The sun comes out from behind the clouds and I take off my jacket.

'It's lovely at this time of year, isn't it? It almost makes up for the winter.'

'You survived this first one fine,' says Tomas. 'If you are to stay here permanently, you will have to get used to it.'

I see Becca glance at us both as though this is a conversation she doesn't feel a part of. I decide to change the subject. I have an uneasy suspicion that it will end up as two against one if the subject of Christian is raised. I could easily defend him but I don't want to spoil such a lovely day with disagreements.

'I haven't seen half these places,' I say, as we glide past the National Library and Becca stands up to get a better look at the smoked glass structure.

'You have seen them from the streets I expect,' says Tomas absently.

'Probably, but not to recognise them again.'

'Perspective,' says Becca.

'Huh?'

'It affects how you see things. You see them from one angle and you make judgments and then you try a new way and see things completely differently.'

I ignore this. I hope Tomas isn't listening and agreeing with her.

The guide shows us a long building with a sloping roof and tells us admiringly for about the twentieth time this trip that Christian IV made this particular building.

'That was one seriously busy guy,' murmurs Becca and the tension breaks.

We climb back off the boat at Nyhavn and sit outside a café. Tomas goes inside to order and I ask Becca if she has enjoyed her afternoon with him. She pushes her hair behind her ears and gives me the exasperated look I know so well.

'Kate, just knock it off. There's nothing between me and Tomas. There never will be anything between me and Tomas.

Even if you stranded us together for the next fifty years on a desert island, we'd both still be single when they rescued us.'

'So that's an undecided?' I try to smile but I feel oddly disappointed. She is so lovely that it seems a shame for her to stay single and I would also like to see him happy. He couldn't possibly find a nicer person than Becca.

'Pushing him onto me to assuage your guilt isn't going to make things any better,' she says.

'I wasn't.'

'Really? I beg to differ. Honestly, Kate, behave like an imbecile if you really have to but don't try to pull both of us into your little game too, just to ease your conscience.'

I stare at the harbour, not wanting to answer. I have never seen this side of her before, unfair and closed-minded. If this is how she wants to play it, that's fine. But she is wrong.

'Are you OK?' Tomas appears again and sits down next to me and I answer as brightly as possible.

'Just a bit tired. All that sun and then the boat ride.'

'What are you talking about to look so solemn?'

He looks from one stony face to the other in puzzlement. Becca and I glance at each other and I stifle a grin at her unusually serious face. We haven't ever fallen out and I don't intend us to fall out now over a man – or even two men.

'She's on her usual theme of me needing psychiatric help. I'm against it. Don't worry, it's a regular conversation we have.'

'I see.' I doubt that he does but the coffees arrive and we all relax.

Becca and I share a custard slice, while Tomas eats an enormous meringue. He licks the last of the cream from his fork and lays it down.

'How long will you stay here?' he asks Becca and my heart sinks in case, just as she has made her feelings about him clear, he is suddenly getting romantic ideas.

'Four more days,' she says and he nods.

'Will you sightsee?'

'Not if I have any choice in the matter. I did that last time. I just like wandering round new cities and watching people.'

'And eating cakes,' I add.

'I'm happy do my bit for the local economy.'

'She likes weird pizzas,' I tell Tomas. 'The more bizarre the better as far as Becca is concerned.'

'Is that right? You two should come up to mine one evening. I have a place round the corner where they put lettuce on their pizza and no cheese.'

Becca looks interested. 'There's a thought. We'll definitely do that.'

'Are we going to start serving those at our place?' I ask Tomas.

'I think Mette would not approve. Speaking of her, I had a talk with her last night.'

'Oh yes?' I swallow the last piece of pastry and lean back to enjoy the sunshine.

'I have agreed with her my notice.'

'You what?' I sit up and again and cough as the last crumbs go down the wrong way at the shock of his news. Becca doesn't say anything, just watches us both.

'Tomas, you're not serious?' I ask and he nods. 'But *why?*'

'I have been thinking for a little time that I might need some change in my life. You should understand that, Kate, of all people.'

'But I had a reason ...' I break off. I am not getting into the whole stalking Christian thing again. If he and I can put that behind us and move on, so can everyone else.

'I have reasons too. I am thinking of spending some time in Jylland nearer to my family. My course will transfer to the university near to them. After I have finished this year's study in June, I am going back.'

'What about Mette?' I ask. It isn't what I really want to ask but his news has hit me like a blow to the stomach.

'She is very supportive. She will look for someone else to work at the café. You will be in charge.'

'In charge? But I don't want to be. I like things just the way they are. That way, there's always someone above me to blame.'

I try to joke but I am close to tears. I hate change and this year has given me enough of it to last me a lifetime. I know it is none of my business what Tomas chooses to do and I do want him to be happy. But, when I look back on the past year, I realise that it is him who has given me much of my stability. I had hoped that Christian might but it didn't turn out that way. It isn't that I haven't learned to stand on my own two feet but it would have been hugely more difficult without Tomas and I am going to miss him more than I can bear to think of.

'Kate, you're surely not going to stay at *The Cinnamon Snail* forever, are you?' asks Becca. Her face is so sympathetic as she watches me digest Tomas' news, that I almost start to cry.

I choke back the tears. 'I hadn't thought. I've had such a good time there that I haven't needed to make other plans. It's been great for learning Danish and paying the bills. I haven't wanted to look any further.'

I don't add that it has been the perfect staging post for me while I have waited for Christian to come to his senses.

'Mette is not going to be firing you,' says Tomas. 'You have a job as long as you want one.'

'It won't be the same,' I sniff. 'Once you've gone, I can't imagine wanting to stay.'

And this time, to my eternal shame, I do start crying. He leans over and puts an arm round my shoulders and I press my face into his jacket and lean against him until I feel a bit calmer. I had hoped, in as much as I had thought about it at all, that he would be there right to the end, until I have seen things through with Christian. Given his feelings, even I can see how selfish that hope was, but I still can't help feeling betrayed. I straighten up and wipe my eyes.

'Sorry, it was just a surprise. Any more of them up your sleeve? Don't hold back.'

'Just that one,' he says and stuffs his hands into his pockets.

Becca isn't giving up. 'I'm serious, Kate. You weren't planning to spend your entire career in that café, were you?'

'I suppose not.'

'Or supporting someone else's career?' She is relentless.

I glare at her. 'There's nothing wrong with supporting someone else's career.'

'Not as long as it's a two-way thing.'

'Of course. But in principle, when there are two of you, you can't both have exactly what you want all the time. That's what a relationship is all about.'

'And what *do* you want?' She doesn't seem remotely fazed by my frown.

I consider for a second. 'I know it's not what I've always wanted but I've really enjoyed teaching my three little horrors over these past few months. They've completely changed my mind about children. I've been thinking of coming back to the

UK in the autumn and doing a year's postgraduate teaching course — or even getting a qualification to teach English as a foreign language. I think I'd enjoy either of those.'

'Good for you. What's stopping you?' She sees my face. 'You can't think like that.'

'Like what?'

'You know damn well like what. If you and Christian are going to work it out, he'll have to be flexible too. So far it's been you making all the changes.'

I glance at Tomas, who has his eyes fixed on an open air art display around Kongens Nytorv.

'I admit that it has been me making most of the changes up until now. If we work things out, of course Christian will accommodate my needs and wishes. He's not a monster, whatever you might think. He's a decent and kind guy who hasn't got a selfish bone in his body.'

'You think I've got something against Christian? I haven't. You're always on the defensive when you talk about him. I'm just saying he'll need to support your dreams as well as you supporting his.'

'That goes without saying in any relationship.' I turn unthinkingly to Tomas. 'You'd support someone's dreams, wouldn't you?'

He flushes and I regret phrasing it quite like that. This can't be an easy conversation for him to listen to. I plough on, trying to make it better. 'I mean, if you and Susanne had stayed together and she'd wanted to move elsewhere for her career, would you have had a problem?' As soon as the words are out of my mouth, I regret them. Now, as well as reminding him that I am in love with Christian and not with him, I have probably opened all the old wounds that Susanne gave him. But he doesn't give any sign of it, just shrugs.

'Of course I would go. I wouldn't care where I was, just who I was with. If they needed me to make changes, no problem and I hope the same for them with me.'

'There you go,' I say to Becca. 'It's no big deal — just relationship stuff.'

'OK.'

Tomas pushes his chair back. 'I really must go now or Mette will be on her own for the rush. Thank you both for your company and a pleasant afternoon.'

He shakes our hands and we watch him pick his way across the square and disappear into distance. I am saved from any caustic comments Becca might have been preparing, by my phone buzzing in my bag. I dig it out and answer without looking at it.

'Hello?'

'Kate, it's me.'

I smile with pleasure as I hear Christian's voice at the other end, warm and friendly. A whole slew of memories comes flooding back at the sound of his voice, sounding so relaxed and just as it used to. I think back to wandering round London hand in hand, sitting across the table from each other at endless dinner parties, waking up in his apartment in the morning and looking out together across London. It is wonderful to hear his voice sounding so affectionate again, and any doubts I might have cherished are immediately swept away. It's like coming home.

'Hi, you,' I say and instinctively turn away from Becca.

'Am I right in thinking Becca leaves on Friday?' he asks.

'Yes.'

'Then would you do me the honour of having dinner with me on Saturday?'

'OK.' It isn't the most romantic reply but he has caught me off balance. So far, we have only had coffee together. Dinner sounds very committed. It is clearly now or never. Even though I haven't wanted to count my chickens over these past few months, it is surely safe to tally them now.

'I have booked a table at the Hotel d'Angleterre,' he says and I raise my eyebrows and turn my head to peer over the square at its façade. That is an incredibly swish place. He surely wouldn't have chosen a place like that just to tell me that we are finally over. A McDonald's would have done perfectly well for that and he would still have had change from one hundred kroner.

'I'm not buying a new dress. I bankrupted myself once doing that and it all ended in tears. I'm never doing that again.'

'Nor would I want you to.' His voice is full of laughter and I smile reluctantly, the memory of that dreadful farewell party finally falling into proper perspective.

'Just as long as we're clear.'

'Seven o'clock outside the front entrance?'

'I'll be there.'

I click the phone shut and drop it back into my bag. Becca waits for a moment and then, when I don't say anything, shrugs her jacket more firmly round her shoulders. 'Ready?'

'As I'll ever be.'

I follow her back across the square and through the chattering crowds.

Chapter Twenty-Seven

I work on Saturday lunchtime but I have arranged to take the evening off. I am still sad about having said goodbye to Becca after her oddly unsatisfactory visit. It was wonderful to see her again and it was almost like old times but something wasn't quite right. Either it was an unspoken disapproval on her side, or a feeling on mine that I am about to act in a way I suspect she won't like. Not that that would matter on its own. She has no more right to dictate my life than I do hers and, to be fair, has never tried to. But her good opinion has always mattered to me and this seems like yet another unwelcome change in my life – moving on in a way she can't completely empathise with.

On top of the depression about her leaving, is my acute nervousness about dinner with Christian tonight. I suppressed my jitters all through Becca's visit and didn't mention our date. As soon as she had left and I was on the train back from the airport, the enormity of the whole situation flooded over me and left me shaken and depressed. When I came out here in the autumn, I was so entirely focussed on what I had lost and what I wanted, that I had no time to sit and think about what I would do if I ever got it. And now that it looks as though my dream is about to come true, I feel woefully unprepared and unsure how to move on from here. Things aren't the same as they used to be. After all that has happened, they never could be. I have changed hugely and I expect Christian has too. Once we are over the first hurdle of admitting that our feelings for each other are as strong as ever, the challenge will be for us to find a way to move forward together. I am sure we will be able to do that. My feelings have survived eight months of separation and so, clearly, have his. But in some ways, it will still be a leap in the dark for us both and I am so emotionally exhausted that I could probably do without more effort and turmoil. I have to keep reminding myself of what I am gaining and how much I love him in order to make the prospect of more relationship hard work seem even faintly desirable.

Tomas tells me at four o'clock that there is no need for me to stay.

'You seem a little on edge,' he says. 'Did Becca get home all right?'

'Yeah, she rang to say she made it back in one piece. I'll miss her.'

'I can see that. She's very nice.'

I look at his face but he shows no signs of love and longing, nor any tendency to rush off and jump on a plane to follow her. Each to his own, I suppose. I am through with matchmaking. I will need all my spare energy for the foreseeable future, to get my own relationship back on track. I will leave everyone else's alone.

'Are you OK, Kate?' he asks and I nod.

'Fine - it's just ...' I pause for a second while I wonder whether to tell him about tonight. I decide it might be a good idea to prepare him before I arrive on Monday with my big announcement. 'I have a date tonight.'

He doesn't look surprised. 'With Christian?'

'With Christian. I think this is it, Tomas. We've been moving towards getting back together for a while now. You knew that, didn't you?'

'In my head.' He sees my face fall and laughs. 'It's OK. I can congratulate you and wish you very well. You deserve to be happy, Kate.'

He bends down and kisses the top of my head and I hold his hand for a moment, choking back tears. He has been such a good friend to me and I know in my heart of hearts that this part of my life is now over. I can't have my cake and eat it. I can't stay close to Tomas once I am back with Christian.

'Go, then,' he says after a moment, and the last thing I see as I walk out of the café is his face as he watches me leave. He doesn't look upset, more resigned, and his smile is as open as ever.

I caught the bus to work this morning. Now that I have been let out early, I decide to walk home. The trees are in their soft green summer clothing and I realise I am privileged to live in one of the most beautiful cities in the world. I walk slowly, drinking it all in, pursued by the oddest feeling that everything is ending. I give myself a mental shake and walk faster. Nothing is really ending apart from the uncertainties and stresses of the past year. All that is happening is that I am facing a new beginning to match the emergence of the new foliage around me. Tonight is just the gateway between the past and the future and I have never done very well with new things. That needs to stop. I am not the person I was when I came out here and I ought to learn to handle change much better than I used to. And I won't be alone this time, I remind myself, and give a tiny skip as I walk. Christian will be by my side and we will face the future together.

Once back at the apartment, I spend a while going through my wardrobe. Most of my stuff is very casual and would be totally unsuitable for dinner at an expensive hotel but I am determined to be myself as much as possible, within the constraints of minimal smartness. I have been dithering all week between a silky blue-and-white polka dot dress I bought the summer I was going out with Christian, and a dark pink-and-green print skirt with a pink top. In the end, I close my eyes and point. The pink wins and I dress carefully, selecting a pair of cream and gold sandals. I take my lightest linen jacket. It is hot but we will be down by the water and it can get cool in the evenings. I deliberate between a tiny evening bag and a more substantial shoulder bag. My unacknowledged problem is how much I want to take with me and where I think I might be spending the night. Going unprepared looks more romantic and shows I have no expectations of what the evening will bring but I remind myself I am hardly some dewy-eyed teenager. In the end, I choose the larger bag and put a small selection of toiletries inside. I think of Becca's pyjamas and smile to myself. Whenever I stayed over at Christian's, I always borrowed one of his T shirts. They smelled deliciously of his aftershave and gave me a proprietorial feeling. If things should happen to pan out that way, I can do that again tonight.

I arrive outside the hotel with a few minutes to spare but Christian is already there. I try to trace nervousness in his face but have to settle for a look of genuine pleasure when he sees me.

'Look at you. You are beautiful.'

'Thanks, you too.' Of course, that is always a given where Christian is concerned but it must still be nice for him to hear it.

'If only you had thought to ask me for Thursday, I could have brought Becca along,' I say and he nods.

'I thought about it but in the end I decided it would be too expensive to have three meals.'

We sit down at an outside table and he waits until we have ordered before taking my hand.

'The last meal we ate together like this was at that little place outside my office, not long before I left London. Do you remember?'

I know the place he means. A tiny café by the Thames under chestnut trees, where he and I sometimes went for breakfast after I had stayed the night. I remember the occasion he refers to, perfectly. It was the evening before we went to Marie and Jeremy's and he announced his imminent departure. We had a lovely, romantic dinner and after dark the waiter brought out candles and wine and I looked out over the water and longed for the evening never to end. He must have known that he would be leaving the next week but he didn't mention it once. Probably, like me, he wanted to make the evening last forever and not spoil it with sadness. That's why he kept his crushing news for the following day. Marie and Jeremy's dinner parties were obviously not as important to him as his dinner with me. It would have been nice to have had a small inkling of his intentions before he dropped the bombshell on me in public and left me to cope with the fallout with so many curious eyes upon me. But that is all in the past now. He is waiting for me to speak.

'I remember that dinner perfectly. I loved that place. But that wasn't the last meal we had together. There was the awful one at Marie and Jeremy's the next night and then those ginger chicken noodles at Harry's.'

He wrinkles his nose. 'Do you need to be so precise? I meant the last meal we ate together as a couple, just you and me alone together without sadness.'

He reaches for my hand and begins to stroke my thumb. So I was right, that was what he meant. Maybe I am beginning to read him better.

'OK,' I say. 'Just being accurate.'

He doesn't answer and we sit in silence until our meals arrive. I pick at mine, suddenly nervous about the conversation we are about to have. I need to get this sorted, and quickly. We can't spend the rest of our life together not being able to speak at meals. We just need this over with. I lift my head and look him squarely in the eye.

'You obviously brought me here to talk. What did you want to say?'

Something flickers over his face. It isn't annoyance. Christian is never annoyed. It is more discomfort at being thrown off course. He recovers quickly.

'You are killing romance,' he complains.

'Sorry.'

Actually, I realise with mild surprise, I'm not. Things have gone way beyond candles and flowers and bottles of champagne whisked from nowhere at appropriate moments. What we need now is a frank and open discussion. The other stuff can come later if we want it. None of it is the stuff that really matters, although it can be the icing on the cake. The only way we can build this relationship again is with truth and honesty and mutual trust. If we can do that, then I am willing to toast it in coca cola or beer. Something of what I am thinking may show in my face because he looks suddenly serious.

'Since you wish us to be honest, Kate, I will be. Remember that you are the one who didn't want all the romantic extras.'

'Fine.' I watch his face intently, needing to find sincerity and love in his eyes.

'I asked you to come here because I need to tell you we should never have broken up. I made a bad mistake and, believe me, I have paid for it.'

'Me too.'

He nods. 'Indeed, you too, and probably you more than me. It was foolish and very unthinking on my part. But I think the only mistakes to be sad for are the ones that cannot be put right. Can we not put this one right, Kate? I love you still and I want to start again.'

He waits and I study his face for a moment. He hasn't actually uttered words of apology but he has admitted to making a mistake, something I have been longing to hear for eight months. And his eyes just now are filled with unmistakeable anxiety and the sort of tenderness I used to see in them before this whole horrible mess erupted. I could make him sweat for a while and wait for a few weeks longer, but what is the point? I have everything I have ever wanted, right in front of me, and I would be a fool not to grab it. I nod slowly and look into his eyes.

'Despite everything, I still feel the same about you, Christian. So I guess that's a yes.'

His face lights up when I say this. He leans in to kiss me and at last it feels right. His lips are soft and warm and his hair, as I run my fingers through it, feels as silky and springy as I remember. He straightens up and beckons to the waiter, who, like any half-decent waiter, has read the runes and is already there with the bottle of champagne. Christian gestures to him to leave it with us. When the man has gone, he takes my hand again.

'If you would like, we can take the champagne upstairs.' He laughs at my surprised face. 'I have checked in for the night here. It seemed such a romantic hotel.'

'What if I had said no?' I am vaguely indignant that he might have been taking me for granted.

'I still wanted to be here. The pillows are luxury ones for crying into all night.'

'I don't have a nightdress.'

'And that is a problem for which of us?'

'Christian, I'm not sure.'

'Not sure? But you just said ...'

'Yes, I did and I am sure about that. But it seems so sudden to be spending the night with you after all that's happened. I know that sounds odd but it's the way I feel. I just want to take a little time to get my head in line with it all, to adjust.'

He nods slowly. 'Maybe I deserve that. I haven't behaved to you always as I should so now I need to pay the price. How about I book you a room here too and we meet for breakfast?'

'Can you afford that?'

He laughs. 'For you, anything. And think of the money I have already saved on that third meal.'

'OK, if you're sure, that would be great. I can spend some time by myself tonight and get my head in order. I'll meet you here for breakfast and we can make plans.'

He goes off to the lobby and comes back with a key, which he hands to me. I almost don't take it. I feel as though I am being unfair. But it's just the one night and we can surely both survive being apart that much longer. After all, we have a possible lifetime of nights together ahead of us. We stop in the lobby and I buy myself a *Wonderful Copenhagen* T-shirt to sleep in. He stops outside my room and traces my cheek with his finger.

'One night only. After that I want you all to myself.'

When he kisses me, I almost give in. It feels so wonderful to be back in his arms after all this time, and shielded from the pain of the past eight months. But it's one night. It won't kill either of us, so after a moment I slip out of his arms and into my room. When I tiptoe up to peer through the security hole, he has gone. I had half thought he might stick around in case I changed my mind. It is nice to see that he respects my decision, even if it isn't the one he wanted.

I fall onto the bed and run my hands over my burning face. Half an hour after the man I love has told me he loves me too, what am I doing all alone in a hotel room, however luxurious? I have an impulse to ring down to the lobby and ask for Christian's room number but I squash it. I asked for a night to myself, to think. I am going to look pretty stupid if I backtrack immediately. I will just have to stay here by myself. It looks as though it will be a long night.

Chapter Twenty-Eight

I wake at dawn, go over to the window, and watch the sun rise across the city beneath me. I didn't really expect to get to sleep for hours. In the event, no sooner had I pulled on my *Wonderful Copenhagen* T-shirt than I crashed out, which means I suppose that Christian didn't lose out on too much. I lie and survey the ghostlike scene below me, which mirrors the surreal situation in which I find myself. I am like a widow whose husband is still alive, I reflect — a total contradiction. I glance at my watch. We are meeting for breakfast at eight so I have three more hours to wait in this half-world before seeing Christian. I can't think very clearly, try though I might. I compromise by staying very still and letting thoughts drift through my mind, while I watch the very few people who are up, walking across the square below and down to the harbour. My mind is still almost numb, exhausted and worn out with fighting all winter for what has seemed to be almost a birthright. Now I have exactly what I want, yet somehow I feel a little like a child at Christmas who has opened her stocking and got everything she asked for and has no idea what to do next.

I am getting maudlin so I force myself to think about Christian, which feels a whole lot better. He looked very handsome last night and I was touched by the look of anxiety on his face as he asked me to come back to him. *Anxiety* and *Christian* are not words that are often used in the same sentence so I savour the image of him, sitting opposite me and waiting for me to give him my answer. I think of his kindness and of how he only allowed the tiniest flicker of disappointment to cross his face when I said I wanted to spend the night alone. Not many people would be that generous but I have always been able to rely on Christian to be kind and tolerant. It is one of the things that make him so popular. Not only does he not say anything bad about anyone else but I have come to realise that he doesn't even think it. And this is the man who wants to spend his immediate and hopefully his long-term future with me. I pull the thick curtain around me because my legs are chilly in this short T shirt, and sigh in contentment. I can trust him with my future because I have seen him caring for me in my past — apart from his inexplicable decision to break up with me. But everyone is allowed one screw-up and at least he has had the courage to face up to his and admit his mistake. I go through to the bathroom and take a long, hot shower. There is a long row of little bottles for me to choose from and I think back with amusement to my first morning in Denmark and my totally insane hair. Once I am out of the shower, I blow dry my hair carefully and shake out yesterday's clothes, thanking my instinct to pack clean underwear. I repack my handbag and, at exactly eight o'clock, I arrive downstairs in the dining room. Christian is already there. He looks as though he hasn't slept much but he greets me pleasantly and I put my arms round him and kiss him fondly.

The waiter brings us both coffee and I ask for a croissant.

'Didn't you sleep?' I ask Christian and he shakes his head.

'Not very much, no. I don't sleep so well in strange beds.'

'Which is why you booked a night in a hotel,' I tease him.

'I wasn't planning on very much sleep.'

I turn scarlet and bury my face in my cup of coffee. I pretty much walked into that one. The waiter brings Christian his favourite eggs Benedict.

'You said last night that we should make plans this morning,' he says and I nod.

'It seems a good idea. Do you realise I have no idea where you live?'

'You must do!'

I shake my head. 'No, in London I never needed to know your Danish address. When I first arrived here, I think you were too afraid of me sending you a letter bomb, to tell me.'

He laughs. 'I have an apartment in Hellerup, quite near to the station. It is very nice. I thought you might like to move your things in later today.'

I stare at him. 'That's quick work. Yesterday I couldn't have found you on a map and today I'm moving in?'

He is unperturbed. 'You share an apartment with Jens and Lisette, don't you?'

'Yes, it's lovely. You'll have to come and see it.'

'But we don't want to start our new life together sharing with someone else when I have a perfectly good apartment of my own. There is a second bedroom so, if we have a fight, you can always storm out.'

'I like the sound of that but I really hadn't thought about leaving my apartment quite yet. I'll have to give them notice at least. They've been very kind to me. They let me move in without a deposit.'

His eyes lift to mine and lower and I wonder if he thinks I am trying to score a point. He threw me onto the street and they took me in. But it wasn't like that. He didn't owe me anything and we both know it.

'I can pay them a month's rent in lieu of your notice,' he says and I frown.

'Let's see, shall we?'

He reaches for my hand. 'I know there will be a lot to work out but I think if we both have good will we can manage it.'

'I have good will,' I say.

'Me too.'

I finish my croissant and ask for some fruit. I was too nervous to eat much last night and I am ravenous this morning. Christian sips his coffee and looks out across the square.

'How long will you work at your café?'

'I don't know. I haven't really given it much thought. Not for long I shouldn't think. Tomas gave his notice last week.'

'And this means so much to you?'

'Not exactly but it means everything's breaking up and changing so perhaps it's an easier time for a move.'

'I agree. What will you do next?'

I pour myself another cup of coffee and decide this is a good time to tell him about my plans, however vague they might be as yet.

'You know those children you met? The ones you thought were Tomas'?' I suppress a grin at the thought, although Tomas will clearly make a wonderful father one day.

'Uh huh.'

'I've been tutoring them and I've been surprised by how much I've enjoyed it. So now I'm thinking about teaching, either in a school or teaching English as a foreign language.'

He sits for a moment and doesn't speak. I tap his arm. 'I thought you'd be pleased for me. You were the one who always told me I was just drifting in Sawley Brothers.'

'Yes, you were, but I didn't expect you to go in this direction.'

'You couldn't see me in an office, could you?'

'You have a point. How will you make this work?'

Now that he asks the question directly, it is easier than I thought to tell him some of my ideas. I clear my throat. 'I've been looking into courses and I could probably get a place at one of the London colleges to do my post-grad teaching course. It would be for a year.'

'A year? I don't want you to be away for a whole year. I've only just got you back.' He strokes my hair and I lift my hand to hold his.

'I don't want to be away from you for a year either but I thought that you could get another transfer to the London Office for that year so we could stay together. After that, we could see which country we would both prefer.'

He drops my hand. 'No.'

'No? No, what?'

'That wouldn't work.'

'They wouldn't give you a transfer?'

'I wouldn't ask for one. Kate, my work is here. You know that. I chose to come back and I intend to stay here permanently. Any plans you and I make must take account of that.'

'But we're a couple. Couples make compromises.'

'And so we will. We can look for a house together if you prefer it to an apartment. You could perhaps look at courses at the university here. But my job was here before you were and it isn't for negotiation.'

'So, if I wanted to teach in England or even go to another country entirely, to teach English, that's entirely off the table?'

'You are too reasonable to insist on either of those things. I decided we should stop seeing each other because I was coming back here. To be honest, I couldn't see you being able to adapt and to fit in here with my life. You have proved me very wrong and I admit it. For that you have my complete admiration. But you must understand, when you came here to show to me that you could be part of my life, I saw that as the deal we would make. Not that you would come here and make me give up my own life and my career to follow you back.'

What he is saying is perfectly reasonable so I take a moment to answer, remembering his dislike of scenes and shouting.

'I understand what you're saying, Christian, and I'm not saying that I want you to move or do anything you don't want to do. But are you telling me that my only option is to plan my life to fit in with yours?'

'That is not quite a fair way to put it. I thought I had been very honest with you from the start. You came here and changed my mind and now I would like you here with me also. But I never promised anything else. I thought you understood the situation and were happy with it.'

He is quite right and he is being perfectly honest with me. I am the one who needs to take a step back and consider what is on offer and why I didn't fully understand, when he was always so upfront about everything. But I don't want to take even one step back. I lay my hand on his. Without stopping to consider my words too carefully, for fear of not saying what I want to, I look him straight in the eye.

'Christian, you're right. You have been upfront with me. I admit that, six months ago, I'd have jumped at this — but not now. It's not what I want. I want a partnership, not some deal where I can have everything I want as long as I never want anything you don't want to give.'

I see his face contract as I say this and I hurry on. 'I don't mean it quite like that but I'm trying to say I want to be in a relationship where I can tell you my dreams and we might decide they won't work but not just because they don't fit in with yours.'

His face is sad as he looks at me. 'And how about if your dreams, when you decide them, do fit into mine? Could it work then?'

'No.'

I am surprised that I don't need even a second to think. My reactions seem to come from months of subconscious musings and reflection. It is a pity I only understand them now but I refuse to blame myself. I haven't been playing games any more than he has.

'Christian, I love you. In a way I probably always will. If you had stayed in London, we might have worked it out — or we might not. It was never terribly real. But you didn't and I chased after you and things changed. I changed. If you did, it wasn't in a way I could follow so we've ended up here today, both going in different directions and trying to cobble together some sort of compromise that neither of us wants. I'm so sorry.'

I can't look at him so I keep my eyes fixed on the table. He doesn't speak for a moment. Then he lifts my chin with one finger and looks at me sadly.

'I don't think this is something we can fix, is it?'

I shake my head and feel the tears behind my eyes. 'No, it's not. I think we have to let go. You already did that once. It was me that couldn't manage it and, for that, I'm truly sorry.'

'Don't be. This wasn't your fault. You tried so hard and I was just too blind, or too stupid, to see it. It is strange that it is so much more painful to lose you this time round.'

'I'm sorry,' I say again and he nods.

'I have no business to ask you this again but, now that you have decided you do not want me, is that because you have decided you want someone else?'

'Tomas, you mean?'

He nods.

'This is nothing to do with anyone else and everything to do with you and me. I hope you can believe me because it's true.'

'Of course. You are always totally straight. I love that about you.'

'Except when I secretly stalk you across countries.'

'Except that of course.' He is laughing now, although his eyes are wet. 'Kate Merrit, it has been a privilege to know you and I hope you can accept my very best wishes for all your future happiness, wherever you go and with whom.'

'You too, Christian. I mean that with all my heart.' I stand up and lean over to kiss him. 'I won't prolong this. There have been times when I've regretted ever meeting you but that didn't last. I'll always remember this year.'

He stands too and hugs me tightly. 'Off you go and good luck.'

'Sorry about the extra hotel room.'

'I think I will not charge you this time.'

I walk as quickly as possible across the room and out of the door. I don't look back and not because I am scared I'll change my mind — that isn't possible — but I am very fond of Christian and I know I have hurt him, which I never meant to do.

I wonder whether to go home, but Lisette and Jens will probably be there and I don't want to talk to them about what has just happened. I owe it to Christian to keep his affairs private. I walk for a while in the morning sunlight, tucking this final scene with Christian into the past, where it belongs. It isn't actually as hard as I feared. In the end, he too seemed to know that it wasn't right. Wrong people, wrong timing, wrong something. I doubt either of us will be seriously hurt in the long term. He has his job and his friends and a driving ambition I will never understand while I have ... I stop my train of thought here and realise I have stopped walking too. I know where I am headed. I have probably known since last night, when I refused to go back to Christian's room. My legs are carrying me across the street and into the train station. I mustn't over-think this one. I have thought and planned and driven myself half-mad this winter, trying to control events and people, and what have I ended up with? A hurt ex-boyfriend and a lot of wasted time. I clip my ticket and sit quietly on the train until my stop comes up. I emerge from the station and walk across the grass, still not allowing myself to think or plan what I am going to say. It will come to me.

Tomas is alone behind the counter when I push through the doors and he looks up in surprise.

'You are not working today, are you? I thought you had the rest of the weekend off to spend with Christian.'

'Can you come outside for a moment? I don't want to talk to you in here.'

He calls to Mette and she appears from the kitchen and smiles when she sees me. He says something to her in swift Danish and she smiles again and nods. I walk back outside. His face is serious as he follows me.

'You have some news for me and you don't wish me to hear it inside?'

'Kind of.'

My heart is thumping as I turn to face him. After being so blind for so many months, the least I can do now is to tell him how I feel.

'Tomas, what you said to me in Sweden. You haven't mentioned it again. Is that because you don't feel the same or because of Christian?'

He shrugs and his face closes. 'What was the point? I am not stupid, Kate. You made things clear that day. It was Christian for you no matter what happened. It will always be Christian.'

'It was never Christian.' I feel my face turning red as I struggle with the words.

'I don't really know what you are saying.'

'Which makes two of us. When I came out here, I thought it was because of Christian but it wasn't. It was the dream of him, of what I thought he was and of what I thought I could be. Right through this winter, I clung onto that dream because I didn't know what else to cling onto. It was the only thing I could focus on while everything else was changing so fast. But last night, I realised he's not what I want. He probably never was. And I'm certainly not the person to make him happy. So he'll always be a good friend but that's it.'

Tomas straightens up from where he has been leaning against the wall, staring across the water as he listens to me. He takes my hand. 'Kate, I know it is probably too early after everything, but is there any chance ... might there be some chance in the future for you and me to ...'

I shake my head. 'You're too late, I'm afraid.'

He nods and leans back against the wall and I take a step towards him and reach up to put my arms around his neck. Looking into his familiar green eyes, it isn't so hard after all to say what I need to. When he realises my meaning, his arms go round me too and he looks down at me with a half-smile.

'Tomas, it's you. I think it always has been. I just didn't realise it until today. Can you live with that?'

'It is just possible.'

He pulls me towards him and kisses me for a long, long moment. Through the rushing in my ears, I can vaguely hear someone inside the café thumping the glass and clapping. He looks up and waves cheerily at them.

'I came over here with just one Danish phrase,' I say, with my head tucked comfortably into his shoulder. 'I expected to use it really quickly. As it turned out, I never had the chance. I think it was waiting until now. Can you guess what it was?'

He rubs his chin on the top of my head and thinks for a moment. 'What time is dinner?'

I laugh in spite of myself. 'Nearly, but not quite.'

I wrap my arms around him again and whisper it almost to myself. '*Jeg elsker dig.*'

He holds me closer when I say this and we stand in silence and listen to the swish and ripple of the water below.

Also by Rosemary Whittaker

Sunshine State

Emily Martin has spent the past six months putting her life back together after her bitter divorce from Jack. Seeing him every day at work doesn't help, especially as he seems to be trying to date every one of her colleagues.

When she is offered the opportunity to work in Florida for a year, she sees it as her much-needed chance to escape. A year away ought to be enough time to find someone who is different from Jack in every way. That way, he will see that she is the one who has moved on. Nothing could be easier ...

The Wattle Birds

Samantha Forrest has just graduated and is finishing an internship, when she meets Josh Fielding. Within months, they are engaged and planning a future together. But Josh is Australian and his business is over there.

Is Samantha prepared to follow him across the world and make a new life for herself in Sydney? Even if she is, how will she cope with her fiancé's hostile sister and ever-present ex-girlfriend? Maybe some challenges are just too much to take on, even for love.

The Feijoa Tree

At twenty-five, Anna Richardson has her future clearly set out. She has a good job as an English teacher, lives close to her bereaved mother and everyone agrees that her boyfriend Matt is completely right for her.

So what should Anna do when the school suspends her because of an incident in her classroom? Matt has been offered a new job. Maybe it is time to move away with him. But is that really what she wants and is he the man for her? When an unexpected trip to New Zealand is offered, she starts to wonder what exactly is stopping her from starting a whole new life.

Made in the USA
Lexington, KY
30 December 2013